2084

ALSO BY ELLIOT ACKERMAN AND ADMIRAL JAMES STAVRIDIS

2054

2034

ALSO BY ELLIOT ACKERMAN

Sheepdogs

Halcyon

The Fifth Act

Red Dress in Black & White

Places and Names

Waiting for Eden

Dark at the Crossing

Istanbul Letters

Green on Blue

ALSO BY ADMIRAL JAMES STAVRIDIS

The Restless Wave

To Risk It All

The Admiral's Bookshelf

The Sailor's Bookshelf

Sailing True North

Sea Power

The Accidental Admiral

Partnership for the Americas

Destroyer Captain

COAUTHORED BY ADMIRAL JAMES STAVRIDIS

Command at Sea

The Leader's Bookshelf

Watch Officer's Guide

Division Officer's Guide

2084

A NOVEL OF FUTURE WAR

Elliot Ackerman and Admiral James Stavridis

PENGUIN PRESS NEW YORK 2026

PENGUIN PRESS
An imprint of Penguin Random House LLC
1745 Broadway, New York, NY 10019
penguinrandomhouse.com

Book design by Daniel Lagin

LIBRARY OF CONGRESS CATALOGING-IN-PUBLICATION DATA

Names: Ackerman, Elliot author | Stavridis, James author
Title: 2084 : a novel of future war /
Elliot Ackerman and Admiral James Stavridis.
Description: New York: Penguin Press, 2026.
Identifiers: LCCN 2025013015 (print) | LCCN 2025013016 (ebook) |
ISBN 9780593489895 hardcover | ISBN 9780593489901 ebook
Subjects: LCGFT: Fiction | Climate fiction | War fiction | Novels
Classification: LCC PS3601.C5456 A617 2025 (print) |
LCC PS3601.C5456 (ebook) | DDC 813/.6—dc23/eng/20250528
LC record available at https://lccn.loc.gov/2025013015
LC ebook record available at https://lccn.loc.gov/2025013016

ISBN 9798217062737 (international edition)

Printed in the United States of America
1st Printing

The authorized representative in the EU for product safety and compliance is Penguin Random House Ireland, Morrison Chambers, 32 Nassau Street, Dublin D02 YH68, Ireland, https://eu-contact.penguin.ie.

For Scott Moyers, our beloved editor and friend

CONTENTS

2084

A BRIEF HISTORY OF THE TWENTY-FIRST CENTURY THROUGH 2084

Like nature, geopolitics abhors a vacuum . . .

The war between the United States and China in 2034 devastated each nation, upending a fragile world order based on their competition. By mid-century, both were trying to claw their way back to superpower status. Neither nation succeeded; by 2054, civil conflict consumed the United States, stalling its forward momentum, while in China, a demographic time bomb detonated, and the fundamental imbalance between an unnaturally high number of males and a far smaller female population triggered a sociological collapse. Into that vacuum stepped two dynamic new powers: India and Japan. Those countries, rejuvenated by the advent of artificial intelligence and robotics, assumed positions of primacy. But it wasn't only India and Japan that benefited. Nations like Brazil, Indonesia, and Nigeria—with huge populations and dynamic leaders—brought the Global South to prominence. By the end of the 2050s, the balance of power in the world had shifted.

In the decade that followed, a new and powerful force began to make itself felt. It was not a nation—far from it. Instead, it was the earth itself, a huge and tortured ecosystem that had never recovered from ecological abuses inflicted in prior decades when the global community—vibrating between populist movements and economic excess—walked away from efforts to mitigate the effects of climate change.

Massive storms, unlike those ever seen in recorded history, battered the planet in the 2060s and '70s. A traditional "hurricane season" that once peaked between August and October had become a quaint and nostalgic temporal boundary that no longer applied as storms came in unpredictable waves throughout the year. Sea levels rose globally, swamping hundreds of major cities, especially the megacities of Southeast Asia. Superstorms washed away coastlines, hiving off entire landmasses in the Global North and South. Wildfires and droughts struck in those mid-latitude nations clustered near the equator. By the late 2070s, an uninhabitable band circled the middle of the planet. Nations in this ever-widening band—Indonesia, Kenya, Nigeria, Brazil, Colombia, Ecuador, and others—saw a massive and sudden drop in the viability of their statehood as their populations became suddenly unable to sustain basic economic activity. By the 2080s, this march of catastrophic events, each more terrible than the last, consumed the globe and threatened all of humanity.

Economies that had risen in the 2050s now found themselves in the uninhabitable band. Indonesia, Nigeria, Brazil had all invested in highly capable militaries, constructed and maintained at great cost, but these had little utility in the face of such an implacable foe. Such relics of previous decades of prosperity and economic growth seemed to mock the leaders of these nations. To the north, a weakened but still formidable United States and China entered an uneasy alliance full of mutual suspicion, but both countries felt that given the lingering costs of their earlier war they were better in league with each other than operating alone. They had a name for themselves and those who would ally with them: the Consortium.

Meanwhile, the nations devastated by the costs of a changing climate drew closer together. They shared a common grievance: the excesses of those outside the uninhabitable band. They began to discuss reparations and new lands for their people as their landmasses became largely uninhabitable. In the capitals of Indonesia, Nigeria, and Brazil, clandestine plans were laid. They called themselves the Reparationists, and the moment was rapidly approaching when they would need to use or lose the military capability they had so lavishly invested in at the height of their power. A new world for their populations—fully one-third of people on earth—was the object of the great armada of 2084.

A war takes shape, its opponents seemingly fixed:

> ***Consortium:*** *China, the United States, the Republic of Florida*
>
> ***Reparationists:*** *Brazil, Indonesia, Nigeria, other equatorial nations*
>
> ***Nonaligned:*** *India, Japan, the Green Zone of Alaska and Washington—BC.*

But wars, like people, have lives of their own. Sides shift. Minds change. Conviction turns to uncertainty. War is that most unpredictable of human endeavors. As with the weather itself, it can never be perfectly forecast.

PROLOGUE

The Storm of '74

03:47 Aug 07, 2074 (-5 GMT)
Makassar Strait

He was at sea on the day she died. It was another routine storm evasion deployment. The Indonesian fleet made these sorties whenever massive tsunamis approached the coastlines. Joko knew this separation pained his wife, particularly as it would cut into his precious days in port. He reminded Gemi, yet again, that ships needed to be at sea when superstorms lashed the nation's islands. "If we stay at anchor, the storms can smash us against the piers. If the ships are at sea, we can steer away from them and ride out the big waves." Joko arched an eyebrow. His wife knew this protocol. They'd both learned it as plebe midshipmen, though his wife had left the navy years ago.

Gemi sat quietly, looking unconvinced as she held their baby daughter, Citra. In Indonesian, *Gemi* means modest or unassuming. But Gemi had never been either. When they discovered Citra was on her way, Gemi had crammed a three-year advanced degree in engineering and artificial intelligence into two years. Parenthood had proven an unexpected joy to them both. Their child was happy and loud. They loved their home in the port of Banda Aceh. Recently, Joko had started talking about what would come after the navy. Watching his wife and child, a reliable sense of calm would settle over him. The only feeling that came close was being at sea.

After graduating from the naval academy in East Java, the Akademi Angkatan Laut, Joko and Gemi married. The doors of Indonesian society were swinging open for them. They decided on different paths. Gemi declined an officer's commission and took a job in the tech sector, an option the Indonesian government offered to its very best engineers from the academy. She soon found herself at the national physics laboratory, leveraging AI to reverse the environmental damage inflicted on the growing uninhabitable band around the center of the planet. This was desperate work, given the rise in atmospheric temperature, the prevalence of superstorms, and the drastic and unpredictable changes in sea levels.

For Joko, the sea became a second home. The beauty of an evening sunset. The moon rising over rippled water. Languid days when his ship rocked gently on a calm ocean. But he also knew what the sea was capable of . . . storms that stretched thousands of kilometers across the superheated Indian Ocean . . . immense and unstoppable tsunamis spitting up from his home waters.

The ocean could swallow individuals . . . ships . . . cities . . . even nations.

When a typhoon took aim at his ship, he could sail out of its path.

But Gemi and Citra didn't have that ability. Each year seemed to bring bigger and more lethal storm systems. Gemi's parents and siblings lived near the base at Banda Aceh. Forecasters predicted that this latest storm would be worse than all the others. Still, Gemi refused to accept one of the few seats on a government flight to the capital in Nusantara. The family would ride out the storm together in one of the designated government shelters on higher ground, just like they'd done with all the others.

The authorities didn't have a name for this storm. They had stopped naming them. There were simply too many. The government now numbered a storm and appended that number to the month and year it became large enough to track. So, on an August morning in 2074, as Joko stumbled out of his bunk on the destroyer *Sumatra* and headed up to the bridge to take the morning watch, he mumbled to himself the number of the storm system nearing Banda Aceh.

At 0400, he said the words "I relieve you, sir" to the outgoing watch officer, then faced east to observe the first faint traces of a sunrise appear on the far horizon. He asked the quartermaster for the latest tracking information on the storm they were avoiding, 2074-08-36. He considered its massive, oblong form on the satellite feeds: it was the largest he'd tracked in his four years of sea duty, nearly nineteen hundred kilometers across at its widest. Joko trusted that Gemi and Citra had gotten to the shelters by now. At first glance, it looked as if the storm would deliver the city only a glancing blow.

He lifted his head and again looked east. The sun's black rim was breaking over what remained of the horizon when, suddenly, the sky turned the deepest shade of red he had ever seen. A dark, malignant red. Every sailor on the bridge faced the breaking sun while Joko recited the old seagoing rhyme, "Red sky at morning, sailor take warning."

He turned from the bridge wing window and glanced down at the track of the storm. It had changed course, its energy shifting and violently compressing. It was headed straight at Banda Aceh.

1

The Armada

23:47 Nov 09, 2084 (-5 GMT)
New Orlando

The skiff passed over a black sheet of water. The moon was down. Stars appeared as tiny pinpricks overhead. Julia Hunt listened for the shore . . . a stray voice, animal sounds, a car's engine. Nothing yet. She sat in the bow, a cracked chem stick casting a pale glow on the paper map spread across her lap, one of a handful of old documents she'd requested from her office at UN headquarters. She compared it with the up-to-date hologram produced by the implanted visi-chip in her left wrist. They didn't match at all.

Old Florida appeared on the paper map like a welcoming arm reaching out into the Gulf. A terrible season of storms two decades ago had eradicated the coast, turning that arm into a stump after years of rising sea levels. Julia had marked the line of amputation with red pencil. The new coast extended in a diagonal from Daytona

Beach in the east, bisecting Old Orlando, and then on to St. Petersburg in the west. She had spent little time in Florida, but she understood the anger and heartbreak of native Floridians as so much of their beloved peninsula vanished beneath the waves.

Julia had set out from Greenland less than twenty-four hours earlier. She'd left her office in a rush, with hardly time to pack a bag. An unmarked Brazilian transport had picked her up at an FBO outside of Nuuk, flown her south across Greenland's coast, and delivered her onto the carrier deck of a multinational flotilla gathered just outside the Gulf of Mexico. The flotilla's commodore, an Indonesian captain named Joko, had gone over the message Julia was tasked to deliver as envoy. Not long after dark she had departed his flagship on the skiff with a pilot and four-man security detail of Indonesian Marines. Now, many hours later, she wondered if they'd ever find the coast and their rendezvous.

Without warning, the pilot threw the rudder violently starboard. Julia toppled to the deck. The twin outboard motors reversed, churning up the water. Julia caught a heavy whiff of diesel as she stood. As a citizen of a Consortium member nation, she hadn't smelled those fumes in years.

The pilot pointed overhead, gesturing for her to duck.

The skiff passed slowly beneath a steel scaffold arching out of the water. The pilot issued another sharp order. A Marine scuttled up to the bow, nudging Julia to the side. He held a high-powered flashlight. Its beam washed over a tangle of these scaffolds. It was an old roller coaster. Julia glanced once more at her map. She now realized exactly where they were. She placed a red X on what had once been Disney

World. She recalled a childhood trip with her adoptive mother after the war as their skiff made wakeless progress through the wreckage.

The Marine shut off his light and climbed back to the stern as the amusement park passed behind them. The pilot throttled the engines and they hurried toward the coast, a darker band of darkness growing on the horizon.

The pilot idled their engine at a hundred meters out. The current drew them silently onto the beach. Julia could hear the waves lap against the sand as their flat-bottomed hull scraped onto the shore. She leaped over the gunwale, landing thigh deep in the water. The four Marines followed, their rifles tilted at the ready. The rendezvous was less than a mile away, at an abandoned airstrip.

Standing in the Indonesian commodore's stateroom earlier that evening, Julia had asked for more details on the rendezvous, the name of who she'd meet, their description, anything really. But the commodore only repeated the little he knew. Ever since Independence, the Floridians had proven notoriously difficult to work with, uncooperative at best and hostile at worst. Her instructions were to head to a nearby airstrip and wait. An envoy would arrive sometime before first light.

Sand coated Julia's boots as she crossed the beach. Her salt-water-wet trousers clung to her legs as she hurried onto the dirt track that led to the airstrip. The summer before, she'd turned sixty and had already served three years at the UN as the Special Representative for the Future of the Planet. She thought of herself as an environmental scientist first and a diplomat second. She had only this year placed a down payment on a farmstead east of Sarqaq, in Greenland's wine country, only ninety minutes by gravi-train from her condo in Nuuk. Before this assignment, the chapter of her life when she'd been Major Julia Hunt, US Marine Corps, had felt long behind her. But here she was, sandy and soaking wet, marching down a dirt road. She glanced at her watch: a little before midnight, November 9. Tomorrow, November 10, would be the US Marine Corps's 309th birthday.

The dirt road opened onto a clearing dominated by a rough-hewn airstrip. Gutted planes rotted against the black tree line. Julia's four-man escort fanned out across the runway. Using their low-light sensors, they swept the abandoned control tower and waved for Julia to join them. The wait wasn't long. A jet engine whined overhead, rattling the windowpanes in the tower. An old Chinese J-19 flew a single low pass, then it flared up, its engines autorotating as it began its vertical descent. Its landing gear touched down on the airstrip as gingerly as a teacup clinking against a saucer.

When the canopy hinged open, the pilot grunted, shifting his weight around with some effort. He hoisted himself up from his cockpit. Once he'd come to standing, he tottered back and forth, arching his back, as if trying to relieve some unrelievable ache. He removed his oxygen mask to reveal a mustache, ample as a dragoon's and white as a bank of fresh snow. He took off his helmet and his thick, silver hair fell to his collar. He shouted toward the control tower, "You in there, Dr. Hunt?"

Julia could make out the markings of the Floridian Confederation on the jet's gray fuselage. The pilot wore a flag patch on his shoulder with the St. Andrew's cross, its red diagonal bars embroidered on a white background. As Julia approached, he introduced himself: Colonel Mark Dundee, Floridian Air Corps. He didn't bother to climb down from the cockpit.

"I'm here to see . . ."

"I know who you're here to see," he said. "And I'm here to take you to see him." Colonel Dundee gestured to the back seat of his plane. "Hop in."

02:17 Nov 10, 2084 (-5 GMT)
Gulf of Mexico, West Florida Shelf

Commodore Joko sat on the bridge of his flagship, the *Banda Aceh*, waiting for news. When the Marines reported that Julia Hunt had made contact with the Floridians, Joko asked about the composition of their delegation. They didn't know. A single plane had landed on the airstrip—a J-19. The pilot had taken Dr. Hunt with him. It had all happened very fast.

Joko exploded. "What do you mean, taken her with him?"

The Floridian pilot had flown her to a different meeting site, and the Marines didn't know where. They had protested . . . they had advised Dr. Hunt against leaving . . . but she hadn't listened. The pilot, a colonel, had assured them that he was taking her to a second location for security purposes. He would return her to this airfield, and then they could return to their flotilla.

Joko took one long, deep breath followed by two short ones, a technique Gemi had taught him. His anger, like a clenched fist in his chest, eased its grip. They had a mission. Yelling at the Marines would do no good.

Joko thought about the nineteen enormous nuclear-powered ships under his command, three six-ship strike groups. Each one had dozens of strike vessels, almost all unmanned, which constituted the flotilla's combat power. He liked to think of his flotilla as an armada, an ancient word, a grand word, one that conjured invasion fleets from prior centuries. Each of the three strike groups fell under the command of an officer from one of the three largest Reparationist nations, the R3: Brazil, Indonesia, and Nigeria.

Joko's flagship was the only purely amphibious vessel in his armada, designed to place his Indonesian Marines or Brazilian Naval Commandos ashore. He hated that he was stuck on the slow-moving amphib. He craved the freedom and maneuverability of a destroyer or frigate. But he was the commodore, and the amphib possessed the most advanced technical suite for command and control.

Joko ordered the Marines to maintain continuous communication. He strode across the bridge to examine a holographic chart projecting from his work console. His three strike groups were fanned out in a line of battle at the edge of what the Floridians considered their territorial waters, an economic exclusion zone extending two hundred miles from the shoreline.

"Are Captain Duarte's and Gambo's ships holding position?" Joko asked.

The deck officer, a newly arrived ensign, confirmed that all ships were no closer than twelve nautical miles south of what had once been Key West. By anyone's definition their flotilla remained in international waters. If the favorable weather held, Joko calculated they could be positioned in their ops box by tomorrow night, so long as Julia Hunt received the assurances they were looking for from the Floridians.

"Think we'll sail north tomorrow, sir?" the ensign asked.

Joko made a slight affirmative grunt. "We'll have to see." He suddenly noticed how young the ensign was. "When did you graduate the academy"—he glanced at the ensign's name tag—"Mr. Sinaga?"

"Half our class didn't finish, sir. No graduation."

Historically, wars had forced early academy graduations, but these days storms did, as the navy rushed officers into the service to deal with one environmental crisis after the next. Joko now recalled that he'd seen the ensign's name before, on a roster of new arrivals. The ensign's maternal uncle was a general, the chief of staff of the National Armed Forces. Joko appreciated that this young man had joined the navy from an army family, cutting against the grain.

"One of my first assignments was on an amphib," Joko said to the ensign sympathetically. "You'll have your turn on a destroyer or frigate soon enough."

"I'm in no rush, sir. I like it here."

Given the armada's mission, service on the *Banda Aceh* did have a symbolic resonance. A super typhoon had wiped out the Sumatran port city a decade ago, killing almost two million people. No one could've imagined when they'd laid down the hull of this ship that it would outlast its namesake. Poor equatorial nations like his own had paid a hefty price for the environmental excesses of far wealthier countries. The Consortium nations had a debt to pay. They could choose to pay it in blood or in land. This armada would present them with that choice.

12:30 Nov 10, 2084 (+8 GMT)
China World Trade Center Tower VI

Jake Shriver had bought the entire 152nd floor. It was quite a bargain, he told his guest as they ate. Between bites of lobster roll—flown in from Cape Cod—he explained that the most expensive real estate in the building was between the 70th and 95th floors. "Once you get above that," Shriver said, "you've got the wind to contend with. Look there." He pointed to his glass. The water inside pitched slightly from side to side. "It's like being on a ship. Most people prefer to sit a few hundred or a thousand feet above the earth while having the sensation that they're on solid ground. But if I'm going to be up here, I want to feel things moving around. Know what I mean?" He bent forward and took another bite of his roll.

His lunch partner, Zhu De, was a new acquaintance. Shriver's old contact in the Guoanbu, Zhao Jin, had retired the year before after a thirty-year career in Chinese intelligence. This new fellow seemed a joyless sort. He wore rimless glasses with small lenses the size of coins. He hadn't touched his lobster roll.

A well-worn leather attaché case leaned against the leg of Zhu De's chair. A long, uncomfortable silence provoked Shriver to ask, "What do you have in there?"

"Signals intercepts. Highly classified." Zhu De pulled out a tablet, turning it over in his manicured hands, before passing it across the table. "Two days old."

Shriver quickly glanced up from the screen. "What's a flotilla from the R3 doing in the Gulf of Mexico? Hard as those countries have been hit, you'd think they'd spend on rebuilding instead of pouring their limited resources back into defense."

Zhu De gestured for him to keep reading. The signals intercept was an encrypted call the adjutant general of the Floridian Defense Militia had placed to his counterpart, the chairman of the Joint Chiefs of Staff in the United States:

CJCS: What's so urgent, Lucius? I'm in the middle of lunch.

AGFDM: An R3 flotilla has arrived in our territorial waters.

CJCS: Those aren't your territorial waters. How many times do we have to go over this? Old Florida no longer exists. Not one international body recognizes the waters above Old Florida as your "territorial" waters . . .

AGFDM: The R3 say that if we allow them to operate safely from our territorial waters, they'll recognize them as our waters.

CJCS: Operate? To do what?

AGFDM: We're not sure. But we'd be willing to work with the United States to expel the R3 from those waters if given the proper incentives . . . otherwise, we'll have to consider our options.

Raw technical and human intelligence gathered by the CIA, NSA, and NGA, had already led analysts to conclude that this flotilla was an empty threat, a show of force designed to open new streams of humanitarian funding, which the R3 would then siphon off and further misspend on their militaries. The chairman's response was the last line on the transcript: *Until you can show us this threat is real, there's nothing we can do.*

Shriver returned the transcript. "Sounds like the Americans are not taking this very seriously," Zhu De said. Whenever Shriver was being asked to do something because of his Chinese heritage, that person always referred to Americans as "*the* Americans," implying that Jake Shriver was Chinese. But whenever Shriver asked anyone Chinese—particularly those in the Guoanbu—to do something on *his* behalf, he found himself referred to as "*you* Americans." Tiresome as it was, Shriver was adept at this code-switching; he'd built his livelihood on it.

Shriver leaned back in his chair and crossed his arms over his chest. "So what can I do for you?" But he didn't need to ask. A decade ago, while a twenty-year-old wunderkind at Harvard Law, he'd founded the East-West Center, whose mission of "climate citizenship through cross-cultural dialogue" had aligned with the establishment of the Consortium in his two motherlands: China and the United States. His multinational funders paid the bills for this posh office in Beijing and for three others like it in Washington, Stockholm, and Nuuk, where UN headquarters had relocated a decade before, after a superstorm had left the old headquarters in New Delhi permanently submerged beneath the flooded banks of the Ganges. Shriver served as a go-between for Beijing and Washington, the two tentpoles of the Consortium. His diplomatic specialty was crisis management.

"Land reparations or war," Zhu De explained. "The Brazilians, Indonesians, and Nigerians plan to deliver that ultimatum to the United States. You submitted a travel authorization for a trip to Washington, correct . . . ? You're headed there tomorrow?"

Like any citizen of a Consortium nation, Jake was obligated to request a waiver for the trip, as the orbital flight exceeded his monthly half-ton carbon allowance. But being an asset of the Guoanbu had its privileges. The rules were only selectively applied to him. "I'll be there through the week."

"I've set a couple of meetings for you," Zhu De said. "I'm hoping you might deliver a simple message to our American friends."

"What's that?"

"Handle this armada. Or we'll have to."

Jake nodded.

Zhu De began to pack up his things. Jake noted that he hadn't touched his lunch. Zhu De glanced at his sandwich skeptically. "C'mon," said Jake. "At least try it. We burned two hundred kilos of carbon to fly in that lobster roll and put it on your plate."

Zhu De apologized, but under no circumstances would he be having a bite. This extravagant waste wasn't his fault. Had Jake bothered to ask, he would've learned that Zhu De was a vegetarian.

02:17 Nov 10, 2084 (-5 GMT)
Camp DeSantis

Flying at night down here was tricky, Colonel Dundee explained to Dr. Hunt over the cockpit's intercom. The Floridians had built a comms shield to protect them from the Consortium's notorious regime of surveillance and social control. This comms shield—a vast network of frequency disruptors like those deployed in North Korea for decades but vastly enhanced by Chinese and American quantum computing—was one of the few infrastructure projects passed unanimously by the fractious Confederation legislature. It kept others out with incredible efficacy, but it forced pilots to rely on more old-fashioned navigation aids. She'd been calling him Colonel Dundee until she asked what branch of the service he'd learned to fly in. "I was a Marine, like you," he said. Then he told her to call him Tick-Tock.

"Why TikTok? You like those retro little videos?"

"No . . . Tick-Tock, the American way, keeping the *c*'s. That's the crocodile that bit off Captain Hook's hand." He'd earned the call sign in his first squadron, being a native Floridian. "Also, even a broken clock is right twice a day." Had Dr. Hunt asked about that squadron, VMFA-323, the Death Rattlers, she would've heard an earful, particularly about Tick-Tock's first commanding officer, Major Chris "Wedge" Mitchell. It was Wedge who'd given Tick-Tock his call sign. That old Marine pilot would've loved flying down here, particularly under the comms shield. No satellite data. No cell phones. Nothing to navigate from that wasn't a paper map, and no way to talk that wasn't a line-of-sight radio. "Yep," said Tick-Tock as he flared his J-19 back on final approach. "It's a throwback. A simpler way of flying."

The engines revved and the aircraft swooped up like a child flung high in a swing. Tick-Tock glanced out the side of his cockpit. He'd landed here countless times so could recognize the gentle contours of what had once been the golf course's ninth hole, now a concrete V/STOL landing pad. Julia came up on the intercom as he was counting off the last hundred feet.

"I was following our route," she said. "I've got us at The Villages."

"Fifteen feet . . . ten . . . five . . . touchdown . . ." She'd caught Tick-Tock's final coordination with the ground crew, who rushed out to place a set of yellow chocks around the landing gear. He popped the cockpit open and took his helmet off before he turned around and answered her. "You've got the right spot." He gestured out to the darkness, at the vague silhouette of low-slung retirement bungalows in the distance. "It's Camp DeSantis now. That map of yours must be outdated."

Tick-Tock walked Hunt across the airfield to a dimly lit hangar. A pair of halogen bulbs hung suspended by wires over a conference table in the back. A potbellied man sat at its head, slowly shelling peanuts with his thick fingers. His wild tangle of jet-black curls fell to his neck. He had so little gray, she wondered if he dyed his hair. He wore the green-on-green camouflage utility uniform of revolutionaries the world over. His crimson beret rested on the table.

Brigadier Lucius Clay was a general officer, so the banding of his beret wasn't leather but crocodile. Officers like Tick-Tock, who had served careers in the US military, remained under a degree of suspicion by the Floridian Confederation, even a decade after Independence. Tick-Tock would likely top out as a colonel, a fact he didn't resent. Clay and amateurs like him needed Tick-Tock. He and the other professionals would always maintain a seat at the table.

"It ain't every day we get a UN envoy around here." Clay leaned back in his chair, crossing his legs at the ankles in front of him, revealing his python-skin cowboy boots. Tick-Tock noticed Hunt noticing the boots. He had seen Clay strike this pose before, on occasions when emissaries from the Consortium traveled south. Clay would convince Hunt that she was dealing with an inferior, a country bumpkin, lulling her into a false sense of confidence. "You gonna tell me why they sent you?"

"Do you mind?" asked Hunt, reaching for the peanuts. Clay nodded, and she picked a few out and crushed their shells between her strong fingers. "As Special Representative for the Future of the Planet, I'm here as a neutral party."

"A neutral party to what?" Clay started to laugh. He glanced at Tick-Tock, who smiled glumly. Clay added, "That's some fancy name: *Special Representative for the Future of the Planet* . . . You get business cards with that? Maybe a fancy hat?"

Hunt reached into her jacket pocket and removed an old-fashioned business card, which she flung across the table. "Sorry, no hat."

"Well, I'll be damned," said Clay. He pinched the card's corner and ran his fingers over its embossed face. "Been a minute since I seen one of those."

"You don't have a lot of time, Mr. Clay." Tick-Tock noticed she didn't use his rank. "Brazilian, Indonesian, and Nigerian warships plan to enter waters that your government claims are territorial. If you fire on those ships, the UN will interpret it as an act of aggression because we believe they have a right to navigate the international waters over Old Florida."

"So you're here on behalf of the Reparationist armada?"

"Don't play dumb," said Hunt. "You know the figures. Last year, humans burned approximately one hundred gigatons of carbon. Our best scientists estimate that every three hundred gigatons we burn pushes up the planet's average temperature by a single degree. Each degree increase in temperature expands the uninhabitable band by five hundred miles. Do the math. Carbon-rationing measures put in place by the Consortium have helped some, but not enough. Do you know what really wouldn't help? A war. That's what I'm here to prevent."

"Is that so?" said Clay, cracking a peanut shell between his knuckles.

03:40 Nov 10, 2084 (-5 GMT)
Gulf of Mexico, West Florida Shelf

This was taking too long.

"Mr. Sinaga, anything from Dr. Hunt and the Marines?"

"Nothing, sir."

How long was he supposed to sit out here with his ships circling? Joko didn't ask the question out loud, but it's what the entire armada was wondering. His destroyers, frigates, and cruisers bristled with weapons. Guided missiles idled in their silos. Large drones with stubby wings sat racked on their launch slides. Smaller drones the size of dinner plates swarmed in their hives. Nigeria, Brazil, and Indonesia had spent their national wealth on these weapons. And now it was time—*use it or lose it.*

All this military power could reach the Eastern Seaboard. Joko's armada didn't technically need to sail into what the Floridians called their *territorial waters.* Yes, moving farther north would heighten the accuracy of the flotilla's missile systems, lessening civilian casualties around the military and government installations on their target list. But Joko knew that the reason to fire his missiles from Floridian waters was a political one. It would send a powerful message to the United States and other Consortium members: in any conflict between the Reparationist nations and the Consortium, the rest of the world couldn't be relied on for neutrality.

None of the Reparationists actually wanted a war. What they wanted was a new home. The Consortium, led by China and the US, had closed themselves off to the rest of the world through trade regulations, through immigration freezes, through carbon rationing. They had closed themselves off at the very moment when the world needed its leading nations to remain open. Joko stared out from the bridge, into the impenetrable night. He could feel the substantial combat power of his armada, like a spring coiled tight. Its destructive potential could be released with the slightest gesture. The idea of violence filled him with despair. Yet he knew that with each passing year, the combat capability of the Reparationist nations diminished as their militaries were starved of resources.

Sinaga brought him a coffee. "What year did you finish school, sir?"

"I graduated the academy in 2060, but I didn't just go there." Joko took a sip of coffee and looked out to sea. "Perhaps you heard about my family . . . after losing them, the navy wanted to help me. They gave me a chance to do graduate school, to try to get myself together. So I went to Bandung, to the Institute of Technology."

"That's a good school. What did you study?"

"Environmental science," said Joko. "My thesis was on atmospheric sulfates, their potential as a carbon neutralizer, and what were then-cutting-edge theories of high-altitude dispersal as a method to reduce global temperatures." Joko and Sinaga continued to gaze out of the bridge windows, looking at the armada lingering in the darkness. "I never thought any of this would be necessary. Back then I thought . . ."

But Joko stopped. He shouldn't unburden himself this way to a subordinate. An image of his family before the storm flashed into his memory . . . Gemi laughing while making their bed the morning he left on his final sortie . . . Citra crawling on the floor . . . Open windows . . . A gust of wind blowing in the curtains . . . His wife gathering those curtains and latching the windows shut . . . Him reminding Gemi that in a storm a ship free on the ocean was safer than a ship anchored in port.

His grief counselor had encouraged him to track these memory flashes. To write down the dates they occurred and place them on a graph. Over time, she explained, they would occur less frequently, and he would be able to chart his emotional recovery. Eventually, these episodes would hardly occur at all, and when memories of his family returned to him, they might elicit a smile instead of a tear. He'd plotted the episodes for a single year. Then a second. And finally, a third. The memory flashes didn't spread out. They contracted. He needed to do something, anything, to reverse this trend. He remembered after the storm, the arrival of the sailors. They'd rescued entire families. He wanted to be one of the rescuers, so he'd finished his studies and continued to serve in the navy. If he had failed to protect his own family, maybe he could learn to protect someone else's.

But he wouldn't say any of this to Ensign Sinaga. Instead, he asked him to check on the Marines, to see if there was any update from Dr. Hunt. Sinaga crossed the bridge. A petty officer passed him the radio's handset, but before he could transmit a message, the Marines ashore were already transmitting one of their own. "*Banda Aceh, Banda Aceh*, this is shore party, over."

"Roger, shore party, this is *Banda Aceh*," said Sinaga. "Send your traffic."

"Contact re-established with Dr. Hunt," said the Marines. "She is en route back to our position. Please advise on retrograde."

Ensign Sinaga glanced at Commodore Joko.

"Tell the Marines to come back the minute they have her."

14:02 Nov 10, 2084 (+8 GMT)
China World Trade Center Tower VI

After Zhu De left, Jake Shriver placed two phone calls. The first was to his mother, Lily Bao, at her home in the northern woodlands of Vermont. The call rang itself out. They seldom spoke. He imagined her on a walk with the dog, weaving between the birch trees, off the grid and free.

It amazed him that his mother had wound up living this way, in near total seclusion. Lily Bao wasn't a native-born American, but her love for the United States had started early. Her father had served in the Chinese navy and was stationed several times in the US. When war came between the US and China, in 2034, she'd only been a girl. Her father, by then a rear admiral in command of a carrier battle group, was scapegoated for a military defeat, and was ultimately executed by the Politburo Standing Committee. Exiled from China, Lily and her mother had sought refuge in the US. Her mother eventually found work as a maid at a low-rent motel on the outskirts of Newport. For the rest of Lily's life, she would make the bed when she stayed in a hotel.

Lily's academic gifts led to a scholarship at Princeton. This led to a two-year stint working eighteen-hour days at Barclays in Manhattan, on the deal side. Then admittance to Harvard Business School. An associate position at the Carlyle Group followed graduation. Given Lily's talents, success came to feel like a formula, an afterthought. Of course she would come out on top. This sense of control, of inevitability, came to an end when she began an affair with Jake's father, a talented politician. This was during a tumultuous period in the mid-2050s, when the US had been on the brink of civil war. They eventually married, and Jake had come along, and they bought the place in Vermont. But business soon called again. An opportunity arose for Lily to step onto the partner track at the Tandava Group. With some hesitation, she took it, relocating her family to New Delhi. Her rise at Tandava was meteoric, aided by a personal relationship with Ashni Chowdhury, the daughter of the founder. Within a couple of years, every major deal at the firm had to go through the investment committee formally, but would always be judged "on the side" by Lily Bao. The Chowdhury family relied on her judgment and advice.

When the firm needed a new CEO in the late 2060s, the choice was obvious. Lily Bao went on to head Tandava for over a decade. Her commitment was total, and her son grew to resent her frequent absences. The day her husband died after a long illness, she'd been away. Her son had called the ambulance on his own.

By the time Lily Bao retired from Tandava, she was a billionaire many times over. She returned to the property in Vermont, alone, and she resumed her life. She kept up with the current crop of partners at Tandava. The younger generation would call her for advice and counsel about all topics except one: Lily avoided domestic politics. "I had my fill of that in the fifties, with my late husband," she would say.

Jake waited a couple of minutes and phoned his mother again. She answered on the sixth ring. They exchanged pleasantries, then

Jake told her that Zhu De wanted him to deliver a message to Washington.

"Which is what?" she asked.

"That if the Americans don't deal with this armada, the Chinese will."

"I wish Zhao Jin was still around," she said. "And your father too . . ."

Jake needed her focused. "I'm leaving for Washington this evening. If you've got any ideas, I'd welcome them. Otherwise, I'll call you when I'm back."

"The Reparationists aren't wrong," his mother said. "The Consortium has put them in an impossible position. If we won't give the R3 land, and if they can't immigrate to the Consortium, then what can we give them? The Consortium has to give them something."

"And what's that?"

"*Hope*," his mother said.

03:34 Nov 10, 2084 (-5 GMT)
Camp DeSantis

Tick-Tock was surprised. This is what he told Julia Hunt as they waited for the ground crew to finish refueling his J-19. Brigadier Clay and his security detail had just left in a cloud of dust as their convoy of three extended cab F-150s sped north, toward Tallahassee.

"What is it that surprised you?" Hunt asked.

Tick-Tock had expected Clay to grant the armada permission to transit their territorial waters, but he hadn't expected the Floridians to allow the armada to launch their strike on the United States *from* Florida's territorial waters, making any attack against the armada an attack against the sovereignty of the Floridian Confederation. "I didn't think Clay would get us directly involved."

It had surprised Julia too. "I was sent here to avert a war. Now I'm supposed to deliver a message to Commodore Joko that the Floridians are allying themselves with the R3. This puts me in an awkward position."

"It's not your job to deliver that message to the commodore." Tick-Tock could hear the hollow whine of a second J-19 as it fired its engines. "I'll be handling that for you."

The second part of Clay's message had also come as a surprise. Tick-Tock would be heading back to the *Banda Aceh* with Dr. Hunt to serve as a liaison for the Floridians, at least for the duration of the armada's attack against the Americans. The crew of the second J-19 would be flying Tick-Tock's plane home after he and Dr. Hunt linked up with the Indonesian Marines.

While they waited for the aircraft, Tick-Tock pulled a snack from his pocket. He unwrapped the plastic off a cream-filled dark chocolate cake sandwich. "What's that?" Hunt asked.

"We've got cases of them in that hangar." Tick-Tock held up the wrapper: *Devil Dogs*. "Take the other half."

"How old are those?"

"They're full of preservatives. They've got no expiration date . . . kinda like us." He smiled with his mouth full. "You know what? It's November 10 . . . Happy 309th birthday, Marine."

THE ARMADA

05:56 Nov 10, 2084 (-5 GMT)
Gulf of Mexico, West Florida Shelf

Commodore Joko stood on the fantail of the *Banda Aceh*, the Florida air blowing in his face, hair-dryer hot even in November. Dawn brought definition to the horizon. Port and starboard, the gray upswept broadsides of his armada resembled a distant city standing indistinct against the water. Their line of battle traced the border between international waters and those territorial waters claimed by the Floridian Confederation. Joko raised his binoculars and scanned the shore, searching again for the skiff. This time he found it, its bullet-shaped hull smacking against the ocean's warp as it sprinted toward his flagship's cavernous well deck.

Joko handed his binoculars to Ensign Sinaga, who'd come down to the fantail from his watch. "When Dr. Hunt arrives, send her directly to my stateroom."

Sinaga nodded briskly, raised the binoculars, and tracked the skiff's progress.

When Joko entered his stateroom, he was pleased to find that the steward had laid out a full breakfast of juice, fruit, sweet porridge, avocado, and poached eggs. Joko would stick to his usual tea and a single piece of toast, but he was keen to impress on Dr. Hunt his appreciation for her mission. It was important for the nations of the armada to remain in the good graces of the UN. The Reparationist nations were the victims, even if the Consortium would paint them as the aggressors here.

There was a knock at the door. “Enter,” said Joko. He was surprised to see behind Dr. Hunt an older man, quite tall, with a thick white mustache and swoop of gray hair. He wore a green flight suit Velcroed with Floridian shoulder patches. The top of his head skimmed the ceiling. Joko wondered how he fit into his aircraft.

Dr. Hunt and the pilot were wet, their clothes damp with sea spray. They trudged sand into his stateroom. The pilot introduced himself as “Colonel Dundee, Floridian Air Corps,” but insisted that Joko call him Tick-Tock.

“Colonel Tick-Tock,” Joko began. “We weren’t expecting—”

“It’s just Tick-Tock, no need for formality.”

Joko glanced at Dr. Hunt. “Very well, Tick-Tock, we weren’t expecting you, but you’re most welcome here.” Then Joko turned to Dr. Hunt, addressing her directly. “Thank you for conveying our message to the Floridians so *effectively*.” He pressed down on the last word hard.

Tick-Tock was making himself comfortable. He had reclined in his seat and was sipping tea from a bulb-shaped glass and munching a papaya spear taken from the fruit plate. He spooned up a mouthful of sweet porridge, made a face, and returned his attention to Commodore Joko, who had just asked Hunt whether his entire armada would be free to transit the waters over Old Florida. Tick-Tock interrupted them. “We’ll do you one better, sir,” he said with a grand wave of his hand. “We’ll let you operate *in* our waters, so long as you acknowledge that they are in fact *our waters*, not international waters.”

Tick-Tock reached in his pocket and pulled out another black cake wrapped in plastic. "Let me guess," he said, taking a first bite, "you've got an ops box somewhere off the Georgia coast, maybe around Savannah, basically as far north as you can get. You're planning to deliver your ultimatum to Washington—demands for territory, open immigration, economic subsidies, exemptions to per capita carbon emission guidelines set forward in the Nuuk Accords—basically a bunch of stuff they'll never agree to. Then you'll wait a few hours, maybe a day . . . and *bam!* You launch your attack. They'll come after you, of course, and with everything they've got. But you'll be back in our territorial waters, sailing south. You're betting they won't hit you there, not with us on their border . . . that's the plan, right?"

Joko crossed his arms over his chest. "Your point?"

"Do the whole thing from our waters," said Tick-Tock. "Brigadier Clay has convinced the Confederation legislature that the benefits outweigh the risks to us."

"The benefits being . . . ?" asked Joko.

"That Nigeria, Indonesia, Brazil, the whole R3, formally recognize the waters above Old Florida as *our* territorial waters. You ever spent any time in my country, Commodore?"

Joko shook his head.

"I've been to yours, but not since '74." Tick-Tock only had to mention the year of the storm to evoke its catastrophic legacy. "But I'd bet you that my home is about as bad off as yours. Your people are demanding reparations for all that was taken from them, a chance to start over. To do that you need habitable land, a resource hoarded by the Consortium. We Floridians need that same chance to rebuild, though what we need isn't land, it's to extract the natural resources below the water—*our waters.* We need Old Florida. We need the world to concede that what once was ours is still ours."

16:34 Nov 11, 2084 (-3 GMT)
Brasília

Commodore Joko apologized. He couldn't fly Dr. Hunt north as she'd requested. The risk of an altercation with the Consortium air forces was too high, and flight back to Nuuk would take her close to their air space. When the armada launched its strike on the Americans, Joko couldn't have a UN envoy aboard his flagship. His only alternative was to have a Brazilian transport from Captain Duarte's strike group fly her south, to the international airport in Brasília. Joko assured Hunt that she'd be able to return home safely before long.

Joko's vague time horizon of "before long" concerned Hunt. As her transport descended toward the airport, she had the sinking feeling that even though she'd prevented an altercation between the Reparationists and the Floridians, her mission had been an abject failure. She had inadvertently brokered a dangerous alliance. Did Joko and Tick-Tock and the governments they represented really believe that the Consortium would respond well to an ultimatum?

Joko had explained to Hunt the armada's catalog of demands. He'd even allowed her to sit in on a final confirmation brief between his command and the ministries of defense in Nusantara, Brasília, and Lagos, as well as their new allies in Tallahassee. This was only hours before she'd left the *Banda Aceh* and Joko sailed north, into an ops box off the coast of Jacksonville where they'd launch their attack.

The armada's demands were simple. They wanted a fraction of the land they'd lost to decades of rising waters and temperatures. The nations guilty of excess were those now preaching carbon austerity, the Consortium nations. Politicians in Beijing, Washington, Ottawa, Paris, and London had all scoffed when presented with a proposed map from the Reparationists, which carved resettlement enclaves into the coasts of Maine and Nova Scotia that extended three hundred miles inland and as far north as Greenland. The Consortium even had the gall to call these enclaves a form of "colonization."

The Reparationists were also demanding that both the UN and the Consortium grant this and any future resettlement enclaves the status of "innovation zones," where new emission reduction technologies could be pioneered in an environment free of the strict emissions standards imposed by the Consortium. This would be particularly important for the Floridians. Their prosperity depended on extracting the three hundred gigatons of fossil carbons below the waters of Old Florida. They needed the energy trapped in their territory to rebuild, and they needed to figure out ways to burn it cleanly—or at least cleanly enough.

This all seemed a tall order to Julia Hunt. Had any nation in history handed over land and natural resources willingly, without bloodshed?

Her flight descended through a patch of clouds into Brasília. A khaki smog hovered over the urban sprawl, a mix of dust and smoke. Lake Paranoá appeared out her window, its shape irregular as a birthmark placed on the city. It was once one of the world's largest reservoirs and used to provide the thirteen million inhabitants of Brasília with fresh water. The reservoir, like the city, had contracted to one-tenth its previous size. Entire favela neighborhoods had sprouted up on the reservoir's banks, which emitted a stagnant, desperate odor.

When Julia Hunt disembarked, she could smell the reservoir, even inside the airport. Its fetid stench had become the smell of the city. The Brazilian authorities hurried her through immigration. As they drove her to a hotel in the airport complex, they asked if she was hungry. Although she hadn't eaten since leaving the *Banda Aceh*, Julia had no appetite. That smell: she couldn't escape it.

17:47 Nov 12, 2084 (-5 GMT)
OPS Box Yankee

Tick-Tock regretted that Julia Hunt needed to leave so soon. A flurry of activity had awaited them both when they'd arrived aboard the *Banda Aceh*, and he'd had no chance for a quiet moment with her. He had wanted to say that he'd known her mother. Admiral Sarah Hunt had commanded the USS *Enterprise* fifty years before, when Tick-Tock had been a wet-behind-the-ears Marine lieutenant in the Death Rattlers. Two-thirds of his squadron hadn't come back from that deployment. Their tussle with the Chinese and Indians, led by their brash squadron commander, had been the largest air-to-air engagement in a generation. There hadn't been many on that scale since.

It wasn't only the connection with Dr. Hunt's mother. There was something undeniably attractive about her . . . the short-cropped hair . . . her athletic build . . . also, they had much in common . . . they were roughly the same age . . . they were both Marines.

Tick-Tock's thoughts lingered on Julia as he stood on the flight deck of the *Banda Aceh.* They were only a few miles off the coast of Jacksonville. He could smell the beach. He could feel the ship come about, so it was facing into the wind and ready to launch aircraft. He wondered if he'd have another chance with her. The fight he was sailing into right now reminded him of the fight he had sailed into fifty years before on the *Enterprise.* Perhaps that explained his urge to tell Julia that he'd served with her mother. It wasn't that he hadn't seen action since. He'd seen too much.

As he walked past the hived drone swarms and missiles racked in their silos, Tick-Tock counted off a career's worth of engagements: he'd slung Sidewinders from the wing of his F-35 during the War of Indian Unification; he'd spotted HIMARS strikes for the Taiwanese during their war of Chinese Secession; and although it had cleaved him into two broken parts, he'd run low-level close air support from a J-19 against his own kind—US Marines—after leaving the Corps to fight alongside the Floridians during the Consortium Wars.

Tick-Tock was no stranger to a fight.

But this one felt different. Because it felt like his first, he suspected that it might also be his last.

02:34 Nov 13, 2084 (-5 GMT)
OPS Box Yankee

Joko lay in his rack, not sleeping. This would be his final chance to get anything approaching a good night's rest for the foreseeable future. But no matter how tired he felt, sleep wouldn't come. That afternoon, he'd participated in a secure metasphere conference. The foreign ministers of Nigeria, Brazil, and Indonesia had attended, as well as the adjutant general of the Floridian Defense Militia, Brigadier Lucius Clay. As his country's senior military officer, Clay reported directly to the legislature, an arrangement akin to George Washington reporting directly to the Continental Congress, as Clay was fond of pointing out. The three Reparationist diplomats all looked the part, their digital avatars dressed in conservative suits and ties. Clay—or at least his avatar—presented as an overweight, cowboy-boot-wearing Che Guevara lookalike.

Joko wasn't seated around the virtual table with the Nigerians, Brazilians, and Indonesians. He lingered with the staffers on seats one row behind. Across the table, the Consortium delegation was led by the American national security advisor, Dr. Eva Boucher, who had only the week before received her appointment from the president after a successful posting as the assistant secretary of defense for Global Resources and Internal Performance, or GRIP, the office that set Pentagon policy on the enforcement of energy consumption at home and abroad.

The Nigerian foreign minister began the meeting cordially. "My congratulations on your new appointment, Dr. Boucher."

"Thank you," she said with a thin smile. "But my name isn't pronounced *boo-shay* . . . My people aren't Creole. We're German. It's pronounced *butcher*."

The man bowed his head and began enumerating their demands.

Dr. Boucher soon interrupted. "I'll save your time and mine by speaking plainly . . ." She said that the United States did not recognize the Floridian Confederation's claims to the waters above Old Florida. This placed the armada in international waters. Boucher then invoked the Monroe Doctrine of 1823. "Intervention in the political affairs of the Americas," she said, as if reading from a script, "will be interpreted as a hostile act by the United States." She didn't wait for a response. Her avatar vanished from the conference. The meeting was over.

Now Joko lay in bed, his mind racing. He still hadn't received his strike orders. He imagined they would arrive in the morning. Like an athlete before a game, he visualized the next day's action, the series of complex moves he would coordinate as his armada arrayed itself in order of battle. That it had come to this, an attack against the United States, felt incomprehensible. He recalled the sailors the US Navy had sent to his home port in 2074 after the storm, the worst disaster since the tsunami of 2004; those sailors had delivered food, water, and medical aid. But Joko also recalled how those same sailors, in order to enforce international emissions standards, had closed any hospital operating off a fossil fuel generator, turning the sick and dying out of their beds.

Joko rolled over. He glanced at his alarm clock on a nearby shelf. The red numerals came into focus . . . a little before three a.m.

The entire ship lurched violently, like when a driver slams on the brakes of a car. His alarm clock flew off its shelf and hit him on the bridge of his nose. His stateroom rattled and filled with the metallic whine of steel ripping in half.

Joko hopped out of his rack. The ship rocked a second time, knocking him over. He heard an explosion from the direction of the bridge. He returned to his feet and leaped into his coveralls and steel-toed boots. He sprinted down the passageway, past sailors who were donning firefighting equipment—flame-retardant hoods and oxygen masks. The ship's intercom boomed, "General quarters, general quarters, this is not a drill . . ." A bell clanged piercingly between alerts. A canopy of acrid smoke unspooled overhead and grew thicker with each step he took toward the bridge. The stream of sailors coming at him also grew thicker. None of them wore firefighting equipment. They appeared dazed, disoriented, as if they didn't quite know which way to their battle stations.

Joko shouted, gesturing for them to travel in the opposite direction to his. He was determined to reach the bridge, to fight his ship, no matter how badly damaged it was. Nearer the blast, auxiliary power failed to light the passageways. Flames from the impact illuminated Joko's path as he drew closer. He choked on the thickening smoke and the deck became slippery. He fell, got up, and fell again. He worried that perhaps the *Banda Aceh* was taking on water. He passed a compartment engulfed in flames and in the flamelight he glimpsed his coveralls. They were slick with a pudding of blood. So was the deck.

A pair of sailors carrying a litter by its handles stumbled toward him. “You can’t go that way,” the first said, not recognizing their commodore in the dim light.

“Who has the bridge watch?” Joko asked.

The second sailor said, “Ensign Sinaga.”

“Where is he?”

The first sailor glanced at the litter.

A deep gash ran from Sinaga’s hairline to his left eye. One arm was blackened, the other missing, as if he’d reached into the flames. Much of his uniform was burned away, but Joko could still read his name tape above his right chest pocket. The eyes were open and rolled back. Sinaga was dead.

Joko grabbed one of the litter’s free handles. “C’mon,” he said to the two sailors. “I know the way back. Let’s get him out of here.”

02:58 Nov 13, 2084 (-5 GMT)
OPS Box Yankee

Tick-Tock had been belowdecks, in the chiefs’ mess. A few of the senior enlisted had invited him to an off-hours poker game. The entire ship had rocked on its axis, but Tick-Tock remained calm and collected, throwing his winning hand of cards on the enormous heap of cash. He left the cash on the table and scrambled to the *Banda Aceh*’s combat control center.

Confusion met him when he arrived. Captains Duarte and Gambo appeared on the video teleconference. One of the Nigerian destroyers had detected what Gambo believed was a hypersonic reconnaissance drone. When the drone approached inside the flotilla's threat envelope, at a little under thirty nautical miles, the destroyer had shot it from the sky with a laser. As it rocketed out of control, it collided with the bridge of the *Banda Aceh*—a one-in-a-million shot.

Duarte disagreed with Gambo. "It wasn't a drone," he insisted. "That was a hypersonic missile. You never should've let it get that close."

The pair continued to bicker. Gambo was defensive. He wouldn't allow Duarte to insinuate that his strike group had made a mistake. Their disagreement on the teleconference was becoming a distraction to the sailors coordinating damage control. Tick-Tock finally intervened. "Enough!" he shouted at the screen. This silenced them. "Was it a missile? . . . Was it a drone? . . ." Tick-Tock's voice was thick with contempt. "I'll tell you what it was: *a golden opportunity*."

Neither Duarte nor Gambo had a chance to reply. A raspy voice from the back of combat control beat them to it. "He's right!"

Commodore Joko stood in the hatch, his face slick with sweat, his uniform filthy with blood, his voice like gravel from the smoke he'd inhaled. But he was here, ready to fight for his ship, and ready to silence the two bickering strike group commanders who threatened to undermine not only his armada, but quite possibly the tenuous alliance between their three nations. "Whether it was a hypersonic drone or missile hardly matters now. We've been attacked. A response is warranted. We are no longer the aggressors."

Joko limped through combat control toward his raised commodore's chair. The sailors hunched over their stations stole concerned looks at him, but his voice was steady, and it remained steady as he issued orders throughout the morning and into the next day. Twice the ship's surgeon tried to attend to him. Joko waved him away. There would be time for that when the *Banda Aceh* wasn't burning. By the afternoon, damage control had contained the fire on the bridge and all personnel had been accounted for. Joko had provided updates on his flotilla's status, which he categorized as "combat ready" to his high command, including General Adil Suharto, commander of the National Armed Forces—who was also Ensign Sinaga's uncle.

Tick-Tock had seen the casualty list. Word spread fast, and he knew about Sinaga and Suharto. Like the rest of the crew—and Joko—he watched the old general learn the news of his nephew's death. Suharto's response was undetectable. He simply told Joko that his orders would be forthcoming. He also suggested Joko move his flag to another ship, given the damage to the command-and-control systems aboard the *Banda Aceh*.

Reluctantly, Joko agreed. Under a different set of circumstances, he might have protested, insisting to Suharto that sufficient repairs could be made to keep him aboard the *Banda Aceh*, one of his navy's finest ships. But Joko wasn't going to argue with a man whose nephew had been killed under his command. Joko would co-locate with Captain Gambo, aboard the five-hundred-thousand-ton super destroyer *Aradu*.

After the call finished, Joko sat slumped in his chair, his chin practically resting on his chest. Tick-Tock stepped beside him. In a small, almost fatherly voice, he whispered, "It's time to get some rest."

Joko's eyebrows rose, though he didn't move his head.

"You look like shit," Tick-Tock added.

With great effort, Joko sat a little straighter. He regarded Tick-Tock with an unfriendly silence. He then informed the watch officer that he'd be in his stateroom.

In the same quiet voice, Tick-Tock said, "I'll make sure they send the ship's surgeon." Joko nodded. He patted Tick-Tock on the arm, as if to say *thank you.*

A wave of exhaustion hit Tick-Tock. The Americans had delivered the armada an opportunity. He couldn't say what orders they'd receive from the Reparationist high command, but he felt certain they would all need their rest to execute them.

Tick-Tock followed Joko out of combat control, toward his own cramped stateroom. He thought he might lie down for a few minutes. But he had one stop to make first. When he arrived at the chiefs' mess, no one was there. On the table, undisturbed, was his hand, an almost unbeatable full house, kings over jacks, sitting atop a huge pile of cash. Tick-Tock recovered his winnings.

16:34 Nov 15, 2084 (-5 GMT)
Eisenhower Executive Office Building

Boucher was running late, and Jake was annoyed.

After passing through security, which included a retinal scan paired with an analysis of biometric data, a staffer had escorted him to the EEOB's broad and high-ceilinged Indian Treaty Room. Inside it was cold; the ornately tiled floor and long walls failed to trap heat. A single desk with two chairs sat in the center, a small island of furniture in an ocean of space. Sitting at the little desk in the big room made Shriver feel small. He couldn't help but wonder if this wasn't all some power play. If so, he resented it.

Too much was at stake for games. Didn't Boucher understand? Shriver knew from Zhu De that her predecessor—a combat-decorated Special Forces general who'd served a full career with a prosthetic leg and missing eye, and who was no snowflake—had lost his job for being "too soft" on the Reparationists. Boucher had a mandate to treat the R3 more firmly, which she apparently intended to uphold. News of the strike on the *Banda Aceh* had surfaced in the media the day before. Details remained spotty. Narratives conflicted. The armada claimed an unprovoked attack. The United States denied this, characterizing the incident as an accident between two navies.

Jake Shriver had been waiting the better part of an hour on Boucher when the heavy, multipaneled mahogany door at the far end of the room creaked open. A young staffer poked his head inside, his postpubescent voice creaking like the door. "Excuse me . . . are you Jake Shriver?"

"Yes, and you are?"

"A member of Dr. Boucher's staff." The young man stepped into the room cradling a briefcase. "Unfortunately, due to a scheduling conflict, she'll need to take this meeting holographically." He unlocked the briefcase and removed a government-modified headsUp, an older model the size of a hockey puck with quantum encryption. An apparition of Boucher projected upward in a cone of light from the headsUp.

"Good morning," she said. "I've got fifteen minutes, so let's get to it."

Boucher sat behind a desk. Shriver recognized the room. She was only a few hundred yards away, in the West Wing. Obviously, Boucher couldn't be bothered to make the walk over.

Shriver offered some preliminary remarks, delivering Zhu De's message. "Our mutual friends in Beijing asked me to convey how important it is for the Consortium that this armada is dealt with. Or else, they will be compelled to—"

Boucher cut him off. "*Or else?* . . . Mr. Shriver, if you've come here to deliver ultimatums from Beijing, I think we're through. Please convey to our Consortium allies that we're more than capable of dealing with this threat. If you don't believe that, just ask the crew of the *Banda Aceh*." Boucher nodded to the staffer, who motioned to shut down the headsUp.

"Wait," said Shriver.

The staffer glanced at Boucher, who nodded, granting Jake a last chance to speak. "What if there's a nonmilitary solution?"

"Like what?" asked Boucher with a heavy dose of skepticism.

Jake outlined several of the Tandava Group's research projects.

"I'm familiar with their work," said Boucher, cutting him short. "I read their quarterly investor reports. We can't innovate our way out of this crisis. The Reparationists don't understand this either. It's not the land they want that poses the biggest problem; it's their determination to use that land to create innovation zones, abandoning the regulations that have thus far prevented a mass extinction event."

"What about the environmental impact of a war?" said Jake. "Have you considered those metrics?"

Boucher was annoyed. "Ten years ago, we were at atmospheric CO2 levels of around 460 ppm. Today those levels have dropped to 412 ppm. Consortium nations have committed to per capita energy rationing of 1,800 watts. Do you know what energy consumption was in the United States before we entered the Consortium? 12,000 watts. We expect to bring this number down to 1,700 watts. Reaching that number is what will save us, not some carbon-reducing Hail Mary pass developed by the Tandava Group."

"War is also a mass extinction event," said Jake.

"Let's hope it doesn't come to that," said Boucher.

Shriver repeated the message Zhu De had sent him to deliver: the United States needed to deal with the Reparationists flotilla if it wanted China to remain out of the western hemisphere—that was all. "And Beijing would appreciate advance notice of any further strikes."

"The incident with the *Banda Aceh* was an accident, a hypersonic reconnaissance drone shot off course." Boucher pinched the bridge of her nose as if she'd said this so many times it was giving her a headache. "But yes, we'll provide advance notice in the future. If it proves necessary."

As Boucher uttered this last word, a hollow siren went off inside the Indian Treaty Room. The siren echoed with a slight lag, as it was also going off in Boucher's office. Her connection cut as she stood from her chair. The staffer she'd sent over opened the door to the hallway. Others were confusedly pouring out of their offices. A panicked voice echoed down the corridor. "To the basement! To the basement!"

Shriver glanced over his shoulder, at the eastward-facing window.

Outside, earth fountained up in a pillar, followed by a terrific crash.

Shriver jerked backward, as if he'd touched a hot stove. There was a flash. The window exploded, showering him with glass. Then everything went dark.

2

Homage to Brasília

03:10 Nov 16, 2084 (-3 GMT)
Brasília

Julia Hunt had decided to make a nuisance of herself, something she'd excelled at during her tenure as a Marine Corps officer. For the past five days she'd remained holed up at the hotel airport, a guard posted at her door, eating her meals out of takeout cartons. Each time she asked when her flight back to Nuuk would depart, a representative from the Brazilian Ministry of Defense—a mid-level officer or civilian who rotated daily—insisted that it would be the next morning. Because each day brought someone new, she found herself receiving the same empty assurances.

That night, she decided she was done playing these games. She stood at her door, eye fixed to the peephole, waiting for the guard to doze off. When he did, at a little after three a.m., she unlatched her door and proceeded to the hotel's emergency exit, down a flight of stairs, and out the back.

Her plan had been to wander the streets until morning, eventually making her way downtown, where she'd present herself at the Ministry of Defense around noon. She would demand a firm answer on her date of departure after having made her Brazilian hosts sweat a bit as to her whereabouts. She had momentarily considered the option of going to the American embassy, but suspected it would be closed given the deteriorated relations between Brazil and the United States.

She boarded a complimentary airport shuttle, which took a circuitous route, heading east. She was midway across the Ponte JK, a steel and concrete bridge, as the sun broke the horizon. The bridge's three arched spans rose and then plunged into the reservoir's shallow water, a remarkable piece of architecture that reminded her of the submerged roller coasters she'd passed a few days before.

Her shuttle bus continued north, juking through residential neighborhoods until it arrived at the Eixo Monumental, a thoroughfare of monuments that formed the spine of the city, much like her own National Mall. She tried to imagine what it had looked like decades before, carpeted by a green lawn instead of stubby patches of brown grass and dirt. A smattering of cafes had opened, their proprietors sweeping the sidewalks in front. She wandered into one, ordered a coffee, and found a table. A television in the corner fluttered with static like a flag no one saluted. Eventually, it picked up snippets of news. Here she saw the first images out of the United States.

Emergency workers pulling bodies out of the rubble of the West Wing . . .

Sailors fighting towers of smoke and flames on ships anchored in Norfolk . . .

Ground crews scrambling to repair cratered runways at Pope Airfield . . .

Julia struggled to comprehend this collage of devastation. The armada under Commodore Joko's command had attacked with a ferocity that surpassed her every expectation. And if it surpassed her expectations, it surely surpassed those of the Consortium.

What role had she played in this? The question felt like a hand on her throat.

Julia left her coffee half finished on the table. She couldn't wait until midday. She headed directly to the Ministry of Defense, a nondescript rectangular building off the Exio Monumental with a single entrance, the type of building a mid-sized corporation would use for its headquarters. She threw open its front door. Before she reached security, a naval officer intercepted her. He wore a gold-braided aiguillette looped around his shoulder, indicating his status as an aide-de-camp.

"Dr. Hunt," he said, "please come with me. The minister is expecting you."

04:34 Nov 16, 2084 (-5 GMT)
Walter Reed National Military Medical Center

As soon as Lily Bao heard news of the attack, she'd dropped her dog at the neighbors' and driven south, calling her son over and over. But Jake Shriver wasn't answering.

The hospital's trauma ward was overwhelmed, the corridors crammed with litters, a triage not only of those awaiting treatment but also those who could not be treated, those who were simply waiting to die. Lily found Jake wandering the corridors with his head swaddled in a bandage, holding a plastic bag with his personal effects. Lily simply asked: "Are you okay?" Jake blinked twice, as if he needed a moment to recover from the surprise of seeing his mother after so long.

Jake attempted to reconstruct events for her. The meeting with Boucher. The flash of light. The glass blown into a thousand shards. A great blast of air that toppled his body end over end. He'd blacked out in the rubble, awakening to voices calling out for survivors. Jake had shouted, "Here!" but wasn't certain how far his voice carried, or if it was even escaping his body. He'd felt no pain, just weight, an incredible weight pinning him down. He'd spotted a single beam of light from where the grand but now splintered mahogany doors of the Indian Treaty Room had once stood. He'd shouted a final time, "Here!" with all the strength he had remaining. When he received an answer, "I've got one!," Jake felt his body go limp.

They lifted him from beneath the collapsed ceiling. Firefighters, police officers, and EMTs expressed their amazement that he was alive as they passed him one to another in a human chain. A cursory examination in the back of an ambulance revealed that he had nothing more than a concussion, cuts, and minor bruises.

Jake and Lily stepped into a room the hospital had provided. News played on a muted television in a corner. The president was giving a speech from Camp David, addressing the nation. But Jake didn't want to hear her or anyone else obfuscate the truth, which was that a massive and preventable miscalculation had led to this disaster. The administration's strike on the *Banda Aceh*, which Boucher and others had downplayed, had provoked the Reparationists. The armada had responded with overwhelming force, an escalation the Consortium had not expected.

"C'mon," said Lily, "we're getting out of here."

"Out of here?" asked Jake. "To where?"

"Back to New Delhi."

08:56 Nov 18, 2084 (-5 GMT)
OPS Box Yankee

Midworld was on fire with enthusiasm for the armada's strike. For the past two decades, those equatorial nations had taken the brunt of the climate crisis, absorbing disaster after disaster. Now it was the Consortium's turn. Congratulatory messages had poured in to the Reparationist armada from Nusantara, Brasília, Lagos, and Tallahassee, to name a few. Commodore Joko had passed these messages along to his subordinates, and Captains Duarte and Gambo read the praise aloud to the crews of each ship over the 1MC. Joko could hardly stand to listen. *It is well that war is so terrible—we would grow fond of it.* Robert E. Lee had spoken those words after Fredericksburg, a one-sided victory that mirrored his own. Joko brooded in his stateroom on the *Aradu*, not sleeping. He wondered if history would cast him as a villain, as it had done to so many once victorious commanders.

His armada had struck over two dozen strategic targets along the Eastern Seaboard, using a variety of platforms and ordnance. They'd thrown everything in their arsenal at the Americans—drone swarms, hypersonic missiles (conventional and thermobaric), electromagnetic disruptors, cyber—everything and anything in their possession aside from tactical nuclear weapons, which they'd held in reserve. In the strike's aftermath, the resulting confusion had allowed Joko to send a half dozen suborbital unmanned reconnaissance flights to penetrate the American air defenses and canvass the destruction. His intelligence section had hastily put together a twenty-minute highlight reel of the footage. Joko found himself watching the reel in a loop.

The smoldering Capitol Dome and West Wing . . .

The cratered foundation of the New York Stock Exchange . . .

The rows of stamped-out barracks from Camp Lejeune to Fort Tubman . . .

The distorted, burning hulks of American warships twisting at anchor in Norfolk . . .

Yes, congratulations were in order, though Joko wished to forgo them.

That morning, a delegation from Tallahassee landed on the *Aradu*. Joko stepped outside the skin of the ship, onto the aft helicopter landing pad. Tick-Tock was already there, puffing an enormous cigar, exhaling blue cones of smoke. He reached into the leg pocket of his flight suit and pulled out a second, with a band from an excellent Floridian manufacturer, the prime zone for growing tobacco having moved north from the Caribbean, one of the few ways where the Floridians had benefited from climate change. Joko waved the cigar away. “It is haram,” he said. “My religion doesn’t allow it.”

Tick-Tock shrugged.

An old-model UH-60 helicopter appeared on the horizon, its rotors beating the air in a *whump*ing rhythm. It flared as it entered its final approach, while an escort of two Floridian J-19s circled overhead. Joko and Tick-Tock turned their backs as the helicopter’s downwash gusted against the deck. Its engines cut to idle. Before either of them could face around, a voice boomed, “Now, that’s how you open a can of whoop-ass!”

Brigadier Clay leaped out the helicopter’s side door and did a little celebratory two-step, knocking the heels of his cowboy boots across the flight deck. He ambled over to Commodore Joko while smoothing and shaping his beret down over his oily black hair. “Well done!” he said, pumping Joko’s hands. “I wasn’t sure you boys had it in you. Guess I was wrong.”

Joko accepted the backhanded compliment. He escorted Clay belowdecks, to his stateroom, where the three could meet in private. Tick-Tock stubbed out his cigar, planting its unlit nub in the corner of his mouth. Joko began their meeting by showing Clay the highlight reel of battle damage. Clay watched in rapt silence, only interrupting with low whistles. When the reel finished, Clay grew pensive. He didn’t say anything at first, and Joko thought that the degree of their success might have spooked him. Eventually, Clay said, “Y’all might be asking for reparations, but shit, the smackdown you just gave doesn't look like reparations . . . not to me. This looks like revenge. Fellas, it's time to put in our mouthguards. The Consortium's gonna come back at us swinging."

Joko agreed. He toggled on a holographic chart that projected from his work console. It was annotated with the armada's current order of battle, including the concentric rings of sensors his reconnaissance teams had emplaced as far north as Myrtle Beach, extending nearly one thousand miles eastward into the Atlantic. "Whatever the Consortium sends against us will be formidable," Joko said. "However, there's one weapon that they won't be able to muster, one that I believe has already proven decisive . . ."

"Okay, I'll bite," said Clay. "What weapon is that?"

"Surprise," said Tick-Tock, answering before Commodore Joko could. "Like the Japanese at Pearl Harbor, right? This war is inevitable, so we had no choice but to leverage surprise to our advantage."

"I suppose that's right," said Joko. A comparison to Imperial Japan wasn't one he relished. He showed Clay the disposition of his forces, how he'd arrayed his strike groups in depth, the overlapping threat envelopes of his weapons systems, the spot on his chart where he anticipated an engagement with the Consortium.

In return, Clay used Joko's chart to outline the preparations made by the Floridians, whose navy was little more than a glorified coast guard, but whose air and ground forces remained formidable. Tick-Tock had already reviewed these particulars with Commodore Joko—the composition of Floridian fighter aircraft, the disposition of their ground forces along the Georgian border, the number and range of their shore-based cruise missiles. Clay stumbled over some of the details. Tick-Tock tactfully filled in the blanks, adding his own assessment: "We're as well-positioned as possible to repel whatever the Consortium throws at us."

Joko agreed with that assessment, as did Clay, who added, "But you won't be here, Tick-Tock." He turned to Commodore Joko. "I'm sorry to do this to you, but we need Colonel Dundee for another priority mission."

"Sir?" Tick-Tock's voice was strained, as if trying to keep the frustration from brimming over. "What could be higher priority than this?"

"I received a call from my counterpart, the defense minister in Brasília. It seems your friend Julia Hunt has made a bit of a nuisance of herself. She's demanding to return to UN headquarters in Nuuk, despite the obvious dangers posed by that journey. It seems she won't take no for an answer, and now wouldn't be a good time to alienate a senior UN official. But she needs an escort, someone who can fly her north. The two of you seemed to get along well, so I volunteered you."

An uncomfortable, even hostile silence passed between Clay and Tick-Tock. Commodore Joko turned off the holographic chart. He grazed over some papers scattered across his desk in a half-hearted effort to appear as if he wasn't paying attention to their disagreement.

"A battle is about to be fought, sir. My place is here."

"Your place is where I say it is, Colonel."

Tick-Tock jawed his unlit cigar from one side of his mouth to the other. "Very well . . . and who, may I ask, are you going to swap me out with?"

"No one," said Clay. "I'm staying on the *Aradu* to coordinate the Floridian response with our allies."

Joko glanced up, but before he could say anything, Clay added, "This has all been arranged with General Suharto in Nusantara." The helicopter that had brought Clay out to sea would take Tick-Tock back to Tallahassee, where he'd board a flight to Brasília that evening.

20:25 Nov 18, 2084 (-5 GMT)
K and 20th Streets

All ten thousand square feet of the East-West Center's Washington, DC, headquarters were dark and empty aside from the corner office where Jake Shriver sat at his desk, its surface illuminated by a single lamp. Zhu De's flight from Beijing had touched down an hour before, at the only operable runway on Andrews Air Force Base. Two days ago, as Jake and his mother had been scrambling for a flight of their own to New Delhi, he'd received a message from Zhu De, a single word: *stay*.

His obedience to this command infuriated his mother. "Stay?" she asked. "What are you, his dog?" Lily Bao had long since regretted her decision to grant Jake dual US-Chinese citizenship when he was a newborn. She'd assumed he would become a thorn in the side of the People's Republic, the great antagonist of her life; instead, he'd become their asset. That wasn't how Jake viewed his relationship with either the United States or China. He had always believed himself to be "uniquely positioned to effect a cross-cultural dialogue between the two nations." His mother despised that sort of bureaucratic word salad. When he'd deployed the phrase at Dulles, as they debated whether he would be accompanying her to New Delhi, Lily Bao gave up. She boarded the plane and left her son on the tarmac.

Zhu De let himself into Jake's office. He wasted no time with pleasantries. He sat heavily in the seat opposite Jake's desk, not bothering to take off his light rain jacket. "Weren't you supposed to convey to the Americans the importance of *taking care* of the armada?"

Jake could hardly contain his frustration. "Delivering your message nearly cost me my life . . ." This hardly seemed to matter to Zhu De, who removed his small, round glasses as Jake spoke. He massaged their lenses with the hem of his coat, examining them at arm's length before hooking their wire arms back behind his fleshy ears. ". . . so don't tell me that I didn't deliver your damn message," Jake said, leaning forward across the desk.

Zhu De rubbed the groove of his cleft chin. "Are you finished?" he asked.

Jake leaned back in his seat and took a breath. "Yes."

"Good," said Zhu De. "No one is blaming you for this. The Americans miscalculated. They thought a strike against the *Banda Aceh* would deter the armada. They didn't expect such a fierce response."

"What now?"

"Now it's time to turn the tables. You and I are going to pay Boucher a visit."

"Boucher? It was her miscalculation that had resulted in this catastrophe." He was surprised she still held her job, that the administration hadn't scapegoated her.

"Quite the contrary," said Zhu De. "She's the most powerful person in Washington."

"What about the president? Where's she?"

"In a secure wing at Walter Reed, in critical condition."

Jake thought back to his time at the hospital, the television playing on mute. "But I just saw her speech at Camp David on the news . . ."

"No," said Zhu De, "what you saw was Boucher's speech. That was an AI rendering of the president, a hologram, nothing more. The Reparationist strike decapitated the administration. Boucher has powerful supporters in Congress, and she's convinced them that it would be a grave national security risk to invoke the Twenty-Fifth Amendment. Without congressional support, the vice president can't assume the presidency so long as the president has a pulse. So Boucher stays in her job, which, so long as the president's condition remains a secret, makes her more powerful than the secretary of defense or state. She's the national security advisor to an incapacitated president in a time of war. Now do you understand why we need to go see her?"

09:30 Nov 19, 2084 (-3 GMT)
Brasília

The Brazilian minister of defense, Retired Rear Admiral Francisco von Hütschler, wouldn't hear of having Julia Hunt locked up at an airport hotel. When she'd arrived at the ministry and he'd learned how his subordinates had sequestered her, he was ashamed and embarrassed. He insisted that Julia spend the rest of her time in Brasília with him and his wife, in the guest cottage of their sprawling official residence. Short in stature, big in heart, von Hütschler reminded Julia of her beloved godfather, the late vice admiral and accidental president John "Bunt" Hendrickson. She took him up on the offer.

The defense minister's wife, Greta von Hütschler, was from the same Bavarian village as her husband's ancestors, who'd fled Germany at the end of the Second World War. The two had met when Francisco was a young lieutenant posted to NATO headquarters in Brussels and he'd made a weekend excursion to his ancestral home. When Francisco had rung the bell to the address his family had given him, it was Greta who had answered the door.

That first night at dinner with Julia, while taking his wife's hand from across the table, von Hütschler boasted, "Our alliance has outlasted NATO." He pivoted to the strategic shortsightedness of NATO's expansion into the Americas and Africa. The overexpansion had ultimately resulted in NATO's collapse and the eventual establishment of the Consortium as the world's predominant military alliance. "It's not the American wing of the Consortium that I'm worried about," he concluded. "It's the Chinese."

Julia spent three days as von Hütschler's guest while she awaited arrangements for her follow-on travel to Nuuk. After the first night's meal, which was formal and served by the staff, every other night she had dinner with the minister and his wife at a small table in their kitchen. She told him about her time in the Marines, her decision to leave the Corps, and the legacy of service in her family, from her godfather, whom von Hütschler had once met when he himself was a junior officer, to her adoptive mother, Sarah Hunt, whose story had become a widely known cautionary tale.

For their final night together, Greta was told by her husband that they would be four. Greta was laying an extra place setting on the table when a set of headlights swept up the driveway. Soon, von Hütschler's voice burst through the door, mid-argument: ". . . Even if the Chinese don't counterattack, we've still overplayed our hand!"

He kissed his wife on the cheek, greeted Julia, and then glanced over his shoulder at his interlocutor, whom Julia was now staring at with her mouth slightly agape. "I believe you two know each other," said von Hütschler.

"What are you doing here?" asked Julia.

"Looks like I'm your ride." Tick-Tock wore a flight suit and carried a green kit bag slung casually over his shoulder the way a businessman might sling his jacket on a summer day. Tick-Tock leaned toward von Hütschler's wife, placing a kiss on her cheek. "Nice to see you again, Greta. It's Sunday. You making feijoada?"

"Yes, and that thing scratches," she said. "Only a bachelor would have that ridiculous mustache."

"You three know each other?" Julia asked.

"Yes, of course," said von Hütschler. "When did we first meet?"

They ticked off the various security conferences and training exercises they'd attended over the years. This history went back three decades. Finally, Greta interrupted. "For the past several years, my husband and I have been trying to convince Tick-Tock to settle down here in Brazil and retire."

"What the hell would I do in retirement?" asked Tick-Tock. Julia thought of the property she'd bought outside of Nuuk, in wine country. She was struggling with that question herself.

The four of them sat around the table, passing the dishes family style, a blend of Brazilian and German recipes, including the feijoada adorned with Alsatian sausages. "Given recent events," said von Hütschler, "I suspect that what to do in retirement is not a question you'll have to deal with anytime soon."

Tick-Tock wasn't so sure. Unlike the defense minister, he believed in the possibility of a negotiated peace. This seemed to be the point the two of them had been debating as they came into the house. "You're overestimating the Americans' military capability," said Tick-Tock, "as well as the Consortium's appetite to fight the Reparationists, particularly if the Chinese don't have their hearts in it. In the end, the Chinese will fight to the last . . . American." Tick-Tock laughed and reached across the table to fork a Frisbee-sized Wiener schnitzel onto his plate.

"Article 5 of the Nuuk Accords leaves the Chinese with no choice." Von Hütschler had become exasperated, as if he could hardly stand to make this point once more. "An attack against one Consortium member is an attack against all. It's dangerous to believe we can avoid a fight."

"Has it ever occurred to you that the Chinese might *want* the Consortium to lose?" asked Tick-Tock. "If our alliance is able to carve out innovation zones in the Americas, it's less likely we'll try the same in China. The Consortium with its charter and binding security measures may no longer be convenient for the Chinese."

This got Julia's attention. "Are you suggesting the Chinese might ally themselves with the Reparationists? Switch sides?"

Tick-Tock dumped a heaping spoonful of fried plantains onto his plate, adding a generous portion of green hot sauce. He took a bite and answered with his mouth full. "Who knows . . . but if I was the Americans, I wouldn't be so trusting of the PRC."

Von Hütschler changed the subject. He asked about Captain Duarte, whom he knew well. He wanted to hear how he and his Brazilian sailors had acquitted themselves. Although Tick-Tock complimented the Brazilian crews, his assessment of Duarte was more measured. He offered only faint praise, using adjectives no greater than "effective" and "competent" to describe him. Julia could tell that Tick-Tock was holding something back about Duarte. The Consortium might not be the only alliance under strain.

"I need to get back to the armada as soon as possible," Tick-Tock said. He turned to Julia. "And we need to get you back to UN headquarters, to help de-escalate this situation." For the journey, the minister had offered them his Learjet 910, a third-generation hypersonic. Tick-Tock would pilot them north, to Nuuk, with a layover in New Vancouver. To avoid Consortium airspace, they'd need to skirt the coast of Washington State–British Columbia until they reached the Alaskan Protectorate, a neutral Green Zone nation. They'd refuel a last time in Juneau before the final leg of their journey across the remnants of the polar ice cap.

Julia was puzzled. "I didn't know you could fly a hypersonic Learjet."

"I can fly anything with wings," said Tick-Tock. "When I was assigned to your mother's carrier, the *Enterprise*, we once flew old model F/A-18s with all the avionics torn out so the Chinese couldn't track us. All we had was a map, compass, wristwatch, and line-of-sight radio."

This got Greta's attention. "You flew with Julia's mother?"

Tick-Tock glanced nervously down at his plate, pushing his food around with his fork. "That was decades ago," he said haltingly. "In another war and another time. I'm not sure how much it matters now."

Greta clasped Tick-Tock's hand. "If it wasn't for 'another war in another time,' I never would've met him." She glanced at her husband.

The next morning, not long before first light, the minister's Learjet was wheels up.

17:56 Nov 21, 2084 (-5 GMT)
OPS Box Yankee

Already Brigadier Clay was causing problems. When Clay had requested that another half dozen of his staff embark with him aboard the *Aradu*, Joko recommended against it, but ultimately accommodated him. When Clay and the Floridians complained about their tight living quarters, Joko suggested that perhaps some of Clay's staff move to another ship like the *Banda Aceh* or even back ashore. Instead, Clay suggested that the junior officers on Joko's staff move belowdecks, to a cramped enlisted berthing. Joko ignored him.

This disagreement was minor compared with what came next.

Joko had kept his fleet in a strong defensive posture, bracing for the inevitable Consortium counterattack. Clay felt that Joko was being overly cautious, that he "shouldn't hesitate to go in for the kill." Clay had first said this to Joko privately in the wardroom one evening after dinner. Joko thanked him for the advice, said he would take it under advisement, then excused himself.

The next evening, Clay hadn't been at dinner. When Joko went up to the bridge after his meal, he found Clay waiting for him. He was quizzing Joko's subordinates, including Captain Gambo, as to the disposition of the armada. He floated the same idea to Gambo about "going in for the kill." Gambo was a careerist. He considered Clay a superior, and his first instinct was to pander to him, so he told Clay that he thought this was a good idea. "Yes, sir, very intriguing indeed. The best defense *is* a good offense."

Joko had arrived on the bridge right as these words were passing Gambo's lips. Clay made a point of loudly repeating them. "The best defense sure is a good offense . . ." The words hung in the air.

The next morning, shortly after Commodore Joko awoke, his orderly presented him with his day's schedule, which included a previously unlisted meeting. "Who added this?" Joko asked.

It had arrived late the night before at the behest of Brigadier Clay's chief of staff. The meeting, scheduled for just twenty minutes, included only him, Clay, and General Suharto, who would be calling in via secure holographic conference from Nusantara.

When Joko arrived at Clay's stateroom, he found several members of Clay's staff lingering inside. The meeting was already underway. General Suharto was listening, rapt, as Clay ran through a series of slides proposing a combined operation: the Floridians would send a flight of land-based J-19s north with support from the armada. This raid force would harass and interdict any American counterattack on their forces in the Gulf.

Suharto massaged his chin as he considered the proposal.

Joko was aware of the other demands on Suharto. Already, the bulk of the remaining warships in the Indonesian Navy were mobilizing to escort a massive fleet of barges toward landing beaches in Nova Scotia and the northeastern United States. Those barges would disembark, not an invading army but climate refugees, hundreds of thousands of them. Given that Clay had scheduled this meeting behind his back, Joko proceeded with caution. He didn't reveal to Suharto his unvarnished opinion: that he thought a raid was a terrible idea; that they'd yet to consolidate their gains against the Americans; that they shouldn't engage in any further provocations and should instead remain in a strong defensive posture.

Joko said only, "I have my reservations. But it's your decision, sir."

Suharto muted the line. He turned and conferred silently with his staff. Then he unmuted himself. "Given the pace of our preparations here, a raid would seem premature."

Joko glanced at Clay, who was staring right back at him.

But Suharto wasn't finished. "However, it would seem prudent to make all possible preparations for this contingency. If we decide to strike before launching the resettlement fleet—or even while the resettlement fleet is underway—it will be a decision we have to make on short notice, so we'll need to be ready. Commodore Joko, how soon could you have a reconnaissance mission up?"

"We could launch a hypersonic as soon as tomorrow morning."

Suharto nodded. "Very well. Run that mission. Let's see what we find."

10:25 Nov 22, 2084 (-5 GMT)
Camp David

The administration was no longer working out of the White House. Boucher had moved all critical personnel to Camp David. Ostensibly the move was for security purposes. The Oval Office was cratered. The Eisenhower Executive Office Building had its east wall torn off. Bodies were still coming out of the rubble and people were scared. But really, the reason for the move was political. To exercise power most effectively, Boucher wanted to remain far from Washington. Far from congressional grandstanding. Far from lesser government agencies who might obstruct her agenda. And far from a hostile, unforgiving press who would give her precious little credit for being the fighter she knew she was.

Jake Shriver knew Boucher was a fighter. He recalled the *Washington Post* profile that accompanied her appointment as national security advisor. The writer had done a workmanlike job of cataloging Eva Boucher's life, including the loss at age ten of her pararescueman father—a member of the Air Force's 24th Special Tactics Squadron, an elite "PJ"—during a mission in the South Pacific. The writer had tracked her relentless, almost pathological, list of achievements: Boucher's appointment to the Air Force Academy at seventeen; serving as cadet captain and an all-American tennis player at Colorado Springs; a Rhodes Scholarship; her passage through grueling pararescue training; military decorations and deployments before resigning her commission and being accepted at Stanford Business School; her appointment as the youngest partner in the history of the Carlyle Group. Jake had struggled to finish the bland, two-dimensional profile that read like a resume, wondering idly if she had crossed paths with his mother at Carlyle. He was rewarded with the kicker quote in the final paragraph: "I live every day like payback for those days taken from my father."

If a spirit of revenge animated Boucher, Jake thought, her moment had arrived. He and Zhu De had driven up to Camp David that morning from Washington. The Secret Service had waved them inside the perimeter after a cursory search, sequestering them in an anteroom at the main Aspen Lodge. The White House stewards had set out an elaborate breakfast buffet for them, but it soon became obvious that this was less an act of hospitality than a stalling tactic. Finally, after two hours, just as Zhu De was suggesting to Jake that they return to Washington, a Secret Service agent appeared at the door.

The agent led them outside to a golf cart and drove them across the property. He pointed to a trail. "She's a hundred meters down that way, by the stream."

"Are you making a joke?" asked Zhu De.

The closest thing he got for an answer was a loud, steady beep as the Secret Service agent flipped his golf cart into reverse.

Shriver and Zhu De picked their way down the trail. Up ahead, the steady gurgle of water grew louder. An escarpment of granite boulders jutted out at a bend where the water pooled. Boucher sat on its edge, her legs dangling beneath her. She clasped a fishing rod, the embodiment of ease, Huckleberry Finn in the middle of a national security crisis.

"Hey, you two!" She waved her hand over her head.

A tackle box sat behind her on the rock, with two other fishing rods. When Shriver stepped out onto the rocks, Boucher handed him her rod. She knifed a worm in half and threaded it on the hook, her fingers slick with blood. She offered the rod to Zhu De.

"No, thank you," he said. "I don't fish. I am vegetarian."

"Okay," said Boucher. "Come have a seat then." She cast the second line out into the middle of the stream, where it bobbed alongside Shriver's.

Zhu De took tentative shuffle steps in their direction like a man walking a plank. When he finally sat, he breathed a sigh of relief, removing a handkerchief from his pocket and wiping his forehead. Boucher and Shriver both suppressed a grin.

"Apologies for dragging the two of you out here," Boucher said. "We have some items to discuss, and privacy is tough to come by these days."

"Do you usually discuss critical matters of national security while fishing?" A sharp edge had returned to Zhu De's voice.

"My father used to take me fishing," Boucher said. "When he had some decision to consider—like another move or an upcoming deployment—he'd grab our rods, drive me to the nearest creek or pond, and tell me about it. He knew that if we stayed at home and the conversation didn't go well, I could storm off to my room. Out on the water, I couldn't really do that. I was stuck. I had to hear him out. Except you don't fish," she added, glancing at Zhu De. "But you'll stay, won't you?"

Boucher offered Zhu De the freshly baited rod. "Whatever I catch," he said, snatching the rod from her, "I'm throwing back. Agreed?"

She agreed.

The three of them sat on the rock spaced a few feet apart. The stream came fresh and slightly cool into their nostrils as their lines played lazily against the surface of the water. Shriver could see the fish below, a string of tapering shadows stirring as if about to take shape. Boucher explained that the creek was populated mostly by trout but included a smaller number of largemouth bass. Water levels had fallen off, decimating the other varieties of fish, but the staff at Camp David kept an upstream fishery populated. "A few times a year, they let the fish run," Boucher said. "This stream has a special history. FDR and Churchill once fished on this rock. There's a photo of it up at the main lodge. They were taking a break from planning the D-Day landings."

Zhu De appeared utterly disinterested. His eyes remained fixed on the surface of the water, as if willing a nibble on his line.

"That was the beginning of the *special relationship* between the Brits and Americans," said Shriver, picking up Zhu De's end of the conversation.

"A special relationship . . . Yet a person couldn't think of two nations whose early history was more acrimonious than Britain and the United States," added Boucher.

"And yet, they crafted a new world . . ." Shriver was getting going now, falling easily into talking points: global environmental security was assured through the Consortium; the war between a previous generation had not precluded subsequent generations of Chinese and Americans from finding common ground and peace; cross-cultural dialogues had assured that peace. Chinese and American leadership was being called upon again, to lead the Consortium against Reparationist aggression.

Boucher nodded. "Our response to that aggression is what we have to decide."

"*Our* response?" Zhu De finally looked away from his fishing line.

Boucher glanced at Shriver, who seemed as startled as she did.

"Dr. Boucher," added Zhu De, "our government's position has remained consistent throughout this crisis. We could not have been clearer. We said that either you dealt with the armada or we would deal with it for you. We are preparing to do just that now, on our own. The Politburo Standing Committee has approved a plan. I am now authorized to inform you about the specifics."

Boucher shot an accusatory glance at Shriver.

"He knows nothing about this," Zhu De added. "But our forces are assembling. There is some coordination that must occur. Perhaps it would be best if we returned to the main lodge to discuss—"

Zhu De's line snapped tight. A fish had snatched his bait, tugging with such force that the bail arm on his reel had knocked loose and line was spooling out freely. Zhu De shot clumsily to his feet. When the fish pulled again, he lost his balance, as if he might pitch forward into the water. Boucher grabbed him from behind. She placed both her hands on top of his, the two of them grasping the reel as they slowly brought the fish in.

It was an enormous largemouth bass, the largest Boucher had ever seen, perhaps the largest ever caught in this stream. Boucher wanted to bring it back to the lodge, to fix it up that night for dinner, but Zhu De reminded her of their agreement. While she protested, he adeptly slid the hook from its mouth and allowed the fish to return to the water, where it vanished.

13:22 Nov 24, 2084 (+5:30 GMT)

New Delhi

When the international board of the Tandava Group discovered that Lily Bao had arrived in New Delhi, they asked to meet with her. They had an offer to make. Given the turbulence to both global markets and supply chains caused by the armada's strike, the board wanted a chair with a deep history at Tandava. A consensus emerged: Lily should return.

The board was so large that it took Lily Bao ten separate sessions over three days to meet with them all. They had cycled into headquarters in groups of twelve, each individual board member a well-paid eminence in their field. The coterie of executive staff and lawyers who attended Lily was even larger than the board. She struggled to keep straight the names of this impeccably credentialed crew who, like minor nobles attending a regent, seemed unduly delighted to bring her any trifle, from coffee to a freshly sharpened pencil to a detailed analysis of global shipping distortions caused by the escalating climate war.

Her message to the board was simple and delivered without equivocation: *a steady hand is needed on the tiller.* She repeated this message in meeting after meeting like an actor shooting multiple takes of the same scene. While her energy never flagged publicly, she knew she was operating on borrowed time. At some point, she thought to herself, I'm going to need help. And so far, I haven't seen anyone around here who can provide it. As she was flipping through various research files in the board chair's suite, she saw an entry that caught her attention: *Beginner's Mind.* She sent a coded text to her acting chief of staff, an obsequious Greek named Yorgos.

"What's Beginner's Mind?"

"I do not know," he said. "Although Beginner's Mind fell under my resource division, access was restricted to the board chair."

"And now I'm the board chair."

"Yassou, Madam Chairman." He smiled and turned to his holographic displays. "It is for you to find out."

06:42 Nov 24, 2084 (-5 GMT)
OPS Box Yankee

Commodore Joko had recommended they wait for ideal conditions before launching their reconnaissance. That morning, the first rays of the sun streaked a cloud-banked horizon, painting it red; the sky soon cleared; the temperature cooled. Suharto ordered the launch.

A spread of six hypersonic drones, each with a two-hundred-mile observation envelope, departed at 0700 up the Eastern Seaboard traveling a little faster than Mach 3. They passed over Nova Scotia where they transmitted their data before self-incinerating at altitude over the North Atlantic. Joko reviewed the final slide on his confirmation brief. *Total mission distance: 2,147 nm . . . Time on target: 47 min 56 secs . . .*

The mission footage would arrive for upload at any minute. Suharto, Clay, Joko, and a host of other high-ranking officers and officials aboard every ship in the flotilla and at the defense ministries in every capital were awaiting the footage. The US response to the armada strike had remained muted, uncharacteristically so for the Americans, who typically responded to a "day of infamy" with reflexive violence. But not in this case. At least so far.

The raw footage arrived. An intel tech aboard the *Aradu* fed it through an AI, which condensed the trove of data into a single fifteen-minute video. Immediately, it became clear. The Americans hadn't responded because they couldn't, at least not adequately. Carrier strike groups lay sunk at anchor. Air wings had been pulverized in their hangars. Armored divisions had been reduced to charred and rusted hulks. An animal is most dangerous when it's wounded, and the Americans were certainly that, but this reconnaissance settled the question of why the Americans hadn't yet launched a counterattack. However, one question it hadn't answered was why no other Consortium nation had taken up its banner.

As Reparationist ministers and senior officers exchanged congratulations on the secure line, Commodore Joko interrupted. "Where are their allies?"

The line drew silent.

Brigadier Clay piped up. Just as the Reparationists had overestimated American military power, they had overestimated the strength of the Consortium, particularly the willingness of its members to enforce Article 5 of their collective defense treaty. "Now's the time to go in for the kill."

The Brazilian defense minister von Hütschler coughed. "Our mission all along has been to convince the Americans and other Consortium members to listen to our demands, which are reasonable. Another strike could work against us if it seems unnecessarily punitive. If the Consortium isn't united in its desire to evoke Article 5 against us, let's not give them a reason to reach a consensus."

The debate soon rose to matters above Commodore Joko's pay grade. Neither he nor his subordinate commanders would weigh in. The leaders of the original three Reparationist nations—Brazil, Indonesia, Nigeria—plus the Floridians would ultimately decide on his armada's next move. They would either launch a final strike, hold in place to keep options open, or return east so their flotilla could be absorbed as escorts in the much larger resettlement fleet that was assembling. Further deliberations would be needed, but those wouldn't involve Commodore Joko. General Suharto congratulated him and his crews on a successful reconnaissance and ordered them to hold position pending guidance.

By nightfall, that guidance still hadn't arrived. Joko couldn't sleep, so he sat on the bridge of the *Aradu* reviewing the disposition of his armada. They were arrayed in a line of battle that projected combat power into the Atlantic, ready to intercept any reinforcements that might arrive from the Consortium. If his high command chose to launch another strike on the Eastern Seaboard, it would require him to reposition his flotilla, as his southernmost strike groups would have to leapfrog north. This would weaken his ability to focus on the most likely Atlantic approach, which was southern, a Chinese fleet coming up from either the Cape of Good Hope in Africa or Cape Horn in South America. He was weighing these variables when the watch officer interrupted his train of thought. The commodore had an incoming call.

Joko stepped into a private conference room off the bridge. General Suharto was on the secure holographic line. None of the general's staff attended him. He looked exhausted, worn out after a day spent negotiating with his counterparts.

"I apologize that I don't have your orders yet, Commodore."

This threw Joko off. He wasn't used to having very senior generals apologize to him, particularly one as gruff as Suharto. He answered, "Not a problem, sir," and then began updating Suharto on the current disposition of his forces.

Suharto listened patiently before interrupting. "Napoleon used to say that in battle, he always wanted to face off against an alliance. Do you know why?"

"Because an alliance has no unity of command, sir."

"Exactly," Suharto said. "Napoleon knew that if an army—no matter how large or well-equipped—lacked unity of command, it would be at a disadvantage. I don't have your orders because we have no unity of command. The Floridians and Nigerians support another round of strikes against the US. The Brazilians don't. And I don't. So we're at an impasse, at least for now."

"We've got the southern approaches covered, sir. We can continue to hold our position."

"Yes, but you shouldn't have to, not without clear orders. The danger of remaining in a static position grows." A slight tremor came into Suharto's usually steady voice. Joko couldn't tell if it was fatigue, emotion, or both. Suharto added, "My hope is to have definitive orders to you tomorrow."

A young sailor opened the hatch behind Joko, interrupting the call. "Sir, it's urgent. You're wanted on the bridge." General Suharto told Joko they could finish their call later.

When Joko arrived on the bridge, the watch officer reported that their picket of sensors had picked up a small strike group, not even a dozen ships, sailing out of Norfolk. They'd headed east, into the open Atlantic. Then they'd vanished.

"Which ships?" asked Joko.

The watch officer presented a partial list.

Joko was soon back on the line with General Suharto, updating him on the situation. "It doesn't make much sense, sir. We outgun them at least five to one."

Suharto agreed, it didn't make much sense. "Which ships?" he asked.

Joko went down the list that the watch officer had provided, including the largest, most powerful ship in the Americans' otherwise understrength strike group, a super destroyer comparable to the *Aradu*.

"Did you say the *John Paul Jones* . . . ?"

"Yes, sir."

"Fifty years ago, which was the last time the world went to war, it was started by an incident in the South China Sea involving an American destroyer named the *John Paul Jones.* She was sunk off Mischief Reef."

General Suharto looked off-camera and thought for a moment. "Napoleon also used to say, 'If you set out to take Vienna, take Vienna.' To turn back now would be foolish." He hopped off the call.

By the next morning, Joko's orders had arrived from Suharto's headquarters. He assembled his officers in the wardroom. The armada would reposition itself immediately for a second strike.

08:30 Nov 24, 2084 (-8 GMT)
Juneau, Alaskan Protectorate

Tick-Tock had offered to sleep aboard the plane, but Julia thought that was ridiculous. It would only be for one night, and their hotel room had a sofa. In both Vancouver and in Juneau, her assistant at the UN had struggled to find them two vacant rooms. This had surprised Tick-Tock, who hadn't traveled to the Green Zone since before Partition, a process that had proven far more peaceful than his own country's fight for independence. The population explosions in Vancouver and Juneau over the past decade mirrored what had occurred in subpolar cities like Nuuk, so it came as little surprise to Julia that it was difficult to find a place to stay.

Julia and Tick-Tock had spent several days hopscotching north from Brasília. On their flight into Vancouver, the weather had been perfect. They could see for miles, including Old Vancouver, whose submerged outline passed beneath them. As with the Floridians after Independence, the Consortium and UN had refused to recognize the old, pre-flood borders of the Green Zone nations after Partition. The policy was economically punitive, converting the sovereign territory of those nations into international waters. If Julia had ever wondered how Tick-Tock could turn his back on his country, on the Corps, and then fight for the Floridians, she only had to hear the edge in his voice as he railed about the fundamental unfairness of the Consortium and UN.

"It's a morally bankrupt position," he'd said that night as they'd settled into their room in Juneau, "an act of punitive aggression."

Tick-Tock had emerged from their shared bathroom wearing a baby-blue set of pajamas and slippers. Julia smirked.

"What? What's so funny?"

"Nothing." She was wearing her workout clothes to bed. As she climbed under the sheets, she said, "I like your PJs."

Tick-Tock glanced down at himself. "Thanks . . . a man's got to find a little comfort in this world, right?" He plopped on the sofa and crossed his arms behind his head on the pillow. He stared up at the ceiling. His large feet dangled over the armrest of the sofa. Julia shut off the lamp. Moonlight poured through the window, landing in a column on Tick-Tock, who spoke in a half voice that barely hovered above a whisper. "Guys in my first squadron threatened to make that my call sign, 'PJ.' That's back when I was on the *Enterprise*, with your mom. Small world, eh?"

"Sure is." Julia rolled on her side and shut her eyes, trying to sleep.

"Can I ask you a kinda personal question?"

Julia made a drowsy, affirmative noise.

"You ever have dreams about her?"

"Who? My mom?" Julia sat up in the bed.

"Because sometimes I do . . . It's been fifty years and I don't dream about the guys in my squadron from back then or the other guys I flew with later, but sure enough, every few weeks, I have a dream about her."

His voice possessed a vulnerable, tortured quality. It was as if he'd had to draw from some inner reservoir to reveal this. Julia was tempted to ask what happened in these dreams, but she thought it better not to pry. Instead, she said, "I dream about her too." This seemed to be all that Tick-Tock needed to hear. Julia listened to his breathing deepen. He'd fallen asleep.

Tick-Tock was still asleep the next morning when Julia snuck out of their room to the hotel gym. She hopped on the treadmill and ran a hard five miles. It had been thirty years since her mother's first vivid appearance in her dreams. Although these days Sarah Hunt appeared less regularly, Julia still felt vulnerable to her, as if she never had and perhaps never would possess complete control of her own consciousness.

Over the years, Julia had convinced herself that her mother's appearance wasn't anything particularly unique. What child isn't marked unalterably by their parents in ways that they may or may not desire? Parents drop by uninvited; that's what they do. But her mother had appeared this way in the consciousness of another . . . and hearing this left Julia unsettled. It also left her feeling a surprising and unsettling closeness to Tick-Tock.

When she returned to their room after her run, Tick-Tock was dressed in his flight suit, his kit bag packed, the blanket folded neatly on the sofa. "I grabbed you breakfast." He gestured to a coffee and a muffin. "Meet you downstairs in twenty minutes?"

Julia thanked him, and later that morning they were back in the air, traveling east across the southern Arctic, on their final leg toward Nuuk. Shortly after takeoff, Julia had knocked on the cockpit door. She wanted to know if she could sit up front.

"Sure," said Tick-Tock. He cleared some papers and snacks off the copilot seat. He seemed pleasantly surprised to have company.

"Looks much different from up here." Julia leaned forward, her gaze dipping down to the Hudson Bay and the northern Canadian floodplains.

"Sure does," said Tick-Tock. He held the jet's yoke with one hand and its throttle in the other. His knuckles were white. He was gripping the controls as he might grip the handholds on a mountain face he was trying not to fall from. They exchanged stray sentences, the conversation turning awkward. Julia commented on the glacial melt below, how vast it'd become. She struggled to find something else to say until Tick-Tock blurted out, "I'm sorry about last night, that stuff about your mom . . . it's none of my business."

As soon as Tick-Tock made his apology, he fixed his eyes out of the cockpit and onto the horizon. Julia leaned forward, so he would look at her. "It's okay," she said. "I don't mind. I'm glad you asked." Tick-Tock faced Julia, and she continued, explaining how it seemed like her mother had taken control of her dreams in the years after she'd vanished, placing either herself or Julia's birth parents into them. Julia spoke about her mother's work on the Singularity thirty years before, and the permeability between biological and technological intelligence, but also biological and technological consciousness. "Even though that technology hasn't proliferated," Julia said, "even though my mother threw up obstacles so no one could replicate her work, her discovery is still out there. Every time I dream about my mother, I'm reminded of it. Every time I dream about her, I'm not sure if I'm the one generating the dream or if it's someone or something else that's doing it."

"A strange thing happened last night." Tick-Tock was staring very intently at Julia, as if he'd only in that moment decided to tell her. "For years, for decades, the dream I've had about your mother has always been the same. We're in a plane, the same F-18 that I used to fly. I'm up front, she's in the back, and I need to land her on the carrier, on her flagship. I'm on final approach when suddenly I find myself completely out of position. I'm either coming in too low, too high, too slow, or too fast. The landing signal officer is screaming bloody murder over the radio, and so is the air boss. The flight controls are nonresponsive; they feel like they're stuck in sand. My vision is out of focus. Nothing makes sense. I know I'm gonna crash. Then I wake up."

Tick-Tock was squeezing the controls again, his knuckles turning white.

Julia reached over. She rested her hand on the throttle, on top of his.

"But here's the thing," he said. "Last night, I caught the three-wire. I landed perfectly. In thirty years of having this dream, that's never happened, not once."

Julia kept her palm on his hand. They flew like this, in silence. She asked him how long he would stay in Nuuk. Tick-Tock looked out the port window of the plane and said that he didn't know. He'd probably get his orders when he landed. Julia said she hoped his orders didn't come through too soon. He said he hoped the same. Then Tick-Tock noticed something below: a convoy of ships stitching its way through the water of the floodplains, zigzagging south. Julia saw the convoy too. She asked if these were Consortium ships, counting more than two dozen before they disappeared over the southern horizon. Tick-Tock said that they were.

"American?" she asked.

He shook his head. "Chinese," he said. "Christ, they must've risked the weather and crossed the Pole. They're headed toward the St. Lawrence River."

"The St. Lawrence River? How is that even possible?"

"It feeds into the Great Lakes. Which goes to the Mississippi. Which empties into the Gulf." He pulled his stick back hard, changing their course. They needed to land.

3

Beginner's Mind

09:22 Nov 26, 2084 (+5:30 GMT)

New Delhi

Lily sat in her office at the Tandava Group's corporate headquarters. She was barricaded behind an enormous desk, a gaudy monstrosity bought from Versailles at auction during the most recent French debt crisis. Yorgos hovered over her. The only thing in front of her on the desk was her personal cube, projecting a hologram. Lily entered a succession of passwords followed by a retinal scan and skin scrape as she logged on to Tandava's walled-off intranet, a bespoke quantum computing platform.

"Reopen that screen," said Yorgos, pointing to the browser. "Wait . . ." He began to read intently.

"What have you got?" asked Lily.

"A performance review for our last director of environmental research. I could never get a straight answer on why he was fired . . ."

"Can we stay on task, please?"

Yorgos glanced away from the screen. "Sorry, it's hard to resist. With the chairman's password and clearance, you're holding the keys to the kingdom." He gave her a few more instructions as they trawled the databases, dipping into active and long-shuttered program interfaces in Tandava's environmental portfolio. Although Yorgos found references to Beginner's Mind in a few places, he couldn't find the program interface itself. "Every vertical in Tandava has a program interface," he explained. "It's a community workspace where contributors to any given program upload their work, chat with each other, and collaborate on research in progress. We then scan all of it with a benign AI that connects ideas, suggests new approaches to unsolved problems, compares thinking to early ideas, that kind of thing. It's very effective." He got Lily to enter a series of program interfaces, but Beginner's Mind wasn't listed.

"Maybe we shouldn't be doing this," said Lily, losing patience.

"Maybe," said Yorgos. "But then what else can we do? Mind if I drive?"

Lily pushed the cube across the desk and leaned back, arms crossed. When she glanced back at the interface, Yorgos was reading the same performance review. "I didn't share passwords so you could go snooping around for gossip about old colleagues," she snapped.

Yorgos continued to type, his eyes widening.

"If you want to keep looking, fine," said Lily, "but no more of this—"

Yorgos interrupted her. "There . . . look there."

Buried in a block of text on the performance review, which spoke glowingly about the talents of Tandava's last director of environmental research, was a single line: *Reason for termination—refusal to participate in military programming.*

"Beginner's Mind is why they fired him," Yorgos added. "The Tandava Group doesn't have the program listed under its environmental vertical. It's a black program within the company."

Yorgos backed out of page after page on the intranet until he landed on the Tandava Group's main portal. He moved from the environmental to the military vertical and logged in again. When he reached the program interfaces of the military vertical, he found Beginner's Mind buried at the bottom. Unlike the other programs, which counted dozens if not hundreds of "authorized users" in an icon beneath the program title, Beginner's Mind had only three authorized users. The previous chair had been one. Yorgos and Lily had no idea who the other two were: they were only identified as "mind2" and "mind3."

"Well," said Yorgos with a flourish. "Time to find out who else knows about Beginner's Mind."

He typed in the chairman's password and hit enter.

System error.

Yorgos typed it in again; same error.

Lily leaned over the laptop. She typed in the password herself. He suggested they look around the office for any clues; perhaps there was an unaccounted password written on a scrap of paper. They opened desk drawers. They flipped through notebooks. When the phone began to ring, Lily and Yorgos were so intent on their search they let it ring itself out. It rang again, and still neither answered.

"Let's think," said Yorgos as he flopped down in a chair by the desk. "If someone had a second password, where would they keep it? Or what would it be?"

The two sat in silence.

Lily's secretary knocked on the door. "Ms. Bao, you have a phone call."

"Not now," Lily growled.

"It's from the Indian Ministry of Defense, a Major General Patel. I told him you were busy, but he says it's urgent, a matter of national security." Yorgos shot Lily a glance. "He keeps calling. He says it's about some files you are trying to access . . ."

09:26 Nov 26, 2084 (-6:00 GMT)
St. Louis

Zhu De had insisted, and Boucher had agreed, that Shriver should accompany the Chinese fleet on the final leg of its journey as a liaison. That morning, Jake and Zhu De had landed on the fleet's flagship, the carrier *Zheng He*. He had received assurances from Zhu De that the Chinese navy would fly them off the *Zheng He* before the possibility of any action against the Reparationist armada. Zhu De wanted Shriver to see firsthand what the Chinese were in the process of undertaking: a fleet's circumnavigation of the globe across the North Pole and into the Gulf of Mexico through the flooded intracoastal waterways of the United States.

The Mississippi was by far the largest of them. Never in its history had the "Father of Waters" been so uncontained, its banks so swollen, deep enough to sustain the thirty-seven-foot draught of the *Zheng He*. The river had long ago swept away the hundreds of bridges that had once spanned its banks. Their welter of iron girders now poked up from the water, twisted from exposure to the current, marking what had been the riverbank but was now a broad estuary. Given the unpredictability of flood cycles, ad hoc pontoon crossings had replaced mighty bridges. Hard-hatted state workers on flat-bottomed barges disassembled those pontoons as the Chinese fleet—a forty-carrier strike group with the *Zheng He* at its center—processed deeper and deeper into the United States, averaging over twenty knots toward the Gulf.

Shriver stood on the flight deck amid dovetailed rows of J-37s, the last manned fighter aircraft in the Chinese navy. Their stubby wingtips were lashed to the deck, their canopies and fuselages draped with the weatherized tarps that had protected them when they'd crossed the Pole. It had been more than a decade since Shriver had traveled anywhere near what could be considered the heartland of the United States. He'd become a creature of elite cities, New York, Boston, Washington, DC. For him, seeing the country meant a flight to Los Angeles; in fact, he'd stopped thinking of America as a country, but as a lost floodplain contained between two coasts.

"I've been looking for you." Zhu De had crept up behind him.

"Sorry," said Jake. "I didn't think we had anything scheduled until lunch."

"The admiral heard you were aboard at his morning briefing," said Zhu De. "He asked that you pay him a visit . . . Looks like your reputation has preceded you."

The St. Louis skyline appeared in the fog-banked distance. The city had rebuilt itself away from the river that had destroyed it. Jake had never been to St. Louis before, neither the old city nor this rebuilt one. Passing by on a warship was the closest he might ever come, he remarked to Zhu De, who said, "I lived in St. Louis for a year, when I was an exchange student."

"I didn't know that . . ."

"Oh yes, at Washington University, before the flood, on their old campus." Zhu De pumped his hand up and down, as if he were honking the horn on a big rig. "Go Bears," he said a little wistfully.

Jake laughed and Zhu De averted his eyes, as if he'd maybe revealed a little too much of his history. "That's the problem," said Jake. "You know more of this country than I do."

"That's not *my* problem," said Zhu De. "It's *your* problem . . . If you Americans knew your country and each other better, it wouldn't create opportunities for people like me to know you better than you know yourselves . . ." Zhu De opened his mouth as if to say something else, but he cut himself off.

Jake thought he knew what Zhu De was going to say, and he was glad he didn't say it, which was that if Americans had known themselves better, a Chinese warship might not be sailing down the Mississippi. But it was too late for that. They were here now.

Jake followed Zhu De into the skin of the ship. The crew was frantic with activity as they prepared to enter the Gulf. The atmosphere reminded Jake of a high-end restaurant, where the dining room was serene and orderly, while on the other side of the door, in the kitchen, it was barely controlled chaos. After climbing up two decks, they arrived at a highly polished mahogany door. An expressionless sailor, so tall that his Dixie Cup hat scraped the ceiling, was posted outside as a sentry. The sailor acknowledged Zhu De with a downward glance. Just then the door flung open, and a clutch of officers stepped into the passageway. Behind them was the admiral. He recognized Zhu De immediately and gestured for him and Jake to come inside.

An aide was sanitizing the office of classified materials as they entered, switching off the holographic projector and rolling up the old-style paper charts that littered every surface. The admiral installed himself behind a large desk. "It's a great honor to have you on this ship, Mr. Shriver. I know we've only just met, so excuse me for saying this, but I feel as if you're an old relation, a distant relative."

Jake smiled, confused.

"You haven't made the connection yet, have you?" The admiral leaned over his desk, rolling his broad shoulders forward. His dark eyes narrowed and tracked Jake closely. He was compact and fit, a lithe coil of energy. "Our grandfathers both commanded this ship, Mr. Shriver. Ma Qiang, who fought against the Americans, was my grandfather. He was an academy classmate of your grandfather Lin Bao. We're practically related." He smiled, revealing large, slightly stained teeth.

Jake glanced at the placard on the desk: *Admiral Ma Fen*. He'd seen the name before, but hadn't made the connection. Admiral Ma spoke at length about Jake's grandfather, about his work as China's military attaché to Washington fifty years before, about the professional rivalry that once existed between their grandfathers, and how Lin Bao's memory had always been revered in his family, a model of service—even though the Politburo had smeared Lin Bao's good name after his "untimely death."

"I've followed your career for some time," the admiral continued. "The work you've done bridging the gap between our two nations honors the memory of your grandfather. It's part of the reason our countries can cooperate today." The admiral leaned back in his chair. His gaze roamed the wood-paneled cabin, its walls hung with mementos of the *Zheng He* through its many iterations, including when the admiral's grandfather went down with this very ship in the Pacific fifty years before. "One might say there's enough of my family's blood spilled into the *Zheng He* to make the ship a relative."

Before Jake Shriver could reply, Zhu De blurted out, "Crossing the Pole with a fleet this size is an unprecedented achievement, Admiral, one worthy of history's greatest military commanders, like Hannibal's crossing of the Alps or Zhukov's winter counteroffensive against the Nazis. And now you and your crews are poised to strike a great blow against the Reparationists, to end this aggression to our allies and our planet." Zhu De stood, his own soaring rhetoric having lifted him from his seat, as if he were delivering a toast—yet no one held a glass. "Our only regret," he added, gesturing to Shriver, "is that we'll have to leave before you deliver the decisive blow."

Admiral Ma clasped his hands together on the desk. He gave Jake Shriver a knowing look, as if Zhu De's obsequious little speech were a joke the two of them might share. "Your presence honors every sailor in this strike group," said the admiral. His voice was detached and formal, as if he were reading from a script. "But where is it you think you're going?"

Zhu De explained that he had pressing matters to attend to in Beijing, and Jake had business to attend to in Washington. After the admiral's inevitable victory in the Gulf, the Reparationists would need to understand the futility of their claims. "This will be a diplomatic effort," Zhu De said. "One the two of us will play a role in. So, you see, we must return before your flotilla enters the Gulf. Also, neither of us are fighting men. We'd only get in the way."

Admiral Ma crossed his arms over his chest. "I'm quite sorry, but you'll have to stay here." He pressed a button on his desk and the sentry from outside appeared, ready to escort Jake and Zhu De from his office.

Jake wasn't sure what to make of this. There must be some mistake, Zhu De protested. When the admiral assured him that there was no mistake, Zhu De became furious. He peppered the admiral with words like "unacceptable" and "outrageous" and threatened to inform the Politburo Standing Committee of their unwarranted detention. The sentry reached for Zhu De's arm, to restrain him, but the admiral waved him away. "Place yourself in my position," he said. "The Politburo Standing Committee sent you to check on me, correct? When you return, you're to file a report on what you've seen here, correct?"

Zhu De opened his mouth to speak, but the admiral silenced him.

"Don't deny it—they sent you to spy on me. If I send you back, they'll use your report to meddle in my affairs or, if our plans aren't successful, to make me a scapegoat later." He glanced from Zhu De to Jake Shriver. "That's something your family understands," he added, evoking the memory of Jake's grandfather, who'd disappeared after the Politburo held him accountable for a military debacle of their own making. "If I keep you with me, there's nothing they can do about it until after the battle. If I'm victorious, they'll hardly care that I detained you both for a few days. If for any reason we aren't victorious . . . well, I'll have greater things to worry about than the two of you."

A panicked expression settled on Zhu De's face.

"You'll be completely safe," said the admiral, as if to calm him. "Our plans are perfectly laid; our adversary is unaware of our approach; right now, they're tracking a small American flotilla in the Atlantic, a decoy led by the *John Paul Jones*. They'll be taken entirely by surprise when we appear in their rear, in the Gulf, and this engagement will be taken care of swiftly, almost before it begins. You'll be in no danger."

The admiral explained that, in the meantime, the two of them could have the run of his ship. They could speak to any crew member they wished and see anything they wanted. He had nothing to hide; he simply didn't want anyone meddling in his affairs, not now. Zhu De was silent. Jake couldn't tell if he were too angered at being detained or too terrified of the impending battle to respond, so Jake took it upon himself to thank the admiral "for being so accommodating."

Admiral Ma nodded appreciatively. "I only wish we were meeting under better circumstances," he said. "When this is over, you'll pass along my regards to your family, won't you?"

22:17 Nov 26, 2084 (-2 GMT)
Nuuk, Republic of Greenland

No one would listen to them. Tick-Tock had called Tallahassee from a conference room in the private terminal's business center. After an operator transferred him several times, he found himself on the line with a rear-echelon staffer in Brigadier Clay's office. He described the convoy of ships they'd seen streaming across the Pole, south toward the Gulf. He made the staffer promise to relay this information to Clay aboard the *Aradu*. Several hours later, the staffer called back. A brief encrypted response had arrived from Clay: *Information inconclusive.* Tick-Tock was beside himself. The next morning, he decided to go outside his chain of command and call his old friend von Hütschler in Brazil, who promised to relay the message himself.

At Julia's urging, Tick-Tock finally left the airport. She offered him the guest room in her diplomatic residence. Tick-Tock awoke the next morning to a message to call von Hütschler back.

"I've relayed your message," von Hütschler said, "but the response I received was identical. The information is inconclusive."

"Joko told you that?"

"I spoke to Captain Duarte about the matter."

"Duarte?" Tick-Tock reminded himself to breathe . . . breathe . . . But instead of breathing he found himself barking down the line. "You needed to speak to Commodore Joko . . . Duarte doesn't have the balls to go around Clay . . . and Clay's determined to launch this second strike . . . I can't believe you would—"

Von Hütschler would only take so much abuse. “Colonel Dundee,” he said formally, in a tone he had never used with his old friend. “I don’t have time for this. You should take up the matter with your own chain of command, not your allies.” He hung up.

Julia returned from work to find Tick-Tock sitting on the edge of the living room sofa, staring off into space, a glass of rye whiskey in his hand. He explained what had happened. He still thought that if he could speak directly to Commodore Joko, it might make a difference. But he’d exhausted his options. What if Julia reached out to Joko in her capacity as a UN official . . .

“You know I can’t do that,” she said. She sat next to him on the sofa and put one hand gently on his knee.

“I know.”

“The UN can’t appear to take sides.”

Tick-Tock’s head dipped like he was staring into a hole in the floor in front of him.

“I’d help if I could,” Julia added.

“I know you would.” His eyes met hers.

Julia took a sip of whiskey from his glass.

He looked down at the floor again. “Have you ever thought about quitting? No more responsibility, living just for yourself?”

“All the time,” she said. “I think about it all the time.”

“Then why haven’t you quit? A sense of duty? A need to matter?”

“I never had something to quit for.”

Tick-Tock leaned over and kissed her on the mouth. “I quit,” he said.

Julia felt as if a flashbulb had gone off in her face. She blinked several times, and when her vision came back into focus she saw that he was watching her. Only then did she know what she would do.

"I quit too," she found herself saying. She kissed him back, hard. They collapsed into one another. Awkward and limb-tangled, they undressed.

Although Julia's diplomatic residence contained many well-appointed bedrooms, they spent the night under a single blanket on the sofa, their bodies fitted tightly together. They slept late into the following morning.

07:42 Nov 28, 2084 (-4 GMT)
400 nm east of OPS Box Yankee

For four days, the dozen-odd ships of the *John Paul Jones* strike group had engaged the armada in a game of cat and mouse. Each time Commodore Joko pinpointed his adversary's location—whether by sensor or reconnaissance flight—they vanished. They would reappear just as he was ready to break off his chase. He could never get a clean shot. Joko couldn't help but feel as if the Americans were toying with him.

Brigadier Clay had convinced General Suharto that the one-two punch of destroying the *John Paul Jones* strike group combined with a second missile strike against the Eastern Seaboard would incapacitate the Americans, forcing them to accept terms of surrender.

"We can win right here," Clay said. "For all time and forever. We just need to keep after them."

Now, four hundred nautical miles east of OPS Box Yankee, the Americans once again popped up and then vanished. Commodore Joko and the armada faced a difficult choice. They gathered on another call to decide whether to continue their pursuit, extending themselves dangerously far into the Atlantic, or to simply let the *John Paul Jones* go, conduct the strike on the East Coast, and prepare to support the resettlement fleet.

Joko thought it was time to let the *John Paul Jones* go. It was too risky to continue their pursuit. Clay vehemently disagreed, pounding fist into palm as he reiterated his belief that a decisive victory was within their grasp. When his argument was met with silence, he added, “History will hold us accountable if we allow this moment to pass.”

“Ah yes, *history* . . . ,” said General Suharto from his desk in Nusantara, half a world away. With his chin cradled in his palm, he looked like a student forced to sit through an interminable lecture. “The Russians at the gates of Kyiv. The Japanese at Pearl Harbor. The British at Trafalgar. The Spanish Armada. When there’s everything to lose and everything to gain . . . *history.* Alexander at Gaugamela . . . do you know that one?”

Clay shrugged.

“The Persians had been invading Greece for centuries, so the Greeks invaded them right back, not unlike what we’re doing against the Consortium. After several years of campaigning, Alexander had chased King Darius into Persian territory. Their two armies met on a dust-covered plain—Gaugamela. A hundred thousand Persians faced off against half as many Greeks. With their superior numbers, the Persians performed a double envelopment. The Persians, convinced of victory, weakened their center, pouring soldiers onto the flanks of the Greek army. But the Greeks proved a hard nut to crack. The Persians couldn't quite break through the Greek hoplite phalanxes.

"That's when Alexander struck. He took his bodyguard and charged right at the Persian center, right at Darius. Alexander had him within his grasp. He could see the Persian king. He could end the war right there. But, at that very moment, Alexander received an urgent dispatch from Parmenion, one of his most trusted generals. His right flank was crumbling. Parmenion couldn't have been clearer: If Alexander didn't break off his chase and reinforce his right flank, it would collapse. Alexander would lose his army. But if Alexander captured Darius, he would gain an empire."

"Why don't you just tell us what Alexander did." Clay smirked.

"He was overextended, with his army disintegrating around him . . . he did the only thing he could: He reinforced Parmenion. He let Darius go."

Clay laughed dismissively. "What a pussy."

"What?"

"You heard me."

"Who? . . . Alexander?" Suharto was incredulous.

"Yeah," said Clay.

"You know he conquered the known world . . ."

"Maybe later he did," said Clay, unwilling to absorb the lesson of this old story worn smooth with the telling. "But he pussed out when it came to Darius."

"Give it a rest." Von Hütschler couldn't take much more. "Brigadier

Clay, what do you make of a report that a Chinese fleet is moving into the Gulf?"

"What?" asked Joko. "Who reported that?"

Clay slitted his eyes at von Hütschler.

"Our sensors in the Atlantic would have picked them up," said Joko. "They'd have to move straight through us. What report?"

"Not if they came across the Pole and down the Mississippi," said Suharto. He understood the threat intuitively. "That'd be quite a maneuver . . . if it's even possible. How sure are we?"

"This is single-source reporting," said Clay. He made sure to answer before von Hütschler could. "When Colonel Dundee was flying into Nuuk, he thought he saw something, some ships traveling south from the Pole."

"*Chinese* ships," von Hütschler said firmly.

"We don't know that," answered Clay.

Joko asked Clay why he hadn't passed this along. Clay hadn't thought it merited dissemination. "Am I supposed to report to this group every time one of our pilots thinks he sees something?"

A junior sailor entered the room where Joko and Clay were seated, interrupting the conference. He placed a situation report in front of Joko, who immediately relayed its contents. "The *John Paul Jones* has reappeared. They're about two hundred nautical miles east of their last position."

General Suharto leaned forward, his ghostly holograph flickering as the communications uplink weakened. "Commodore, can you give chase while effectively deploying a reconnaissance to our exposed flank in the Gulf?"

Joko did some quick calculations in this head, solving for time and distance. "Yes, sir, think so. I'd say we can go another three hundred miles into the open Atlantic before our reconnaissance assets fall out of range."

It was agreed. The armada would continue its pursuit of the *John Paul Jones*, at least a little farther, while simultaneously conducting a reconnaissance in the Gulf, just in case. When the holographic conference was over, Joko and Clay were left alone at the table.

"Don't ever withhold information from me again," said Joko.

Clay stood to leave, ignoring him.

"Did you hear me?" repeated Joko.

"Yeah, I heard you," said Clay. "But sometimes you boys just can't get outta your own way. You got the whole damn Consortium by the balls, and you want to let 'em go? Unbelievable. How do you think that's gonna work out? How'd it work out for Parmenion?"

"For who?"

"For Parmenion, son of Philotas, commander of the right flank at Gaugamela, general to both Phillip II of Macedon and later to his son Alexander. You think I don't know this shit? Don't you and your general let *this*," and he gestured at his appearance from head to toe, "confuse you as to my competence. And don't confuse being able to win a round of military *Jeopardy!* . . . 'Er, I'll take Ancient Battlefield Fuck-Ups for $10,000' . . . for sound generalship and decision-making. As for Parmenion, things didn't work out so great for him. Alexander never forgave him for Darius's escape. A year after Gaugamela, Alexander had Parmenion's throat slit."

The sailor reappeared in the doorway. "Sir," he said, "begging your pardon, but Captain Gambo wants to know your orders for the *Aradu.*"

"Tell Captain Gambo that we'll be setting a course for the last known position of the *John Paul Jones,*" Joko said. "All ahead full."

08:30 Nov 28, 2084 (+5:30 GMT)
New Delhi

Major General Sandeep Patel, the director of India's defense innovation lab, summoned Lily Bao to his office. He hadn't elaborated on the purpose of their meeting. Lily felt uneasy about this, so she'd brought Yorgos. The defense ministry's outer layers of security appeared normal, but as they drew closer to Patel's office, their progress slowed. Every door required a fingerprint or a retinal scan, or in one case a DNA sample swabbed from their cheeks.

A young officer escorted them. She held a key card to another pad on another door. The pad flashed green. Three heavy locks opened with a sound like soda cans crushed underfoot. The door slid into a thick wall, opening onto an unlit corridor. A single red-colored fluorescent strip, the width of a tape measure, ran the corridor's length. The young officer explained that she wasn't authorized to proceed any farther; the two of them should follow the strip on the floor.

"To where?" Yorgos asked.

The officer wasn't quite sure. She'd never been through this door. Lily and Yorgos stepped into the corridor and the door throttled shut behind them.

Aside from the fluorescent strip on the floor, the corridor was impenetrably dark. Lily counted their strides as if this might help them find their way back. When her foot touched the ground on its fifty-seventh step, she heard the familiar noise of locks shuttling out of their casements. A rectangle of white light appeared ahead. She and Yorgos paused, then proceeded. They walked through the door and into the light. It took a moment for their eyes to adjust. Lily heard Patel before she saw him.

"Madam Chairman," he said. "Are you ready for a little trip?"

12:42 Nov 28, 2084 (-6 GMT)
Vicksburg, Mississippi

True to his word, Admiral Ma granted Zhu De and Jake Shriver the run of his ship. They could go anywhere and do anything they wanted, except leave.

Shriver had taken their detention aboard the *Zheng He* in stride. He explored every corner of the nuclear-powered supercarrier, from its aircraft to its combat control center to its reactor and propulsion systems. The crew knew about their visitors, and Jake simply had to open his mouth with a question to find it eagerly answered by sailors pleased to entertain a rare outsider, and an American at that, who spoke their mother tongue as if it were his own. And the sailors had their own questions for Jake. They had seen the United States, or at least its floodplains, from the deck of their ship. What surprised them most was how poor the country was. Jake explained that this wasn't the case in all corners of America. Near the coasts, wealth congregated.

"How can a country survive like that?" one sailor had asked. Jake hadn't entirely understood.

"Like what?"

"With its heart ripped out."

Zhu De had little interest in exploring the *Zheng He*. He didn't see the point. By the time he could transmit his observations on the readiness of the ship and the morale of its crew to his superiors at Guoanbu headquarters, the information would be irrelevant, their engagement with the armada concluded, its result—a victory or defeat—known. Zhu De stayed in his stateroom, brooding. He appeared in the wardroom only at meals and, using a takeout container, brought his food back to his quarters to eat.

"Why does he behave like this?" Admiral Ma asked Jake. They were sitting at lunch with a handful of other officers when Zhu De arrived in line. Jake didn't have a good answer, except for the obvious one: Zhu De resented his temporary confinement. Admiral Ma crossed the wardroom, and Jake watched as he invited Zhu De to join them. Zhu De shook his head and shuffled back to his room. When Admiral Ma returned to their table, he called Zhu De a fool. "Just because he insists on staying in the dark," he added, "doesn't mean you should." He motioned for Jake to follow him.

They went into a conference room where a briefing was underway, voice-only over a secure line. As Jake settled into the back row of seats, behind the admiral, he recognized the speaker; it was Eva Boucher.

"How certain are you?" she asked.

An American voice, whom Jake assumed was the captain of the *John Paul Jones*, replied, "One hundred percent, ma'am. The *Aradu* has taken the bait. They haven't changed course. They're continuing their pursuit."

"How much longer until our ally's last ship enters the Gulf?"

Admiral Ma announced himself on the line before answering Boucher's question. They would need another day.

Silence met this assessment.

"Admiral Ma," said Boucher, "I'm not sure we have another day. We're lucky the armada has followed the *John Paul Jones* this far out to sea. We need you in position now."

"We need a day," repeated Admiral Ma.

"Can the *John Paul Jones* hold out another day?" Boucher asked.

Silence. Jake could imagine the captain and crew, isolated on the open ocean, conferring among themselves. Static intermingled with the captain's voice, giving it a far-off sound, as if his words were coming down a long tunnel. "If we go farther east, it's unlikely the armada will continue to follow us. If we maneuver in any other direction, they'll locate us immediately. We're boxed in."

Admiral Ma still needed another day.

"I don't see how another day is possible." Boucher sounded defeated. "If the *John Paul Jones* broke contact, Admiral, could you initiate an attack with a portion of your fleet? Otherwise, the armada will have nothing to prevent them from launching a second strike against our targets on the East Coast."

Jake was sitting among Admiral Ma's staff. From their murmurs he could tell that a partial attack wasn't an option. Before Admiral Ma could break the news to Boucher, a staticky transmission from the *John Paul Jones* filled the room. "We'll get you your one day, Admiral."

Admiral Ma leaned forward. "How will you do that, Commodore?" He paused as if suddenly realizing that he didn't even know this American officer's name.

"We'll turn course and attack. That'll do it. That'll get you your day."

The room went silent.

Admiral Ma promised him that they'd use it well.

07:47 Nov 29, 2084 (-2 GMT)
Sarqaq, Republic of Greenland

Julia had alerted her colleagues at the UN: the Chinese fleet was descending the Mississippi into the Gulf of Mexico. No one doubted her, but they refused to do anything about it. They wouldn't confront the Chinese or any other Consortium nation, and they wouldn't warn the Reparationists.

When Julia relayed the response to Tick-Tock, he'd bitterly muttered, "Hypocrites." But that didn't seem quite right to her. A hypocrite says one thing while doing the opposite. Few inside or outside the UN considered it to be more than a deliberative body, an organization with no teeth. If the UN had no teeth, could Julia really fault them for not taking a bite? No, they weren't quite hypocrites, but something else: *irrelevant.*

Julia was feeling the weight of the UN's irrelevance—and by extension her own—when she suggested to Tick-Tock that the two of them get away, just for a night. She wanted to show him the place she'd bought outside of Sarqaq, a sleepy fishing village that was experiencing a real estate boom. She'd gotten a good deal on a two-bedroom stone cottage sitting on ninety irrigable acres with a fallow vineyard and garden.

Instead of the gravi-train, Julia suggested they travel by ferry. It would take twice as long and use twice as much of their monthly carbon allowance, but it would give Tick-Tock a chance to view the explosion of gentrified residential development along Greenland's intercoastal waterways. He'd said little as they embarked; neither of them had addressed what'd happened the night before, what their lovemaking had meant. Julia hadn't wanted to raise it, though she hoped he might. During the first awkward hour of their journey, she'd interpreted Tick-Tock's extended silences as having to do with his mixed feelings.

They sat on the crowded port side of the ferry, which had the best views. Newly built glass and concrete mansions mixed with older, weather-beaten homes with each season's worth of repaired wooden slats striping their sides.

"You know, this is what used to be called a *posh* journey." Julia was searching for any toehold into a conversation.

Tick-Tock glanced up and down the length of the ferry, the torn vinyl seat cushions, the sickly orange rust blotches that stained the white paint, the galley that sold coffee with powdered creamer in paper cups. "Doesn't seem too posh to me."

"Posh didn't originally mean fancy," Julia explained. "The term's a relic from Imperial Britain, an acronym: *port out, starboard home.* When they'd travel from Britain to India by ship, there was a consistent north-to-south breeze that would blow during the hot summer months. On the outward journey east, this made the cabins on the port side of the ship more expensive because a person could open a window and enjoy the breeze. On the journey home, that breeze was felt in the cabins on the starboard side of the ship. So if a person was upper-class, they traveled posh: *port out, starboard home.* The best views on this ferry are posh."

Tick-Tock's droopy mustache bracketed his mouth as he smiled. The two sat in a silence that Julia could hardly stand. "Did I say or do something that upset you?"

"Upset me?" He took her hand. "No, that's not it." He was pressing his fingers through hers, braiding them together.

"Then what is it?" As soon as the question escaped her mouth, she felt uncertain of it. Perhaps she was pushing him too hard. She hadn't been with someone in a very long time. The simple fact was that being on her own for so long had left her not knowing how to be.

"It's good to see people building homes beside the water," he said. "It's good they have that confidence. It reminds me of how things once were, all the way back when I was a kid . . . this place is beautiful . . . really beautiful . . . I guess climate change has had some winners."

"But you seem upset."

"I'm not upset," he said.

Julia relented. She didn't need him to put a word to what he was feeling. And so they sat, sharing the silence for a while longer, their fingers entwined as they drew closer to their destination.

Eventually, Tick-Tock said, "I'm scared. If you really want to know, that's what's going on."

She didn't ask *Of what?* Instead, she got up, went to the canteen, and returned with two coffees. They sipped their coffees as they pulled into Sarqaq, the ferry threading its way between the islets that led to the old port. She described her place to him, the cottage where they'd spend that night and the plot of land she'd bought on what had then seemed an impulse and now seemed like a decision that might determine the remaining years of her life.

That night, after a day spent at the property together and a simple dinner with a bottle of wine from a neighboring vineyard, they readied for bed. Tick-Tock sat on the edge of the mattress in his powder-blue pajamas, his feet tucked in his slippers, his left hand on his left knee, his right hand on his right knee, his back straight, his eyes forward, his body as rigid as if he were in the cockpit about to be catapulted off the carrier deck. Julia emerged from the bathroom in a silk nightgown, one she'd bought years ago but had never worn. Like the cottage, she'd bought it on impulse. She sat beside Tick-Tock, her arms looped around his neck.

Their day had been perfect, she said, and she wanted to end it that way.

His body remained rigid, as if he were still braced in his cockpit.

"What's the matter?" she asked.

"I'm not sure you'll understand."

Whatever it was, she would try, Julia said.

"I want to stay here with you. I want it so much, and that's scaring me."

"I want that too," she whispered.

"It'll get taken away." He shut his eyes like a child who believes that if he can't see the evil thing, then the evil thing can't see him. Julia lifted the blankets and climbed into bed with him. They left the bedside lamp on as if they weren't quite ready to call it a night, but they drifted to sleep.

Julia dreamed of her mother for the first time in years.

When she awoke the following morning, she still hadn't pieced together the particulars of the dream. But she had a strong sense of foreboding. Tick-Tock was right. Julia felt certain. The little they had together would soon be taken away.

18:17 Nov 29, 2084 (+5:30 GMT)
Shimla

Lily Bao was struggling to adjust to the altitude. When they arrived at the defense ministry in New Delhi to meet with Major General Patel, Lily had assumed they would visit the research lab dedicated to Beginner's Mind. Lily hadn't been wrong. What she had been wrong about was the location. It was in the Himalayas, more than two hundred miles north, in a clandestine facility in Shimla.

The town itself, with its Alpine-style chalets and Anglophone churches nestled among Hindu temples and Mughal forts, was a paean to a stubbornly persistent colonial legacy. With its temperate climate, Shimla had once served as the summer seat of the British Raj. Now an international jet set of Consortium elites had taken up residence. They considered Shimla a safe harbor in the event of a mass extinction event—climate related or otherwise. Their private wealth had become the great colonizing force in Shimla, turning it into a destination that had snatched the mantle for over-the-top luxury once held by mountain redoubts like Aspen, Gstaad, or St. Moritz. To Lily, it seemed an unlikely location to house a sensitive research program. But Patel had explained that residents of these uber-wealthy enclaves were always incubating some utopian initiative or another, so hers hid in plain sight; Beginner's Mind was one more to add to the pile.

The secure room inside the defense ministry, where Lily and Yorgos had arrived, hadn't been an office, or lab, but rather a terminal for the gravi-train, which connected the most sensitive sites in India's defense infrastructure through subterranean high-speed rail. The gravi-train they boarded took them directly from New Delhi to Shimla, to an underground entrance to Wildflower Hall, a luxury hotel built on the site of Lord Kitchener's summer home. The Indian military had built a modest but comprehensive lab into a lower floor. That night, the three of them had congregated in a private dining room off Wildflower Hall's main restaurant for dinner. In the morning, Patel would return from Shimla to New Delhi. He'd originally planned to stay through at least the following evening, but reports of heightened activity between Consortium and Reparationist navies in the Gulf of Mexico and mid-Atlantic were drawing him back to the defense ministry.

The dining room, which was well-appointed with Wildflower Hall monogrammed silver, generations-old crystal, twin chandeliers, and a polished mahogany table, required a retinal scan to enter. This modern security measure notwithstanding, the décor suggested a gilded, high-society dining room from Imperial Britain's past. As they sat, Lily noticed that the waitstaff had discreetly set the evening's meal on banquet tables in the back of the room. The three of them would serve themselves and so remain undisturbed.

After they found their seats, Patel stood at the head of the table. He had chosen to wear his formal military uniform with its vibrant rows of colored ribbons and medals pinned over his chest. A light dusting of gray on his sideburns and the subtle cat's cradle of wrinkles that framed his mouth were all that betrayed his age. He declared, as if for the record, that the public-private partnership between the Indian Ministry of Defense and the Tandava Group entitled Lily, as its chairman, to a full briefing on Beginner's Mind.

In simple terms, he explained that Beginner's Mind was an effort to fuse a biological and technological consciousness, to give the human mind the power of God's mind. The world had edged close to this thirty years ago, around the time of the near civil war in America. A handful of humans had a chance to achieve this singularity, a fusion of a human mind with quantum computing. But ultimately, the power unleashed by the singularity was deemed too much of a risk. Those who achieved this advanced knowledge had buried it where they found it. Or so it was thought. The Indian defense ministry had since managed to replicate certain of these advances through a partnership with the Tandava Group.

"Your predecessor took Beginner's Mind further than many believed possible," Patel told Lily. "This current crisis places us at a moment when we must consider the role such a capability might play in stopping this climate war before either side escalates further, or perhaps goes nuclear, as the US and China did half a century ago. If there is a path to de-escalating this conflict and reducing the effects of the climate on Midworld, we have an obligation to explore it." His rows of medals made a clinking noise as he sat back down.

"The name," said Lily, "I'm not sure I understand the relevance of Beginner's Mind."

"*In the beginning*," said Patel. "That's Genesis 1:1; it opens both the Torah and Bible. We assume that technological breakthroughs are always forward-looking, the result of accretions of human knowledge. But if we're looking for a godlike consciousness, perhaps human instinct is what's holding us back. Let's not forget, cavemen are the ones who invented the gods. To draw closer to God's mind, we must return to an earlier, beginner's version of consciousness. Beginner's Mind allows us to strip away what we know, to get out of our own way."

Yorgos interjected, "If Beginner's Mind has been used to enhance our environmental research, why house it under Tandava's military vertical?"

Patel folded his hands on the table. A brief and awkward silence ensued before he answered. "This was long a point of contention between the defense ministry and Lily's predecessor. After some time spent in the lab, I'm hopeful you'll come to appreciate the ministry's view on the matter."

05:42 Nov 30, 2084 (-4 GMT)
525 nm northeast of OPS Box Yankee

Commodore Joko adhered to "stand-to" as a military protocol, a belief that the most likely time for an enemy attack was the hour before dawn and the hour before dusk. He made sure to position himself on the bridge then, particularly in the morning when everyone not on watch was asleep. Alongside his crew, he would wait out the hour when an attacker could place the sun at their back and strike unseen. The practice had begun 170 years before, the first time the world had gone to war, in the trenches of the Western Front. At dawn, the Germans could attack with the rising sun at their backs. At dusk, the French and British could attack just the same. Some things never change, thought Joko as he stood on the bridge of the *Aradu*, flanked by two Nigerian petty officers. The younger sailors hovered over a suite of sensors while Joko scanned the horizon with a set of binoculars.

It was only yesterday, as the armada continued their pursuit of the *John Paul Jones*, that they'd sent the unmanned reconnaissance flight west. They'd lost contact with the flight over Alabama, near Mobile. They assumed a malfunction. Before that flight had gone dark, it had mapped two-thirds of the Gulf, showing no unusual activity. They would launch a second flight today, just to be safe. It was the first item on the ship's schedule, after stand-to.

Joko glanced down onto the deck of the *Aradu*. Three hypersonic drones sat cradled in their launchers, angled upward at forty-five degrees, ready to fire. By that evening, Joko expected to have the armada repositioned in the center of OPS Box Yankee. From there, they'd launch their second strike on the East Coast, reducing a few final strategic targets before returning to friendly waters to augment the resettlement escorts.

A band of water along the horizon was turning iridescent as dawn broke. Joko couldn't help but think of his wife Gemi, his daughter Citra, and that other sweet, long-vanished life of his. He stared into the shimmer. The ships under his command had proven that the United States was a paper tiger. The Consortium wouldn't hold together when tested. Reparations seemed a foregone conclusion. Those whose only crime was being born in countries ravaged by the environmental excesses of wealthy Consortium nations could now be safely resettled and spared the loss he'd experienced. Joko allowed himself the thought that his family would have been proud of him.

The *Aradu* cut a wake due east.

"Sir," said one of the sailors as he hovered over his suite of sensors. "I'm catching an unusual amount of atmospheric interference. It's washing out our radar, thermals too . . ."

Joko felt the hairs on the backs of his arms raise as if a balloon charged with static electricity had passed over his skin. A blizzard of static washed out all the sensors. Joko glanced at his watch. The second hand had frozen. To check the time, he glanced at the sun, which hovered half a palm's width above the horizon. This old mariner's trick told him that half an hour had passed since dawn. He searched with his binoculars through a veil of early morning mist. A thicker shape appeared, its slate-gray sides sharpening into a solid object.

He observed a flash, a meager blossom of light.

"Contact off the bow!" he shouted.

The sailor watching his sensors also saw it. General quarters sounded, its nervous siren booming from the bridge down into the bowels of the ship. The close-in weapons system, CIWS, affectionately known as the sea-wiz, with its six-barreled 20mm Vulcan cannon, juked from side to side on its swiveled base, tracking the incoming missiles. The ship's more sophisticated lasers swung toward the threat as well. Joko could see the spread of three main missiles darting toward them surrounded by a cloud of decoys. He could tell two of the main missiles would go wide, one splashing to port and the other to starboard. But the last one was on target. "Brace for impact!" he shouted. The crew took cover, huddling on the deck. Joko's small inner voice said, *Stand tall on the bridge.* He forced himself to stare straight ahead at the incoming missile.

A swarm of armor-piercing tungsten penetrator rounds, like a beaded veil, appeared to his front, only a few yards off the bow. Laser beams flashed and danced in front of his ship. The disparate speed of light and sound created a bizarre incongruity in this universe of hypersonic combat. Events appeared in mute only to have their attendant sounds catch up as a later irrelevance, like an unnecessary comment in an argument that has already been won. Joko saw the sea-wiz's defensive cannon intercept the missile, then he heard the missile's inert remnants splatter across the deck of the ship.

Joko gave two orders. First, the *Aradu* would turn to port so its starboard faced the enemy *John Paul Jones* strike group, whose ships had evaded their sensors and now loomed close on the horizon. Joko needed his flotilla to position itself for a rapid broadside of responding fires. Before launching that broadside, the *Aradu* would execute Joko's second order, releasing the hypersonic reconnaissance drones racked in their launchers. As Joko was giving this order, Clay ran onto the bridge with a half dozen of his staffers in tow.

"Get back down to your stateroom," Joko barked. "That's your battle station."

"Like hell it is," said Clay. He bent over to catch his breath. "The enemy's right there and you're launching a reconnaissance?"

Joko ignored Clay. Captain Gambo began supervising the crew's final launch sequence while Joko kept watch on the horizon.

". . . three, two, one, fire!" The petty officer flicked a switch. An ascent of contrails uncoiled from the launcher on the storm deck as the hypersonic drones traveled skyward, angling into their suborbital flight pattern. Joko started the timer on his watch, which was again working. They could expect the first of the reconnaissance footage within the hour.

Gambo commanded the bridge, barking out orders. His gunners were readying a salvo of older-generation, Russian-made Zircon anti-ship missiles. While Gambo handled the particulars—registering the targeting data, refining the charges for each rocket, adjusting the speed and heading of his ship—Joko coordinated with the *Banda Aceh*. They needed to launch aircraft armed with an assortment of air-to-air and air-to-surface munitions.

Joko also had orders for Captain Duarte. Instead of prepping nearer-range, lower-tech Zircons like Gambo, he was to maneuver in trace of the *Aradu* with his full suite of hypersonic over-the-horizon anti-ship missiles at the ready. When the *Aradu* hit the *John Paul*

Jones strike group with the full complement of Zircons, Joko expected the Americans to try to break contact. Duarte would be in position and ready to hit them a second time as they ran.

These preparations had to be handled, second by second, via an intricate, highly technical, and choreographed set of commands. But Clay kept interrupting. *Was it a good idea for the* Aradu *to use the Zircons? Should they hold fewer aircraft in reserve?* At first, Joko ignored him. There was no time to answer his questions. But Clay became more intrusive and more esoteric in his concerns. He began to prattle on about the threat of unmanned torpedo boats and submersibles. Joko swiveled on his heels. He couldn't take it anymore.

But as Joko opened his mouth to speak, Gambo interjected. "Brigadier Clay, the unmanned surface and submersible threat is a concern of mine too." Gambo was multitasking as he spoke, double-checking firing tables, confirming his ship's speed and heading as they entered their missile launch sequence. "After we deploy the Zircons, we could be vulnerable. We don't have enough crew to man our near-range defensive weapons. We could use you and your staff on the aft guns." He gestured behind them to a pair of largely irrelevant DShK heavy machine guns typically used for security when in port. "We have body armor and ammunition below. It would be critically important to have you and your men back there."

Clay glanced skeptically at Joko, who eased his mouth shut, as if uncocking a pistol. "Sure, why not," said Clay. "Happy to pick up some slack for you."

The *Banda Aceh* was launching aircraft. Captain Duarte reported that his ship had maneuvered in trace of the *Aradu* with its over-the-horizon munitions ready for a follow-on strike. Captain Gambo reported that his sensors were tracking the *John Paul Jones* as well as four other targets. "Commodore Joko," Gambo said, standing to attention. "We're ready to launch at your command."

Joko raised his binoculars a last time, leveling them on the horizon, where he could make out the vague impression of the American flotilla. "Very well, Captain Gambo. Fire!"

03:16 Nov 30, 2084 (-2 GMT)
Sarqaq, Republic of Greenland

Julia Hunt awoke in the middle of the night. She reached for Tick-Tock, but her hand found only his empty impression on the bed. They'd spent the day before on her property, reading, strolling around the ninety acres, driving into town to run errands. Tick-Tock had needed a change of clothes, so he'd bought a pair of jeans and two flannel shirts. She teased that he looked like a farmer. He asked if she liked what he'd picked. She said that the clothes suited him, that he made a good-looking farmer. He smiled. Those jeans and flannel were now folded neatly over a chair in the corner.

Julia opened the bedroom door and stepped into the sitting room, lit by the small lamp on the desk at which Tick-Tock sat, facing a window framed with a timbered lintel. He was hunched over a single sheet of paper, writing. Softly, she asked, "Are you coming back to bed?"

He startled. "Jesus, you scared me." He set his pen on the page and swiveled in his chair, facing her. She straddled him, looping her arms around his neck. She leaned her weight against him, pinning him to the chair. "What's this?" she asked, picking up the sheet of paper.

"Hey, I'm not done with that." Tick-Tock reached awkwardly above his head as if for the ejection handle in an aircraft.

"Is this a resignation letter?"

Tick-Tock reached his hands under her thighs and came to his feet carrying her, like a parent carrying a sleepy child. He walked back through the door, flung her onto the bed, and snatched the paper from her hand. "I'm not done with that yet." He walked back to the desk.

Julia came up behind him, sliding her hand under his shirt and onto his chest. "We've got to get up early," she said. They had to take the ferry back to Nuuk. Julia was due at her office in the morning. "Why don't you sleep on it?"

He glanced down at the sheet again. "I'd like to stay with you."

"And I want you to, but let's get to bed. Tomorrow's going to come early."

Tick-Tock shut off the lamp and followed Julia into the darkness. They lay beside one another. Neither slept.

08:25 Nov 30, 2084 (-4 GMT)
450 nm northeast of OPS Box Yankee

The damage reports sent by the *John Paul Jones* strike group to the *Zheng He* were sounding increasingly desperate. Zhu De and Jake Shriver stood shoulder to shoulder in the back of the crowded combat information center listening to the transmissions as Admiral Ma praised the valor of the American sailors while taking his time to maneuver his ships into position. His plan was coming together. The Reparationists had taken the bait, blowing through their ammunition stores as they pilloried the *John Paul Jones.* Aside from a second hypersonic reconnaissance flight, which Admiral Ma's crews had disabled with electromagnetic disruptors, just like the first, the armada's attention was focused solely on the *John Paul Jones*, to their east. The Reparationists were looking in the wrong direction.

The first wave of Admiral Ma's attack would consist of a dozen unmanned stealth torpedo boats with a nearly invisible radar signature. They would strike the Reparationist armada from behind, making interception unlikely. Admiral Ma had selected the *Aradu* as his first target. He suspected this was the armada's command ship. A frenzy of activity consumed the combat control center as the *Zheng He* strike group crossed the seventy-five-nautical-mile threshold, their trigger line for launching the torpedo boats.

The crew's focus was interrupted by another transmission from the *John Paul Jones.* They'd already lost their starboard screw and rudder, and could only turn in circles. They were about to lose their port screw. A fire in the magazine had grown out of control. Even if the armada didn't attack again, secondary explosions meant their own ordnance would soon sink them. The captain had ordered his surviving crew to abandon ship. "Very well," said Admiral Ma to the staticky, discombobulated voice on the other end of the radio. "That's understood, the crew will abandon ship . . . What are your plans, captain?"

"Say again the question?" Radio static and a background of panicked voices blended with the captain's voice.

"*Your* plans, captain? The crew will abandon ship. What about *you*?" Admiral Ma's eyes narrowed. He listened intently, but in return came only static.

Admiral Ma returned the radio handset to its cradle. He surveyed the clutch of sailors around him, until his gaze found Zhu De and Jake Shriver. Both had been listening to the exchange. "Very disappointing," said the admiral to the two of them. He came up on his tiptoes as if this would allow his words to carry above the heads of the others. "A captain stays with his ship, even to the end."

Admiral Ma plopped down into his seat and gave the command to launch. The crew set the stealth torpedo boats on course for the *Aradu.* A live stream of their progress projected on one of the half dozen screens hung across the combat control center. From a camera mounted to the bow of one of the torpedo boats, the stern of the *Aradu* came into view. "There!" shouted Admiral Ma, pointing to the screen. He leaned in closer. "We've got them." The profile of the *Aradu* grew larger and larger on the horizon as the torpedo boats rapidly approached. On impact, Admiral Ma would launch a second salvo of missiles at multiple targets within the armada, but this first blow would be a sucker punch from behind.

The weapons officer began a countdown to impact . . . "One minute . . ." The *Aradu* took up nearly the entire frame of the first torpedo boat's onboard camera . . . "Forty-five-seconds . . ." The torpedo boat had drawn so close that it could observe movement on the deck, what looked like crew members scurrying into position . . . "Thirty seconds . . ." A pair of sustained flashes came from the stern of the *Aradu*, where they'd gotten a gun into action . . . "Fifteen seconds . . ." A skirt of turquoise water churned up around the *Aradu* and white spray mounted its bow as the ship began evasive maneuvers. Little geysers were kicking up all around the torpedo boat. Then its camera feed turned to static.

Admiral Ma shouted for a status update. Gunners manning an old-style DShK on the stern of the *Aradu* had sunk the lead torpedo boat. The weapons officer toggled up the positions of the others. Two had also disappeared like the first. The *Aradu* was maneuvering aggressively now, swiveling around so its main defensive weapons systems could meet the remainder of the unmanned torpedo boats. Admiral Ma, along with everyone else, watched the live feed as the *Aradu* skidded across the surface of the ocean like a sports car in a tight turn. They glimpsed the defensive weapons bristling from its bow. The sea-wiz, with its snub-nosed six-barreled cannon, twitched once on its swivel base. Then every live feed on every torpedo boat went to static.

Silence enveloped the command-and-control center.

Zhu De stepped toward the back hatch. "Where do you think you're going?" the admiral asked, catching him in mid-stride. Zhu De muttered that the command-and-control center was getting crowded. "Nonsense," said Admiral Ma. "You'll miss our hour of glory." He turned to the crew. "Set course for the *Aradu*. All weapons and ships modes: full attack."

11:47 Nov 30, 2084 (-4 GMT)
370 nm northeast of OPS Box Yankee

Brigadier Clay sprinted up from the aft gundeck and barged his way onto the bridge. He and his staff had single-handedly saved the *Aradu*, and he wanted everyone to know it. The *Banda Aceh* and three others in their flotilla hadn't been so lucky; they had suffered direct hits. Clay announced himself with a raucous "Did you see that shit!" His voice drowned out the panicked damage-control updates coming from the other ships.

Commodore Joko needed to organize the *Aradu* and the remnants of the Reparationist armada into a line of battle to fire another salvo. Although Joko appreciated Clay's fighting spirit—he was now whipping up the crew with the energy of a revivalist minister—Joko needed calm on the bridge.

"Brigadier Clay," he said. "Let's get you back on those aft guns."

With Clay off the bridge, Joko issued firing commands throughout the armada. Unmanned torpedo boats and submersibles splashed into the water. They fanned out in a broad arc, each with a specific target, and headed directly toward the *Zheng He*'s line of battle. Joko's crews prepped hypersonics. Joko checked his watch. If the timing worked out, the hypersonics, unmanned torpedo boats, and submersibles would arrive simultaneously.

Unlike in centuries and even decades past, the speed and violence of naval combat had made it the modern-day equivalent of a duel. Pistols at dawn. Both sides turned and fired. Whoever was left standing won. The *Zheng He* had taken its first shot. Had it not been for Clay scuttling those torpedo boats with the aft guns, it's doubtful the *Aradu* would have been able to reply. But Joko had been given that chance. He wouldn't get another. After this salvo, he'd need to break contact.

Joko raised his binoculars. The *Zheng He* strike group was deployed over the horizon, so he couldn't get a visual. The *John Paul Jones* had sunk thirty minutes before. It had burned for nearly an hour as its crew abandoned ship. Joko could make out clusters of life rafts bobbing ten miles to starboard. An oily, metallic odor carried itself on a steady breeze; this was the smell of a sunk ship. Joko swallowed the odor and faint taste away. He wouldn't allow himself to associate that fate with his flagship, the *Aradu*.

Captain Gambo was on the ship's phone, taking in the last reports from his department heads. "Commodore Joko," he said, "the hypersonics are ready."

"Very well." Joko gave the command to fire.

Dozens of missiles loosed skyward from their launchers, wreathed in smoke, corkscrewing into their suborbital flight patterns.

Joko glanced at his watch. This would all be decided in minutes.

A drone provided a live feed of the *Zheng He*. Joko observed the several dozen ships of the enemy strike group begin evasive maneuvers, churning up the water around them as their counterbattery radars tracked his incoming salvo of missiles. He also watched as the *Zheng He* fired a quick, retaliatory salvo. Joko's fires officer shouted across the bridge that one of these missiles was heading for them. Joko barely registered the news. His attention remained fixed on the

Zheng He. His flotilla was outgunned, but if he could sink the strike group's flagship, it might create enough disarray to allow him and his diminished armada to escape from this trap and sail back across the ocean to their home ports where they could regroup.

Captain Gambo barked out orders for a series of evasive maneuvers. Sirens blared, a warning to brace for impact. Joko glanced out from the bridge, to belowdecks, reassured to see the crew scrambling inside the skin of the ship to safety, as they'd been trained.

Joko returned to the live feed. The *Zheng He* was immersed in a parallel set of evasive maneuvers, its crew similarly bracing for impact. Joko's attention narrowed to a pinpoint, the voice of the weapons officer counting down the seconds until their strike landed on the *Zheng He*. "Twenty seconds to impact . . . ten seconds . . . five, four, three, two . . ."

The spread of missiles exploding up and down the *Zheng He* strike group caused an atmospheric shock wave. The live feed shuddered, momentarily scrambling to static, then recomposed.

A hole appeared in the superstructure of the *Zheng He*, its sides molten and seeping. Joko could glimpse into the gutted, cavernous belly of the ship. Then it was overcome by smoke, an enormous pillar billowing exultantly into the highest reaches of the atmosphere.

"Direct hit!" shouted the weapons officer.

Joko grasped him by the arm and shook him joyfully, even as the missile defense officer on the other side of the bridge was now shouting his own countdown, followed by "Brace for impact!" Despite their countermeasures, one of the missiles fired by the *Zheng He* was about to find its mark.

"Right full rudder!" shouted Captain Gambo. The ship lurched and violently swiveled, like a motorcycle turning donuts on pavement. The aft section of the *Aradu*, which contained fewer critical systems, was placed directly in the path of the missile.

The impact threw Joko and the crew to the deck. The shriek of splitting metal filled their ears and an oily metallic odor filled their nostrils and mouths. A bluish smoke, snapping with molten flecks, consumed the bridge and billowed out the shattered aft storm window. When the air cleared, Joko found the weapons officer lying on the ground, his hand at his neck, gasping for help as blood soaked the front of his coveralls like a spilled bowl of soup. Crew members straddled him, rendering aid, but his pleas became weaker and weaker until his voice fell silent.

Joko forced himself to step outside the bridge onto the weather deck to survey the damage to the rest of the ship. It looked like Gambo's maneuvers had the intended effect. All the forward weapons systems remained operational. The missile had impacted on the aft section of the ship, which is where Joko's gaze now traveled. The *Aradu* was still churning a wake, so its propulsion systems hadn't been compromised. Joko's relief ebbed as his gaze traveled aft and he noticed the space where the twin DShK machine guns had been mounted. All that remained of them was a tangle of twisted metal. No trace of Clay or any of the Floridians.

Joko ducked back inside the bridge. A blanket in the corner covered the body of the young weapons officer. Joko averted his eyes. He would deal with his feelings later. Gambo called his attention to the live feed. The *Zheng He* was consumed by flames, taking on water.

The first of the crew had begun to board lifeboats. "They're sinking," Gambo said with a quaver in his voice. "What are your orders, sir?"

Joko's mind flipped through the possibilities. They could launch another attack on the *Zheng He*. They could try to pick up survivors. They could sail closer to the East Coast and strike at the United States a second time, their original plan. But to Joko the decision seemed obvious.

"Home," he said. "Set a course."

4

Dead Hand

08:15 Dec 01, 2084 (-2 GMT)
Nuuk, Republic of Greenland

News of the battle awaited Julia when she arrived at UN headquarters. Already, her colleagues were referring to it as "the Battle of Yankee Station," using the Reparationist term for the square of ocean where the two fleets had clashed. Delegates from the Consortium objected to any Reparationist naming convention. They circulated several emails with draft motions that would strike "the Battle of Yankee Station" from the record. The Consortium wanted to designate the battle in all official UN correspondence as "the Attack on the Mid-Atlantic." What neither side—Consortium nor Reparationist—seemed interested in discussing was how to prevent a broader war.

Julia sat at the desk in her office, while on the other side of the door her modest staff drafted a memorandum, an official statement from the Special Representative for the Future of the Planet in response to the current crisis. While Julia waited to give her final sign-off to that draft, she scanned through details of the battle as they appeared in the UN's internal intelligence reports.

The losses were staggering. The Chinese had suffered thirty-seven ships sunk, one-fifth of their entire navy. This included the eight-hundred-thousand-ton supercarrier *Zheng He*, the fleet's flagship, consigned to the bottom of the Atlantic by a barrage of hypersonic missiles. The Reparationists had fared little better. They'd lost the *Banda Aceh*, which the Americans had already damaged some days before, as well as two dozen other ships. Although their losses weren't as great as those of the Consortium, this represented a larger fraction of their naval forces, and Midworld lacked the industrial base to replace what the Consortium had destroyed. Luckily for the Reparationists, their flagship, the Nigerian super destroyer *Aradu*, had escaped the fate of the *Zheng He*.

When Julia's chief of staff emailed her the draft statement, describing the attacks as "an affront to climate security" and "a direct violation of the Nuuk Accords," Julia couldn't help but feel the futility of the statement's final line, the only action she and her colleagues had the power to take: "We hereby condemn these hostilities in the strongest possible terms." Mere words.

Julia told her chief of staff to circulate the statement. She glanced at the time; it was a little before noon. Crisis or no crisis, her colleagues would soon break for lunch. This gave Julia a free hour, or at least an hour when no one would be looking for her. She rushed back to her residence. She needed to check on Tick-Tock.

When Julia arrived at her front door, she paused and took a

breath. She was afraid that Tick-Tock might already be gone. When Julia stepped inside the apartment, his half-packed kit bag was in the foyer, his powder-blue pajamas folded neatly on its unzippered top. Her eyes tracked to the entry table, where beneath the mirror an envelope rested with her name on it in his slanted, all-caps handwriting. Before she could open the envelope, Tick-Tock stepped out of the bathroom. He was wearing his flight suit.

"You're back early," he said, wiping his cleanly shaved chin with a washcloth.

"Were you hoping to avoid seeing me?"

Under his arm, Tick-Tock cradled the flannel shirt and jeans she'd bought him in Sarqaq, his farmer clothes. He set them on the sofa, where they'd slept together that first night.

"I have to go," he said. "I don't want to, but I have to."

"You don't *have* to." But Julia's words fell flat. She—and he—knew this wasn't true. He had to go, just as she had needed to return to work that day. This is what he'd written in the note on the entry table. He simply had to glance in its direction for her to understand. Only the particulars of their separation—not the cold, hard fact of it—remained in question. She asked, "Did Tallahassee call you?"

"Not yet," he said. "But they will. So better not to sit around and wait for their call."

He zipped up his kit bag and stood by the door.

"I know we can't promise each other anything . . ." Julia's voice trailed off. She felt an urge to reach for him, to hold him in place. She wouldn't, though, and so crossed her arms over her chest, holding herself. "But what if we *could* promise each other?" she asked.

“Then we would.” He leaned over and placed a kiss on her cheek.

After Tick-Tock left, Julia returned to her office. Ten minutes of lunch hour remained. She planned to eat a cold sandwich at her desk; instead, Julia found her chief of staff there, standing beside a secure phone.

“Hold on, she’s just arrived,” said her chief of staff to whoever was on the other end of the line. “I’ll tell her to head right up.”

Julia tossed the paper bag with her lunch on the desk. “Who was that?”

“The secretary general’s office. It seems you’re needed in New Delhi.”

04:20 Dec 02, 2084 (-5 GMT)
The Hay-Adams

Jake Shriver lay awake in a double bed on the third floor of the Hay-Adams hotel. Zhu De snored gently in the next bed. When the FBI agents had checked them in that afternoon, he’d insisted on a room on a low floor and the bed nearest the door.

Every time Jake shut his eyes, he was back on the *Zheng He*, its passageways choked with smoke, his ears filled with screams. The backs of his arms were still smooth from where the heat had singed his hair. He’d been on the bridge with Admiral Ma when the barrage of Reparationist hypersonics impacted. Jake had made the mistake of grabbing the admiral by the arm and pleading with him to join the rest of the crew as they scrambled onto the flight deck in search of one of the few remaining lifeboats. Jake's jaw was still sore from where the admiral had struck him—he refused to entertain any notion of abandoning his ship. The last glimpse Jake had of the admiral, he was standing on the bridge, encased in smoke, demanding updates from a nonresponsive damage control, his commands drowned out by the hull-splitting shrieks of steel tearing and the roar of compartments flooding.

Zhu De had been right beside Shriver as they'd scrambled out onto the flight deck, into the harsh smoking daylight. Trapped by flames and the violently listing ship, they had jumped off its port side. With legs braced together at the ankles and arms crossed over their chests, they had plunged into the water four stories below. When they bobbed up, clawing their way toward the mid-Atlantic light, a lifeboat filled with *Zheng He* survivors had hoisted them out of the ocean, its surface a tabletop of burning oil. Within a matter of hours, a dispatch of US Coast Guard vessels had arrived.

Jake Shriver and Zhu De hadn't needed to announce themselves to the crew of their rescue ship. The Americans had been on the lookout for them, picking them out from among the huddles of soaked Chinese sailors cloaked in foil blankets on the aft weather deck. They were taken by helicopter to Washington. The FBI agents who'd retrieved them at Joint Base Andrews had then driven them in a convoy of black SUVs to Brooks Brothers on Connecticut Avenue for new suits, compliments of the US government, to wear for their debriefings.

That suit now lay folded on the chair of Shriver's hotel room. Zhu De continued to snore in the bed beside him. Their final debriefing was scheduled for that morning, at Camp David, with Eva Boucher.

06:20 Dec 02, 2084 (+5:30 GMT)
Shimla

As the details of the battle became known, Beginner's Mind assembled an increasingly complex set of inputs, running its decision-making intelligence over this new reality, in which the Consortium and Reparationists had fought to a draw. Beginner's Mind pulsed with activity, and Lily Bao kept opening the portal that connected her to the AI. She asked question after question, realizing that like an oracle, this technology could only provide answers to the questions it was asked, so knowing to ask the right questions was imperative. Also imperative was knowing how to interpret—or at least not misinterpret—those answers.

One of the first strategic questions offered to Beginner's Mind had come directly from General Patel at the Ministry of Defense. He'd wanted to know whether the time was right to attempt a mediation between the Consortium and Reparationists, with his government taking the lead role.

Lily had carefully run this question through Beginner's Mind. At first, she had typed out the question, framing it as simply as a child might when asking a question of a fortune-telling Magic 8 Ball. Instead of receiving a simple answer from Beginner's Mind, the question elicited a cascade of data, a torrent of minute lines of code flooding down from the top of the screen. When sifting through this code, Lily entered a state of deep concentration; she became nonresponsive for minutes at a time. Her eyes glittered like two black stones, and her hands moved languidly through the air as she interpreted the data. Lily seemed possessed, in a sort of trance, a spell that was only broken when she found an answer to the question asked of Beginner's Mind.

Lily had reported back to General Patel in New Delhi that Beginner's Mind supported Indian mediation of the conflict. This move, she explained, would lead to "maximum efficiency."

She and Yorgos had been locked up in the lab for days. Yorgos insisted they take a break. "A little fun" was how he framed it. Yorgos's suggestion took Lily by surprise. She seemed at a loss, sputtering out a meager ". . . Okay."

Yorgos grabbed his coat off a peg on the door and helped Lily on with hers. Soon they were walking along a snow-banked street. The freshly piled drifts glowed, their light projecting upward into the night. With each step, they inhaled the cold mountain air. They soon arrived at an Austrian chalet-style restaurant. Inside, shaded lamps cast a warm glow on white table linens. The maître d', a turbaned Sikh wearing a high-collared trachten jacket in velvet, sat them in a back corner. In the dim light, Yorgos asked Lily about Beginner's Mind.

"I'm still learning the interface," she began, "but its technological underpinnings are rooted in the evolutionary sciences."

Yorgos sipped his water. He perused the menu and asked about the term she kept using in her conversations with General Patel: *maximum efficiency.*

"If we go back to the beginning of our species," she said, "we can trace our evolution as a series of conscious and subconscious choices.

The choices that are made with *maximum efficiency* are those that have led to the perpetuation of the species, so good choices. Those that have been made with less than maximum efficiency," and here Lily listed a whole category of *inefficient* choices, with climate destruction and war being paramount among them, "are those that have led us to this and every other calamity that's threatened our continued existence. Our challenge, as a species, is to adhere to *maximum efficiency*."

Their waiter arrived tableside. Lily glanced at her watch. She ordered a single dish with no wine. Yorgos couldn't help himself, and he ordered elaborately, a salad, appetizers for the table, a main course, and the chocolate soufflé. After the waiter collected their menus, Yorgos apologized. "Tonight," he said, "we take a break from efficiency."

12:20 Dec 02, 2084 (+7:00 GMT)
Nusantara

Joko was no longer a commodore. Most of his ships were at the bottom of the Atlantic. The remnants of his once proud armada had sailed into Lagos by ones and twos. A helicopter from the mainland had intercepted the *Aradu*, touching down on the aft landing pad, and one of General Suharto's aides had hopped out the side. Joko was to come with him. The helicopter didn't even power off its rotors. From the deck of the *Aradu*, they'd flown to a nearby airport and departed on an orbital flight. When Joko landed on home soil, military police detained him on the tarmac and rushed him under armed escort to an apartment at the bachelor officers' quarters at Malahayati Naval Base. Malahayati, history's first female admiral, had expelled the Dutch from the Java Sea nearly five hundred years before. She had died in battle, a fate Joko would've preferred to his own.

His room had a view of the bay. Joko stood at the window. He tried to open it, to allow in fresh air. It was locked. When he checked the door, it was also locked—from the outside.

Joko returned to the window. In a few days, he would suffer the indignity of watching the remains of his armada limp into port without him. Spread below were the empty docks they'd departed from weeks before. His returning flotilla would fill less than half the berths it had sailed from. The *Banda Aceh* was the greatest of those losses. Joko knew accounting for that and other losses would be enough to keep him in a room with a door that locked from the outside for some time. The dominant emotion Joko felt wasn't fear for his forthcoming punishment, which would likely include a board of inquiry and even imprisonment, but rather regret.

The resettlement fleet—more than one hundred barges and warship escorts—lay at anchor in the bay, stretching to the horizon. Joko knew he would be sidelined from their next mission. Regret became a physical sensation: a twist in his stomach, a weakness in his knees, a slumping of his shoulders. He thought of his family, taken from him a decade ago in a storm fueled by the economic excesses of the Consortium. He couldn't help it—he wanted revenge.

Joko rarely allowed himself to think in those terms, but standing at the window he had no other word for it. He struck the pane of glass with his open palm. He thought it might break. He struck it a second and then third time, banging it like a drum.

The door behind him unlatched. "Calm down" came a familiar voice.

It was General Suharto.

A military policeman stood beside him, a chain of analog metal keys dangling at his hip. When the policeman followed inside, Suharto waved him off. "That won't be necessary." The policeman backed out the door, leaving the two of them alone.

"Looks like we're both locked in here now."

Suharto glanced behind him. "I guess so."

"I assume there's going to be a board of inquiry . . ."

"Unavoidable," said Suharto, ". . . given the circumstances."

"I'll be reprimanded, forced to retire . . ."

"That's if you avoid time in the brig."

"And the resettlement fleet? Can it still launch? We've lost more than half our escorts."

Suharto stepped beside him at the window. The chunky barges—a mix of cruise liners, commercial ferries, and government-requisitioned private yachts—mingled with their warship escorts. "What other choice do we have?" asked Suharto. "The waters are rising. Our country is vanishing. We have to try."

Joko asked whether this episode was testing the resolve of their allies. Suharto relayed the assurances he'd already received from Lagos and Brasília. "They might not be sinking into the ocean like we are, but Midworld's uninhabitable band spreads every year. They know we're all in the same position. Resettlement and survival, for our three nations, have become one and the same. Less so for the Floridians."

Suharto couldn't predict if the Floridians would remain aligned with the Reparationists, declare neutrality, or even switch sides altogether and try once again to align with the Consortium. If it would secure the Floridians territorial rights to the contested waters above Old Florida, Suharto suspected the leadership in Tallahassee might strike such a deal. "We have it on good recognizance," he said, "that before the Floridians aligned with us, they'd made overtures to the Consortium. They'd offered military support for recognition of their territorial waters. But the Consortium had refused."

"We'll have to see about Florida's new military leadership." Joko left unspoken that the old regime—Brigadier Lucius Clay and his lieutenants—had been killed under his command and in the most questionable of circumstances: an army brigadier general manning a machine gun in the midst of a naval battle was highly unorthodox. Joko didn't need Suharto to tell him that Clay's death placed yet another degree of scrutiny on his own decisions while commodore, to say nothing of the stress it placed on their alliance with the Floridians.

"The legislature in Tallahassee picked Clay's replacement yesterday," said Suharto. "I think you know him, a veteran pilot they'd assigned as a liaison officer."

“Tick-Tock?” The call sign didn’t register with Suharto, so Joko added, “Sorry, do you mean Colonel Dundee?”

“Yes, that’s it,” said Suharto. “Though I believe it’s Brigadier Dundee now. It seems the Floridians have finally come around to putting the professionals in charge, at least for the moment.”

Tick-Tock’s sudden advancement was surprising, but not unprecedented. The peacetime politicking that often defines military promotions—particularly among the most senior ranks—falls by the wayside in war when, as a matter of national survival, the cream of fighters must rise to the top. But Joko couldn’t tell whether Tick-Tock’s elevation would advantage or disadvantage the Reparationists, because he wasn’t certain whether the Floridians could be counted on as allies.

When Joko posed this question, Suharto turned pensive. He looked out the window again, his gaze fixed on the resettlement fleet arrayed in the bay below. “I don’t know what the Floridians will do,” he said. “But I know there’s only one course of action for us, no matter which side they wind up on.” Stepping away from the window, Suharto turned with a flourish toward the door. Like an actor executing a stage direction, he crossed the room in a handful of confident strides. He then placed his hand on the knob, glanced over his shoulder at Joko, and firmly announced, “Our resettlement fleet must be ready.”

When Suharto went to open the door, it wouldn’t budge. He’d forgotten it was locked.

08:30 Dec 03, 2084 (+5:30 GMT)
New Delhi

General Patel requested that Lily return from Shimla for an urgent meeting, though he gave few specifics. She had traveled by gravitrain, her ears popping as she descended from the mountains to the stifling flatlands. She had only just arrived home when Patel appeared at her door. "I thought we might head over together."

His chauffeured car, an anachronism amid the autonomous vehicles that clogged New Delhi's streets, was waiting outside to shepherd them to his office in the defense ministry. Lily knew only that they were meeting with a representative from the UN, but didn't entirely grasp her own role. Once they got into his car, Patel explained how the battle between the Consortium and Reparationist navies in the Atlantic posed a threat, not just to the global order, but to whatever gains the world had made against the climate crisis. "Whether you believe the solution is a combination of land reparations and allowances for innovation zones, or strict adherence to social controls, a war—no matter who wins—would prove disastrous."

If the binary between the Reparationist and Consortium nations defined the current conflict, it didn't define the global order, which was far more complex. Patel hardly needed to explain to Lily how India's apparent neutrality had defined that order over the past fifty years. Neutrality, as a national strategy, wasn't a new concept. The Swiss were the most famous of its adherents. But what India had pursued wasn't quite neutrality. Unlike Switzerland, they were too large for that.

"It's impossible to be neutral when you possess one-fifth of the world's population," Patel said. "We've never aspired to neutrality. What we've aspired to is a policy of nonalignment. The difference is the selective use of national power. You're of both Chinese and American heritage. Those two Consortium nations were once very good at the selective use of national power, the Chinese at the beginning of this century, the Americans at the beginning of the twentieth century—less so today. Of course, it's difficult for a nation to know when to deploy national power. Until now."

The meeting Lily was walking into would be with the UN Special Representative for the Future of the Planet. The subject would be Beginner's Mind. Thus far, this was a capability the Indian government had withheld for its own benefit, allowing it to inform policy decisions as their nation navigated a world in crisis. Although India's policy of nonalignment wouldn't change, this most recent engagement between the Reparationists and the Consortium had convinced India's political leadership that the time had come to deploy Beginner's Mind on a global scale—a decision endorsed by Beginner's Mind itself.

"As the chairman of the Tandava Group," Patel explained, "we need you to attest to this capability. After all, you're the ones who developed it." Lily didn't need to explain that she was a novice in these matters, that she hardly understood the scope of this technology and the help—or harm—it might cause if deployed on a global scale. As the car pulled up to the ministry, she told Patel that she didn't quite know what he meant when he'd described employing Beginner's Mind in this way.

Patel replied, "It means that the UN needs to convince both the Reparationists and the Consortium to accept whatever solution Beginner's Mind delivers after it analyzes the conflict between them."

"What makes you think either side will agree to that?" Lily asked.

They stood at the door to Patel's office. "Because Beginner's Mind said that we should try."

15:20 Dec 05, 2084 (-5 GMT)
Camp David

A parade of analysts from the three-letter agencies had cycled through Jake Shriver's guest suite. CIA . . . NSA . . . FBI . . . DIA . . . NGA . . . he'd spoken to these dark-suited functionaries for hours. They'd clicked their pens, scribbled in their notebooks, and poked at their tablets, asking him all the same questions, extracting from him every grim detail of the battle. Shriver had decided to embrace the repetitiveness of these debriefings, rationalizing them as a type of exposure therapy. He was still having trouble sleeping; each time he shut his eyes, those traumatic events spun out in his dreams. He hoped that if he relived the events enough, they'd gradually lose their grip over him—though he doubted it.

Jake's first morning at Camp David, he and Zhu De had debriefed Eva Boucher who, despite the recent naval disaster, remained at the helm of the US response. At first, Boucher had asked few questions, allowing the pair to unspool their tale. She then asked about Admiral Ma. Why had he insisted the two of them remain aboard the *Zheng He*? Why did he fail to appreciate the threat facing the Chinese fleet? Boucher believed that Admiral Ma's slow progress into the Gulf had placed the *John Paul Jones* in unnecessary danger. Boucher went so far as to say that Admiral Ma might even have acted recklessly. Jake Shriver soon understood what Boucher was after. She needed a scapegoat. Admiral Ma would do nicely; he was both Chinese and, conveniently, dead.

Meanwhile Boucher was fighting for her political life. The president remained incapacitated, but many in the administration—from the vice president's office to a growing conspiracy of cabinet secretaries—were agitating for Boucher's resignation. She could ill afford another misstep.

Shriver and Zhu De's rounds of debriefings in Washington were interrupted by a second summons to Boucher's Camp David office. When they entered, she was tucked behind the president's empty L-shaped desk. She sat with her back to a picture window. Outside, the landscape showed the season's first snow, a pristine dusting. The stubby trees seemed taller and more dignified dressed up in white. Shriver and Zhu De took their seats across from her. She looked up at them. "A little winter storm is cause for optimism about the climate, wouldn't you say?"

Shriver and Zhu De glanced at each another, confused. She got to the point. Julia Hunt, the Special Representative for the Future of the Planet, had arrived unexpectedly that morning. She was waiting in a nearby anteroom.

"And what is it that she wants?" asked Zhu De. His voice was thick with a skepticism that Boucher seemed to share.

"Not sure," Boucher replied, speaking directly to Zhu De. "But I wouldn't want anyone, and most certainly not a representative from the UN, to believe that there's any daylight between our two nations."

Zhu De nodded.

"Shall we invite in our guest?" Boucher leaned over her desk and spoke curtly into an antiquated intercom system. "Send her in."

Shriver had seen photos of Julia Hunt before in the news. He had also heard stories about her from his parents, decades ago. After introducing herself to Zhu De and thanking Boucher for taking this meeting on such short notice, Hunt turned her attention to Shriver, enthusiastically shaking his hand. She declared herself to be "an admirer of your father," whom she called "a patriot for holding the country together thirty years ago," before offering her condolences on his passing, though his death had occurred years earlier.

This convivial display only seemed to add to Boucher's impatience. Several times she gestured to the three chairs in front of her desk while Julia remained standing beside Shriver, peppering him with niceties. Boucher's patience soon ran out. "I only have thirty minutes," she said. "Let's get started."

Julia apologized, took her seat, and thanked Boucher for her time. She entered a diplomatic preamble, which she recited mechanically, acknowledging how busy the national security advisor must be, the challenges facing her and the current administration, and—with a little nod toward Zhu De—those challenges faced by other Consortium member nations.

Boucher clasped her hands together. She glanced once and then twice at her watch. This had the desired effect, bringing her guest more succinctly to the point.

". . . It's because of the Consortium's long-standing commitment to peace and climate security that I'm here today with a proposal, one that could solve our current . . . um, challenges."

"*Challenges?*" Boucher shot back. "Is that how you and your colleagues in Nuuk are framing this situation?"

"How would you suggest we frame it?"

"How about *aggression*," said Boucher. She glanced at Zhu De and Shriver, as if inviting them to add their indignation to her own. "Or *conquest*, that's another good word. A Reparationist attempted conquest of Consortium territory . . ."

"*Punitive assault*," said Shriver, piping up.

"Yes!" said Boucher, clapping her palm against the desk. "A punitive assault, that too. You must understand, Dr. Hunt, that this *aggression*"—Boucher pressed down hard on the word as if to crush its three syllables into one—"isn't a subjective matter, in which the arguments of both sides have merit. The Reparationists believe it's acceptable to invade a sovereign nation, acceptable to lay claim to our territory, and acceptable to flout international norms regarding the climate. Does the UN accept that? Does your proposal accept that they can . . ."

Zhu De calmly interrupted. "What exactly is your proposal, Dr. Hunt?"

Hunt offered Zhu De an appreciative nod. Hunt started at the beginning: an explanation of Beginner's Mind and the technology developed by the Tandava Group. Shriver had heard plenty about the Chowdhury family, the Tandava Group, its vast holdings, and the technologies it had pioneered around climate and around the Singularity, from which Beginner's Mind was derived. The creation of an artificial general intelligence that "maximized efficiency" hardly surprised Shriver. The Indian government, through its alignment with the Tandava Group and Beginner's Mind, had offered a vote of no confidence in the future of human-based decision-making.

Boucher interrupted. "Why would we allow India to mediate our dispute with the Reparationists? On what possible grounds could we offer concessions to those who would invade our homeland and ravage our climate? Fifty years ago, India mediated a dispute between our two nations"—Boucher gestured to Zhu De—"but that's hardly grounds to grant that power to India today. The world has changed."

"The world *has* changed," said Dr. Hunt. "No one is suggesting that India mediate this dispute. What I'm proposing . . . what the *United Nations* is proposing . . . is that the Consortium cede that power to Beginner's Mind."

"Your idea isn't new," said Boucher. "Beginner's Mind is a dead hand."

"A dead what?"

"A *dead hand*," said Boucher. "It's from the Cold War, an autonomous weapons-control system we suspected the Soviets of developing, one that would have retaliated against any American nuclear strike no matter what, with no human involvement. The Russians used to worry how they'd respond if they were all dead. But I suspect they were also worried about not responding if they lost their nerve."

“Why not allow Beginner’s Mind to come up with the most efficient solution?” asked Dr. Hunt. “Not the solution that’s best for the Consortium, nor the Reparationists, but the solution that’s best for humanity. For the planet.”

“Humanity? The planet?” Boucher uttered the words with disdain. “We are defending our nation against an invading armada and you’re lecturing us about *humanity and the planet*? You’ll need a better reason than that.”

Julia Hunt came forward in her seat. Zhu De and Shriver flanked her on either side. She glanced at each of them, then fixed her gaze on Boucher. “Okay,” said Hunt in the same tone a person might say *If you want to play hardball, let’s play.* “How’s this for a reason: I’ve just returned from Nusantara. The Reparationists have agreed to allow Beginner’s Mind to resolve this dispute . . .”

“That’s hardly a surprise,” said Boucher, tossing her arms in the air. “Half their fleet is at the bottom of the Atlantic. I doubt they have the capacity to—”

“Will you let me finish!” snapped Hunt. The persona of a self-possessed diplomat had at last given way to the short-fused Marine that Shriver had heard stories about from his parents. “I’m also in contact with Tallahassee,” she added. “You might want to make sure you can shore up your alliance there before you reject this idea outright—especially with your cities still smoking, your defense industrial base crippled, and much of your own fleet on the ocean floor. With your losses, you may not be a match for the Reparationists.”

With her outburst, Hunt knew the meeting was over. She’d leave empty-handed. She asked if Boucher could arrange a ride for her to the airport. If the Consortium was refusing mediation, Hunt wanted to depart as soon as possible to deliver the news to her superiors. She'd had a hard time getting into Camp David in the first place due to the snow. Boucher, in a conciliatory gesture, arranged a car. She also noted that the weather shouldn't give Hunt a problem on her return journey. Outside, the temperature had increased a few degrees. A light drizzle had begun to fall. Soon it would wash away what was left of the snow.

19:47 Dec 05, 2084 (+5:30 GMT)
Shimla

After Lily's meeting in New Delhi, she returned to Shimla and shut herself up in the laboratory at Wildflower Hall. General Patel had sent her back with a range of scenarios to run through Beginner's Mind. In some, the Reparationists and the Consortium had both agreed to mediation. In others, hostilities between the two resumed and they remained in a state of open war. She also ran through scenarios for every contingency in between. This modeling allowed Beginner's Mind to, as Lily put it, "learn the problem."

After two days of work, Lily was operating on little sleep. She folded her arms across the desk and rested her head on them.

When she awoke, it was night.

The portal she'd been working at had switched off. She touched its display to turn it back on. It remained dark.

She tried again, still nothing.

In a panic, she imagined that she had lost her work.

Before she could reboot the entire system of servers that powered Beginner's Mind, her display inexplicably switched itself on.

At a glance, she could see her work was gone: her notes, the scenarios, the seemingly infinite lines of code. All of it had vanished.

Then, as she sat in front of the portal, a cascade of letters poured down the display. A single word was repeated over and over:

JOKO

07:38 Dec 07, 2084 (+7:00 GMT)
Nusantara

Joko stood beside General Suharto on the airstrip at Malahayati Naval Base. The two men visored their hands above their eyes as they gazed eastward toward the rising sun and the jet coming in on its final approach. Its tires smoked against the runway as it landed. General Patel ducked out of the open fuselage door, blinked at the harsh daylight, and jauntily descended onto the tarmac. He was all smiles greeting the cluster of Reparationists officers. He started with General Suharto but immediately moved on to Joko, whom he addressed as "Rear Admiral" in acknowledgment of the promotion Joko had received only days before.

Joko was struggling to comprehend his dizzying change in fortune. He'd been preparing for his board of inquiry when General Suharto arrived in his quarters along with a judge advocate. The Indian government, Suharto explained, had decided to enter the conflict on the side of the Reparationists. The strategic planners in New Delhi, relying on a program called Beginner's Mind, had reached this fortuitous if unexpected decision. But there'd been a condition. Suharto had reached into his pocket and removed a pair of gold-braided shoulder boards. "You are to lead the resettlement fleet," said Suharto. "General Patel asked for you by name. This was New Delhi's condition."

On the brief car ride from the airfield to the docks, Joko sat in the front seat while Patel and Suharto sat in the back. Patel's easygoing and gregarious display on the tarmac had vanished. He spoke urgently of the preparations the Reparationists needed to make in the days ahead. They spoke about timelines, the consolidation of warships from Lagos, Brasília, and now New Delhi, and they spoke about weapons, the array of conventional and hypersonic missiles, drones, and electromagnetic cannons that they would need to outfit those ships. Patel wasn't rude, but he was certainly direct. He wasn't asking but telling Suharto what must happen in the days ahead.

Joko said little. He couldn't help but feel as though he didn't belong in this conversation, as if his promotion had been a fluke. He was struggling to understand why the Indians placed such confidence in him. Fortunately, the magnitude of the task ahead didn't afford him time to fixate on questions of his own worth.

The three flag rank officers and their staffers arrived at the half-empty docks. General Patel's war planners at the defense ministry had provided General Suharto's staff with a detailed schematic for loading and embarking the resettlement fleet with civilians. Now Patel wished to inspect the facilities. "My staff in New Delhi didn't want me to take this trip," he confessed to Joko and Suharto. "They believed our planning was sufficient and so this trip was unnecessary."

"I believe you'll find our navy up to any task," Joko said.

Suharto nodded in agreement.

General Patel considered the two of them for a moment, crossed his arms over his chest, and rested his boot on a dockside pylon. An offshore breeze was capping the distant waves with fringes of whitewater. "I have no doubt that you are up to the task, Rear Admiral Joko." General Patel gazed at the resettlement barges at anchor, this hodgepodge of commercial ships bobbing on an increasingly turbulent sea. "You're no accidental admiral."

Joko glanced down at his gold-braided shoulder boards.

"Of all the officers here," Patel added, "you're the only one that Beginner's Mind said we couldn't do without. I look forward to discovering why." Patel clapped Joko on the shoulder and then wandered down to the dock. There was work to be done, an inspection to make, and they were short on time.

22:10 Dec 09, 2084 (-5 GMT)
Tallahassee

"You shouldn't have come down here, Julia."

Those were not the words she wanted to hear. By the time Tick-Tock appeared at her door, Julia had been waiting three days inside a ground-floor room at the Country Inn & Suites off Interstate 10. Tick-Tock hadn't asked her to take this trip, so she couldn't fault his response. She explained herself only by saying, “I decided we should get out of here.”

“You decided?”

“Yeah,” she said. “I decided.”

“For Christ’s sake, Julia. Do you even know what’s going on down here?” He’d stepped into her room and sat on the springy bed.

Julia shut the door and sat beside him. “I’ve got a pretty good idea.”

Tick-Tock considered her for a moment before stepping into the bathroom. With the door open, he unzipped his flight suit to the waist. He spoke into the mirror as he splashed water on his face and patted it dry with a washcloth. “I’m already in a jam,” he said. “I’ve got half the Floridian legislature agitating for war against the Consortium, the other half convinced that we should flip sides and fight against the Reparationists, and the other half determined that we should remain neutral . . .”

“Sweetheart . . .” said Julia. “That’s three halves.”

Tick-Tock flung the damp washcloth into the basin. “That’s what I’m trying to tell you . . . This whole thing adds up to stupid.”

“I’ve been waiting here three days,” said Julia.

“I know.”

“I was at Camp David before that.”

“I know,” said Tick-Tock. “I know all of that. The only thing I don’t know is *why* you came.”

“For you, moron . . .” Julia sat on the bed, already defeated. “Because I can get us out of here.”

Tick-Tock crossed the room and again sat beside her. “Listen, I’m sorry. I can’t just up and leave. Things are a mess.”

"Things are a mess everywhere," she said. Her travels hadn't only taken her to Camp David, but also to New Delhi and Nusantara. She explained Beginner's Mind to him, this breakthrough made by the Tandava Group. Humanity had advanced to a point where it could no longer be trusted to make decisions for itself, not regarding climate and most certainly not regarding matters of war and peace. Human dysfunction cost humanity too much.

"What does Beginner's Mind tell you about Florida?"

Julia had been dreading this question. "It doesn't matter."

"What do you mean it doesn't matter?" said Tick-Tock. "If this technology can do everything you claim it can, if it can prevent wars, if it can create models to solve climate change, if it can set humanity on the right path, how can you believe what it says about our decisions doesn't matter?" An old-style television with a film of dust across its surface sat in a corner of the room. As if to emphasize his point, Tick-Tock snatched its remote and tuned into a live broadcast from the statehouse. Only a few miles away, Floridian politicians jockeyed for their allotted time to speak on the floor, pressing against one another in a scrum. "Christ, look at them," said Tick-Tock. "They can't agree on anything, so why not at least tell me what Beginner's Mind says we should do?"

"It doesn't matter. That's what I'm trying to tell you: whatever Florida does or doesn't choose to do won't matter in the end," Julia explained. "*The strong do what they will and the weak do what they must* . . . you've heard that before, right? That's what Beginner's Mind says about Florida."

"What are you saying? Are you calling us weak?"

Julia snatched the remote from him. She clicked off the television, taking some pleasure in silencing the chattering politicians. "The Consortium has refused to enter mediation, so the Indians have chosen to ally themselves with the Reparationists. No one's calling you weak. No one's calling you anything. But who Florida chooses to ally itself with will have no bearing on the outcome of this conflict; that's all I'm saying. Or rather, that's what Beginner's Mind has said."

Tick-Tock stood from the bed. He zipped up his flight suit and smoothed down its collar, fixing himself. "I have to get back to work." His voice was cold, detached. "And you have to get home. I assume your colleagues at the UN don't know you're here. They must be wondering after you."

"I'm sure they are," she said. "But that's what I'm trying to tell you. I'm not going back." Julia was up from the bed. She had slowly maneuvered herself between him and the door. "I want you to come with me."

Tick-Tock shunted her aside. He promised that as soon as he could come back to her hotel room he would. The two of them could then sort this out.

"I won't be here."

Tick-Tock froze with his hand on the doorknob. "Okay," he answered, clearly frustrated by this ultimatum Julia had presented. "Where will you be?"

"Nusantara."

"Nusantara?" He was increasingly annoyed. "Why?"

"Reparationist support from the Indians was contingent on them putting one specific officer in charge of the resettlement fleet, a navy officer requested by Beginner's Mind . . . I know him a bit, and so do you . . . It's Joko. Aren't you curious why he matters so much? Don't you want to know?"

"I can't come with you," he said.

"No, you *won't* come with me."

Tick-Tock promised he'd return tomorrow, and they could talk it over some more. Maybe he could find a way for her to stay in Tallahassee.

After he left, Julia turned on the television again. She lay in bed with a blanket pulled up. She watched the legislators working late into the night. She hoped to catch a glimpse of Tick-Tock as he returned to the statehouse floor. When he at last appeared, it was in the early hours of the morning. She stared at him for a long moment, and then she finally drifted off to sleep.

5

Guests of Guests

13:02 Dec 14, 2084 (-5:00 GMT)
Fishers Island, NY

Jake Shriver had originally planned to fly back to Beijing with Zhu De. A robust defense of the Eastern Seaboard of the United States would require continued Chinese military backing. Jake thought it important for him to help shore up that support. But Eva Boucher had other plans. She insisted Shriver remain in the US. This is how he found himself on the Amtrak from DC to New London, trundling up the East Coast on a rail line that hadn't seen a meaningful update in over a century. From the dock in New London, he'd taken the hour-long ferry that made the twice daily milk run to Fishers Island, an exclusive vacation community where the US Navy maintained a shuttered World War Two–era base. He'd been to Fishers Island before, as a boy. On his father's side, the Shrivers had been one of the island's founding families. But he hadn't returned in decades.

Normally, Shriver would have flown into the small airstrip on a western spur of the island, but it was temporarily closed. Crews were tipping shovelfuls of fresh, steaming macadam across the dilapidated runways and threading a new refueling network into the ground, one that could sustain the six squadrons of Floridian J-19s that would soon be based here, the bulk of Florida's small but capable air forces.

Boucher was presiding over an unprecedented mobilization not only of the American military, but of the entire American population. Every member of the national guard, reserve, and individual ready reserve would defend the homeland. Boucher had even flirted with the idea of a draft, but it would take too long, and given her increasingly tenuous political position, such an unpopular measure would be beyond her power to implement. Nevertheless, Boucher was working with her generals and admirals to stitch together a defense. She secretly suspected these efforts would prove insufficient. The US military had fallen into disrepair in recent decades, which was why she'd needed the Floridians. Their contribution of the J-19s, although small, might be meaningful enough to help tilt the scales in the Consortium's favor.

Boucher knew, given the recent hostilities between the Floridians and the Consortium, that housing those aircraft on the US mainland could prove a political liability, which is why she'd chosen Fishers Island. It was well-positioned, geographically shielded by Cape Cod and just south of the likely landing beaches. Also, placing the Floridians on an island would keep them isolated from those Americans who still viewed them as a national security threat, despite pledges made by leaders in Tallahassee.

Boucher had laid out her concerns to Shriver in a phone call. She needed his help on Fishers Island. "Everyone knows that you can handle the Chinese," she said. "How about a new challenge . . . do you think you can handle the Floridians?"

Shriver was about to find out.

He and Boucher sat at what the locals on the island called the "Big Club." The oak-paneled dining room was littered with silver cups, plaques, and other trophies and overlooked the green undulations of the island's internationally ranked golf course. The course itself remained lush and well-tended in apparent contravention of the water rationing that browned the lawns of less affluent Americans. Boucher had promised Shriver a warm turnover with his counterpart, a Floridian brigadier named Dundee, who everyone called Tick-Tock. But Tick-Tock was running nearly thirty minutes late.

Shriver was beginning to have second thoughts. His East-West Center focused on Chinese–US relations because of his background and expertise. The success he'd achieved couldn't necessarily be replicated. Also, he wasn't a military officer, let alone an aviator. What meaningful counsel could he provide to a Floridian brigadier? Shriver had found himself in this position before, on the *Zheng He*. The open-mouthed sailors screaming their last breaths in flooding compartments . . . the spoiled-wine smell of jet fuel mixed with cordite . . . curlicues of flame rising and crashing across the surface of the ocean like an overhead swell . . . those memories hadn't left him—if anything they were growing more vivid.

Boucher eventually excused herself to the ladies' room. While she was away, Shriver had decided he couldn't do this job. He resolved to tell Boucher that he'd be returning to Washington, that his coming here had been a mistake, that he wasn't the right person.

A commotion came from the front of the restaurant. "Yeah, well, show me where it's *written* . . ." The voice drew out the last word sharply.

Shriver's table was just around the corner from the maître d', whom he could hear mumbling a whispered response. "Sir, it's not incumbent on me to show you anything in writing about our dress code . . . you are not even a member of this club."

"I'm late to see Eva Boucher . . . you need to get outta my way . . ."

Shriver poked his head around the corner.

The green flight suit. The slightly grease-stained hands. The long drooping mustache. No doubt about it, this must be Tick-Tock.

Shriver approached the maître d' and asked if perhaps he might be of some assistance. The maître d', who stood behind his large, black leather appointments book, didn't miss a beat. He explained that Eva Boucher was not a member of the club, that she and other government officials had only been permitted to dine at this club as guests of the club's owners. Tick-Tock's name wasn't on the list the sponsoring member had provided, so he'd have to dine elsewhere.

"Certainly, we can figure something out," said Shriver. "Dr. Boucher might not be a member, but this gentleman is her guest."

"Guests of guests are not guests," the maître d' said crisply, as if for the thousandth time in his professional life. He slammed the appointments book shut.

Tick-Tock jutted forward, as if to throttle the maître d'. Shriver placed a restraining hand on his chest. "Might I show you something, sir?" He gestured for the maître d' to follow him toward a cabinet filled with trophies and memorabilia from the club. Shriver walked the two of them down to the farthest cabinet, which contained the oldest memorabilia: photographs and engraved silver cups and plates from more than a century ago. On a shelf upholstered in forest-green velvet sat a framed sepia-toned photograph of a dozen whiskered men attired in stiff four-button suits with high detachable collars and wearing a mix of pageboy and boater hats, their golf clubs slung over their shoulders. "Second row," said Shriver. "Third from the left."

The maître d' found a youngish man, not more than forty, who with only a slightly lighter complexion appeared to be a facsimile of Jake Shriver. The difference in their appearance was as minor as the difference in their name; this man was Jacob Shriver, a founding member of the club.

"It's my understanding," said Jake, "that according to club bylaws, descendants of founders retain membership in perpetuity . . ."

The maître d' nodded while scowling at the trophy case.

"So, you see that gentleman there." Shriver gestured toward Tick-Tock, waiting at the front of the restaurant. "He is not a guest of a guest; he's simply a guest—*my guest*."

"Your guest still needs a dinner jacket."

Shriver strode across the dining room while removing his blue blazer. He handed it to Tick-Tock. "Put this on."

Tick-Tock laughed, but when he saw the maître d' following determinedly behind Shriver, he put on the jacket.

"But now you'll need a jacket," said the maître d', as if delighted to find a rule that Jake Shriver couldn't flout.

Shriver glanced into the dining room, to Boucher's empty chair. She'd been wearing a burgundy pantsuit, and its jacket—although several sizes too small—was hanging off the back of her chair. Shriver pulled it on with difficulty. His wrists protruded ridiculously through the sleeves as he crossed the dining room. "Last I checked," said Shriver as he returned to the maître d's podium, "jackets aren't required for ladies. We'll be seated now."

The maître d' snatched an extra menu. He escorted Tick-Tock and Shriver to their table. A moment later, Boucher returned from the restroom to find Tick-Tock dressed in a flight suit and blue blazer and Shriver wearing her burgundy jacket. After considering them both, she said, "It looks like the two of you are off to a good start."

07:38 Dec 15, 2084 (+7:00 GMT)
Nusantara

The pace of preparations at Malahayati Naval Base was relentless. The resettlement fleet hadn't even gotten underway and already Admiral Joko was averaging only a few hours of sleep per night. General Patel and his staff had kept operations on a tight schedule, with no room for deviation. Like Noah loading his ark, Joko knew a storm was coming. It was imperative that his resettlement fleet leave on time and fully loaded. And if Noah had taken his instructions from God, Joko was taking his instructions from Beginner's Mind, which was behind the intricate load plans fed to him by General Patel's staff.

Amid these harried preparations, Francisco von Hütschler, the Brazilian defense minister, had arrived. The purpose of his trip ostensibly had been an inspection of the resettlement fleet. His nation's contribution to that fleet was a mix of warships and barges that would comprise less than a quarter of the force. They would rendezvous with the main fleet on the open Atlantic, south of Africa's Gold Coast, along with the Nigerians. Although it made sense that a senior representative from a Reparationist nation like Brazil would want a firsthand accounting of the preparations being made by their allies, it didn't follow that their defense minister would undertake the errand personally—but here he was.

Given the demands on Joko's time, he could only allot von Hütschler twenty minutes for an audience, the same twenty minutes he'd scheduled for lunch. Joko was slurping from a bowl of noodle soup at his desk, the window behind him framing the ship-filled bay, as they began their meeting.

"The time you've allotted is more than enough," said von Hütschler after Joko had apologized for his tight schedule. "Your staff has been most accommodating. They've shown me the preparations you've made, which are quite impressive. But an accounting of your preparations isn't the real reason I'm here."

"I suspected it wasn't," said Joko as he spooned up the dregs of his bowl.

"Our Floridian allies have proven a disappointment," said von Hütschler. He paused and then tented his hands together as he carefully delivered the rest of his message. "It would seem the Consortium is expanding while our alliance is contracting . . ."

"Perhaps."

"Yes, perhaps . . . Brigadier Clay spent time under your command before he was killed, correct?"

Joko nodded.

"And you know his replacement, correct?"

Joko knew Tick-Tock, insofar as the newly promoted brigadier had briefly served as a liaison on the *Banda Aceh*. But Joko couldn't say that he knew him particularly well.

"I *do* know him well," von Hütschler explained. "I've known him for years."

"And?"

"I'm not sure . . . He's fiercely loyal to Florida. But not necessarily to the politicians in Tallahassee. Their ever-shifting alliances don't sit well with him."

Joko gazed over von Hütschler's right shoulder, to the clock on the wall. "What do you expect me to do with that information?"

"I understand Beginner's Mind is the architect of our battle plans . . ."

Joko nodded. He attested to the efficacy of Beginner's Mind, its track record of finding the most efficient solution to any problem. Joko wasn't certain that he necessarily believed all of this, but as the commander of the resettlement fleet he felt obligated to toe the line, especially to von Hütschler. The Reparationist alliance couldn't afford to deteriorate further.

"Yes, yes . . ." von Hütschler interrupted. "I've heard your colleagues' arias about Beginner's Mind. But let me ask you a question... Can Beginner's Mind see into a person's soul?"

"A person's soul? That's a tall order. Can you?"

"No, I suppose I can't. But it's my understanding that Beginner's Mind chose you by name to lead this flotilla. It must have seen something in you."

Joko shifted in his seat. "It's no secret," he explained, "that I lost my wife and daughter to the tsunami in '74. Beginner's Mind must think it's important to have someone in charge of this resettlement fleet who understands the stakes, who has a deeply vested interest in our success." Joko's eyes shifted only slightly, again finding the wall clock above von Hütschler's shoulder. He dropped his soup spoon into the now empty bowl and crossed his arms over his chest.

"I know you're busy," added von Hütschler. "But before you go, I'd like you to consider one idea, which I can't imagine Beginner's Mind knows, or that anyone knows, because I'm not certain of it myself. When I was last with Tick-Tock, he seemed different, troubled, like a man at the end of his rope. You'll be landing on beaches defended by his aircraft. But I don't think his heart is in this. It's important you understand that... because I doubt Beginner's Mind does."

"What leads you to believe this?"

"Let's call it instinct," said von Hütschler. "*Human* instinct."

Joko finished his audience with von Hütschler, who returned to Brasília that afternoon.

A flurry of activity filled the remainder of the day, an uninterrupted stream of inspections, briefings, and conference calls with allies. Exhausted, Joko returned to his quarters after midnight. He would be up before dawn. A litany of details crowded his unsettled thoughts as he sat on the edge of his bed, unlacing his boots. He returned to his meeting with von Hütschler, to the observation about Tick-Tock. Von Hütschler had recognized a blind spot, one he didn't have confidence Beginner's Mind would see.

Joko wondered about his own blind spots. How much would he be forced to rely on his intuition in the days ahead?

He stripped down to his shorts and T-shirt. He slid beneath the sheets of his single bed and propped himself up on a couple of pillows. The lights were off except for the lamp on his bedside table, where an aide had left a folder of documents for him to review before morning.

He glanced at the next day's schedule, which was much like today's . . .

He reviewed a report on crew readiness, which was sufficient . . .

He tabulated armament and fuel delivery levels, which were on track . . .

Lastly, he came across a roster from his lead immigration officer. The government in Nusantara had assigned him a cluster of these bureaucrats. Their job was to screen applicants who wished to join the first resettlement wave. Given the deteriorating conditions not only in the Indonesian archipelago but across Midworld, and certainly among Reparationist nations, demand to embark with the resettlement fleet had surpassed expectations. Increasingly, the composition of the settlers had become an issue of political sensitivity, which was why Joko was kept abreast of any high-profile applicants.

He scoured the list of recent arrivals to Malahayati Naval Base:

several former CEOs and industrialists . . . a politician who'd recently lost reelection . . . two musicians and a film star of some renown . . . and, at the bottom of the list, conspicuously out of alphabetical order as if it'd only just been added, a name he recognized: Julia Hunt, the UN official he'd inserted via small boat into Florida the month before.

Joko made a note of it. As soon as he woke up, he would have his aide coordinate a meeting with her. Joko couldn't say why Julia Hunt had arrived here, but he'd do as von Hütschler had advised; he would trust his instincts and find out.

01:26 Dec 17, 2084 (+5:30 GMT)
New Delhi

Lily was increasingly concerned about her son. He hadn't responded to any of her messages. She'd considered boarding a plane to the United States and showing up at his door, but Patel wouldn't hear of it given India's new alliance with the Reparationists. Lily was running out of time to reach him, and so, in desperation, she placed a final call, one she hated to make.

Zhu De answered on the second ring. "This is an unexpected surprise."

Lily had locked the door to her guest suite so she wouldn't be interrupted. "Let's dispense with the pleasantries."

"As you wish."

"I'm looking for my son."

"Is that so?"

"Where is he?" Lily could hear the vitriol in her words as she spat out the question. Her hatred of Zhu De and the Guoanbu, though causing her to behave irrationally, was a rational response to all that they'd robbed her of over a lifetime, starting with her father and now, perhaps, extending to her son. She took a breath and regained her composure. "I need your help."

"I'm happy to help however I can," said Zhu De flatly. "But I don't know where your son is."

"He was with you on the *Zheng He* . . ."

Zhu De said nothing.

"And you returned to Washington together . . ."

Zhu De's silence felt menacing.

"The Consortium is in crisis . . . surely he's shuttling between Washington and Beijing . . . he wouldn't allow himself to be anywhere else . . ."

"Why is it so urgent for you to speak with him?"

Now it was Lily Bao's turn to be silent.

"Of course, the reason you need to speak with him is none of my business," said Zhu De. "I wouldn't presume to understand what's shared between a mother and a son. But I also wouldn't presume that the services of his East-West Center are still required. My country has paid a dear price for . . . how does your son put it . . . *a cross-cultural dialogue*. Also, we've been briefed on Beginner's Mind. We must take its capabilities into account."

"Beijing has already rejected mediation with Beginner's Mind."

"We did nothing of the sort," said Zhu De. "Our American allies rejected that option. Beijing can't act unilaterally on behalf of the Consortium. We can't force the Americans to enter mediation."

"But they can force you to fight on their side?"

"If they're attacked, yes. Article 5 of the Nuuk Accords clearly states that an attack against one is an attack against all. But some are beginning to say that the recklessness of one allied nation shouldn't force others into war. Those voices are becoming louder in my country."

Lily wasn't getting anywhere. She asked if he would let her know immediately if he heard from her son.

"Of course," said Zhu De. "But might I ask a favor of you?"

Lily asked what the favor was.

"Don't assume that the policies of the United States, or the Floridians, or any other Consortium nation are the policies of the People's Republic. Some journeys are begun with one set of companions and ended with others. You're the chairman of the Tandava Group. It's important you understand that."

She didn't respond, and after a long pause their call ended.

She sat with her hands folded on her lap, in quiet disappointment. She gazed out her window unable to believe that with all the resources of the Tandava Group at her disposal she couldn't find a way to reach Jake. The lights of the city blinked gently, the only movement in the still night. Time had run out. Before this shift in alliances, she had only wanted to speak to him. She had wanted a chance to explain herself.

Then it occurred to her, a way to deliver this explanation. A means of communication so obvious, so antiquated, that she had overlooked it entirely. Lily rifled around in her suite. She found a pen, paper, and even an envelope.

She wrote her son a letter.

08:47 Dec 19, 2084 (-5:00 GMT)
Fishers Island, NY

The runway on the west end of the island was now operational. Shriver had accomplished this in record time, using the same brand of persuasion he'd cultivated at the East-West Center. It hadn't been easy, but he'd brought the local politicians around to his way of seeing things. After some heated negotiations, they agreed to have the construction workers, who were ferried over to the island daily, deprioritize the renovation of several prominent summer homes in favor of a renovation of the airfield and the island's defenses.

That airfield was now home to six Floridian fighter squadrons, nearly one hundred aircraft, the bulk of their force. To thank Shriver for navigating the local politics, Tick-Tock suggested the two take a flight in a J-19. The best view of the Consortium's defensive preparations up and down the East Coast was from a cockpit, Tick-Tock had insisted.

Shriver had never flown in a fighter before. This surprised Tick-Tock. He assumed there were few if any delights this son of privilege had never enjoyed. The morning of their flight, Shriver and Tick-Tock had sauntered across the freshly laid runway to one of the squadron's ready rooms, housed in a Quonset hut with an arch of sandbags framing its door. Tick-Tock explained that this ready room belonged to the Death Rattlers, an old squadron of his, the first he'd ever flown with. They were originally an American squadron, Marine Fighter Attack Squadron 323. They'd been disbanded and later reconstituted within the Floridian Air Corps. Old-timer that Tick-Tock was, he'd endured long enough to become the only living pilot to fly in both incarnations. When Shriver followed him through the ready room, he couldn't help but notice how younger pilots stepped out of Tick-Tock's way, nodding deferentially, and how a few even sported their own versions of his trademark dragoon's mustache.

Riggers from the ground crew had hung Tick-Tock's and Shriver's kit in two adjacent lockers. Tick-Tock's helmet was emblazoned with his call sign, a hand-painted rattler bearing its razor-sharp fangs, and a career's worth of fighter silhouettes—one for each of his air-to-air victories. Shriver's helmet was white as a cue ball with his name scribbled on a piece of masking tape stuck to its side. Shriver felt sheepish putting on his kit, as if he'd been asked to try on a suit of armor for size while standing next to Sir Lancelot.

While they dressed, a radio played the news. Boucher had left the island a few days before. She'd said she had business to attend to in Washington. The details of that business were today's top story. It seemed a growing coalition of appeasement lawmakers in Congress were maneuvering against her. They wanted to revoke the Authorization for the Use of Military Force, which granted the administration broad latitude as to the measures it could take and resources it could use to defend the homeland. The debate, it seemed, was largely symbolic. The dissenting legislators didn't have the votes to revoke the measure. They simply wanted their dissent on the record should the resettlement fleet succeed.

"Spineless politicians, always covering their own ass," Tick-Tock said bitterly. "You ready to go?"

Shriver grabbed his helmet, and they walked outside into the cold winter sun. They climbed into the cockpit and one of the ground crew helped strap Shriver into his ejector seat. The canopy descended and they were soon trundling down the taxiway. As the J-19 swiveled into position at the base of the main runway, Tick-Tock came up on the intercom. Above the roar of the engine, his voice was nuzzled intimately inside Shriver's helmet. "Almost forgot," he said. "Reach into the pocket on the back of my seat. There's a baggie there, just in case."

Before Shriver could ask *In case of what?*, Tick-Tock switched over to tower control, acknowledged they were ready for takeoff, and told Shriver, "Hold on tight. Next stop, the penthouse."

Tick-Tock released the J-19's brakes and Shriver's head slammed against the back of his seat. It took three seconds to reach takeoff speed. Tick-Tock tore back the throttle, so they weren't flying so much as launching vertically, careening skyward in a corkscrew, a wild barrel roll worthy of the mightiest of fighter jockeys. The skin on Shriver's cheeks flapped back toward his ears. What felt like an enormous hand was now pressing on his torso, harder and harder and harder. When Shriver finally managed to breathe, his exhalation escaped him as an inadvertent squeal, a little whine like a piglet.

"You all right back there?" Tick-Tock was laughing. He'd begun to count out their ascent: "Three thousand feet . . . four thousand . . . five thousand . . ."

A creeping darkness preceded by pinpricks of light crowded Shriver's vision. It was as if he'd taken a hot bath and stood too quickly to dry off. His sight constricted into a tunnel and all he could hear was Tick-Tock calling out their ascent, but his voice was growing fainter, as if he'd stepped into another room.

"Remember to squeeze your ass cheeks together," said Tick-Tock. "If you're gonna black out, just keep squeezing."

Shriver could hear himself making primal, grunting noises.

"There you go!" said Tick-Tock, and he continued to count out their ascent. "Seventeen thousand . . . eighteen . . . nineteen . . . Yee-haw, partner, that's twenty thousand feet . . . Level off."

Tick-Tock pitched the stick forward. In an instant they went from perpendicular to the earth's surface to parallel, from pulling three and up to four Gs to normal gravity, which to Shriver felt like a luxurious weightlessness, an immense release. He took a deep, satisfying breath as his vision floated into focus.

Then everything came up from his stomach.

He reached for the plastic bag at the back of Tick-Tock's seat. While he was vomiting, Tick-Tock's steady voice toggled between air traffic control and encouraging Shriver not to spill, to get everything in the bag if he could.

After three or four good heaves, Shriver was done. He'd sweated through the seat of his pants and flung open his visor so he could wipe the sweat that was burning his eyes. Tick-Tock apologized. The vertical takeoff was necessary, he explained, given airspace restrictions and the size of the force currently gathering just off the coast. Maybe he should've warned Shriver, but he thought it better to save him the anxiety. "It'll never get worse than that," Tick-Tock added. "At least not much worse. Whaddya think of the view from the penthouse?"

The glare was blinding at altitude. Shriver squinted into the distance before sliding his visor back down. He could see dozens of ships spread to the north, what he assumed were the four remaining American carrier battle groups. He couldn't pinpoint the carriers themselves, but counted their escorts, which were arrayed in depth, extending eastward into the Atlantic. The J-19 flew tucked beneath the sound barrier, which within a few minutes placed them above the landing beaches in Maine and those farther north, in Nova Scotia. Shriver couldn't help smiling as they flew. He imagined that anyone coming up here would ask themselves if their life might not have been better spent as a fighter pilot.

Tick-Tock pointed out tufts of upturned earth below. They marked the recently dug emplacements of long-range antiship missile batteries. On closer inspection, Shriver could make out breaks in the camouflage netting that hid the largest of these tracked missile launchers. One well-placed hit from these batteries could take out any ship in the Reparationist fleet, including the most expensive and sophisticated of the carriers, to say nothing of the barges that would be crowded with civilians. The same missile batteries were only just now being dug on Fishers Island, with Floridian crews manning them.

"We're going to be reliant on those batteries," said Tick-Tock. "Four carrier battle groups won't cut it, not against what the Reparationists will throw at us, to say nothing of what the Indians might bring."

"Don't forget our allies in Beijing," said Shriver. "Once they regroup, they'll send another two or three carrier battle groups."

Tick-Tock went silent.

"You don't think they'll help us?" Shriver asked.

"Are you originally Chinese or American?"

"I'm both."

"But you must be a little more one than the other."

"I don't like to think of it that way," said Shriver. He'd received his Chinese citizenship the day he was born in Beijing, and he was raised in the United States. His mother was the daughter of an infamous Chinese rear admiral and his father a New Englander to the bone. "Can't a person be from two places?"

"Sure," said Tick-Tock. "But you're always from one place a little bit more than another. And sometimes you're forced to choose. When Florida split from the US, I had to choose. Toughest decision of my life. Would've been easier to keep being from two places. But that wasn't an option."

"Why are you telling me this?"

Tick-Tock didn't answer right away. He was chatting with air traffic control, deconflicting their route. Stacked at altitudes above and below, Shriver could discern the glint of fighters coming and going from the defending carriers and airfields up and down the coast.

Tick-Tock soon finished on the radio. He returned to Shriver's question. "Why am I telling you this? Consider it some friendly advice. If you wind up having to choose, it'll be a rougher ride than our takeoff."

They continued their aerial tour. Although Shriver had read about the preparations made at sea—the numbers and types of ships, the national mobilization on shore, the missile batteries and littoral defenses—he hadn't comprehended the scope of the effort until now, seeing it from the air.

When it came time to return to base, Tick-Tock began making the requisite calls to air traffic control. Between transmissions, Shriver asked if he should brace himself for a landing as severe as their takeoff.

"No," said Tick-Tock. "I'm gonna take us back nice and easy."

True to his word, they bled altitude gradually all the way home.

04:17 Dec 20, 2084 (+7:00 GMT)
Nusantara

A single column of light shone at the tent flap. Julia Hunt slept in the center of the tent, one of dozens hastily erected in every sports field and parking lot on Malahayati Naval Base. As Julia awoke, she glimpsed an Indonesian Marine pacing down the rows of cots. He was shining a light in the faces of those who slept. They grumbled as he asked them a question, one that Julia soon discerned was her own name and whether anyone had seen her. Since landing in Nusantara days before, Julia had kept to herself. She didn't want her name on the lips of every resettler, so she rushed down the rows of cots and presented herself to the Marine.

The Marine brushed her with his flashlight from head to toe. He made a dissatisfied noise, a little grunt, as if unconvinced that this person had been worth the trouble of his early morning search.

Julia waited until she was outside the tent to ask where they were headed. "To see the admiral."

It was still night. Stars spread overhead, but a band of light was brightening the eastern horizon. As they walked across base, Julia could make out the vague impressions of the resettlement barges. Water lapped rhythmically at the sides of their hulls. All day every day since Julia had arrived, those sleeping in tents like hers were filling these barges. Her tent might be empty when she returned to it. She didn't want to miss her chance, having traveled all this way to load onto one of these barges.

After Julia's clandestine visit to Tallahassee, she'd submitted her resignation to the UN. She couldn't help but see the irony. When she and Tick-Tock had been together in Nuuk, he'd been the one flirting with a resignation letter. But she'd ultimately been the one to follow through. She'd done it the old-fashioned way, writing it by hand and posting it by regular mail. It would take a few days before it landed on the secretary-general's desk in Nuuk. Not that it would cause much of a stir. Inside the UN, some might question her commitment to "the future of the planet," as her job description so grandly framed her duties. But she was no longer convinced that the UN would play much of a role in determining that future.

Julia knew that here, among this fleet of ships, the future of the planet would be determined. And she was about to meet one of the most important figures in determining it—at least according to Beginner's Mind.

The Marine led her to a nondescript brick building. Inside, other Marines stood guard at several closed doors. Julia was taken through one of these doors and into a dim anteroom lit by a single lamp. A seam of light framed another shut door, behind which she could hear low murmurs.

The Marine told Julia to wait.

It was nearly noon by the time the door flung open. A gaggle of chattering officers from many nations spilled out of the room. Julia was summoned inside by a more junior officer, an aide who said curtly, "The admiral will see you now."

Joko stood when he saw Julia. He stepped from behind his desk and gestured for her to sit on a sofa while he perched on a chair beside her. When the aide went to sit in the other chair, Joko dismissed him. "Give us a few moments alone, won't you."

Joko crossed his arms over his chest and inhaled deeply, as if to summon from the center of himself what he'd say next. "Most of my staff thinks I should call the UN and tell them that you're here. When I saw your name among the resettlers, I considered alerting them. Having a UN official embarked with us could complicate matters. But I heard a rumor you've resigned . . . is that true?"

Julia said it was.

Joko furrowed his brow. He was confused but also concerned, like a parent worried about their child. Julia's posting at the UN had marked the pinnacle of her career, the validation of her life's work. Why would she turn her back on it?

"I don't think I'm turning my back on anything," answered Julia. "Actually, I'd be turning my back on that work if I stayed at the UN."

"I don't have a position to offer you," said Joko. "There's no room on my staff and I'm not certain I'd even know what to do with someone like you. This is a military operation, not a scientific one."

"I'm not asking for a job."

"Then what are you asking for?"

"Just to come," said Julia. "To resettle, like everyone else."

"You'd give up everything to be part of this?"

"Let me ask you a question," said Julia. "I understand that one condition the Indians made when forming this alliance was that you lead the resettlement fleet . . . I've also heard they made that request because of Beginner's Mind. So why you? Why did Beginner's Mind choose you?"

Joko shrugged. "I don't know. No doubt you've heard about my family, my wife and daughter lost in the storm. Or perhaps it's because unlike most senior officers I've got no ties at home, nothing to lose."

"We're not so different," said Julia. "I don't have anything to lose either."

Joko's aide had left behind a tablet. It sat on the table between them. Joko picked it up and began to swipe its screen. "These are the manifests for the resettlement fleet," said Joko. "Hundreds of thousands of people. You'd be just another name, no special treatment. You sure that's what you want?"

"My mother was an admiral, like you . . ."

"I know who Sarah Hunt was."

"Growing up, when I'd ask her why she'd chosen to adopt me, she was fond of quoting a piece of Old Testament wisdom. It says that the person who saves one life saves the world entire . . ."

"We have the same idea in Islam."

"I hated her for this. She'd been complicit in the deaths of millions. Did she think adopting me relieved her of that responsibility? According to my mother's logic, my life only had meaning as it related to absolving her of her sins. But I was young. And judgmental. I hadn't learned that whether you've got the blood of the world on your hands or have never hurt a fly, we save ourselves by saving others."

"So you've come here to save yourself?"

Julia averted her eyes. "I need a fresh start."

Joko glanced at his tablet. He continued to swipe through the hundreds of manifests, both the resettlement barges that were already loaded and those few that had yet to load. Then he stopped, his finger hovering over the screen. "There's room on this ship. It hasn't arrived yet, but when it pulls in, I can make sure that you're on its manifest." Joko paused. He stared gravely at Julia. He delivered a final warning about the hazards of their journey, the Consortium defenses, and the threat that even civilian ships would face. "You could very well wind up right back here, or worse . . . Are you sure this is what you want?"

She was sure.

"Very well," said Joko. "My aide will arrange it. Here are the details."

He handed her the tablet. She glanced down, committing the ship's name to memory, the *Sakura*.

12:22 Dec 20, 2084 (+7:00 GMT)
Nusantara

The door shut behind Julia Hunt on her way out.

Admiral Joko was again alone in his office. He sat at his desk, composing a message to his aide that Julia be added to the manifest of the *Sakura*. Then his tablet rang with an incoming call.

"Hello?"

A man's voice answered, "Please hold for the chairman . . ."

A handful of seconds passed.

"Admiral Joko . . . do you know who this is?" It was a woman's voice, her words soft and precisely articulated, spoken in no rush.

"Chairman Bao?"

"Yes," she said. "It's nice to be speaking with you. If you're answering my call, it's because I presume that she's left."

"Who's left?" asked Joko.

"Julia Hunt, she's left your office. You were just meeting with her."

"But how did you . . . ?"

"Know that? It's not important or relevant or even that interesting. There's a great deal that's obvious to me, which may not be obvious to you . . . for instance, you are the right person to lead the resettlement fleet—this is obvious. The reason I'm calling is to confirm that you've manifested Dr. Hunt on the *Sakura*."

"I'm about to write the order."

"Good," said Lily Bao. "Please see to it."

"Of course," said Joko. "Might I ask a question?"

"Please."

"What's her importance?"

The other end of the line was silent for a beat, as if Lily was considering whether to answer. Then she said, "I'm not sure . . . I haven't quite figured her out yet. Which is the reason she's so important, or might be. Understood?"

Joko didn't entirely understand so said nothing, except to ask if there was anything else he might do for Lily.

"That you see to this matter is more than enough." Lily noted that "we might not speak again before you depart."

"Wish us luck, ma'am."

"Luck will have nothing to do with it," said Lily. "Of that, I'm certain."

09:58 Dec 20, 2084 (+5:30 GMT)

New Delhi

General Patel stood outside the door to Lily Bao's suite. Increasingly, he found himself relying on her counsel. The insights she derived from Beginner's Mind had become indispensable. He knocked, but there was no answer. He waited a beat and knocked again; still, no answer. He let himself in and found her in front of a Beginner's Mind remote portal, attended by Yorgos and lost in her work. Lily waved her hands in an intricate pattern and the portal closed.

Patel requested an update.

Lily glanced at Yorgos.

He shrugged, and Lily delivered the less-than-ideal news that despite India throwing its weight behind the Reparationists, Beginner's Mind still seemed to believe the odds were weighted slightly against them—though not definitely so.

General Patel's brow furrowed. "Does that analysis take into account whatever resources the Chinese might provide?"

"It does."

"Okay, but that's strictly a military analysis, correct?"

Lily nodded.

"Politically speaking," said Patel, "the Consortium is displaying certain weaknesses. An appeasement movement in the US is gaining ground. It threatens hawks like Eva Boucher. A vote in Congress to nullify the Authorization for the Use of Military Force just failed, but not by much."

"That's all true," said Lily.

Patel was sounding more upbeat. "Boucher is one or two more setbacks away from seeing her power collapse, particularly given the president's condition."

"What's the latest on her condition?"

"Incapacitated, but stable," said Patel. "Remarkable, isn't it? The Americans—fixated as they've always been on their presidency—are also quite content to have the job filled by an empty suit."

"Speaking as an American," said Lily, "an empty suit is often the best you can hope for." She asked how much longer until the launch of the resettlement fleet.

"A few days," said Patel. "A week at the most."

Lily grew quiet, lost in thought.

General Patel observed her silently. Her increasing level of connection with Beginner's Mind was obvious. Like any visionary—artist, oracle, or mystic—Lily seemed to exist in a state of delicate equilibrium. Patel was careful in his speech around her, as if the wrong word or a misplaced gesture might cause Lily's grasp of the future to vanish, as if the future itself wasn't inevitable but ephemeral, like a mist that gathers only to dissipate.

Lily noted Patel's deference and was amused by it. A slight smile curved the edges of her mouth. She kept him sitting across from her. She wanted to see how long his patience would last.

After a couple of minutes he asked, "Is there something else you're seeing?"

"No," said Lily. "Actually, I am hoping you might help me with a personal matter. I need to get a letter to my son."

"I know you've been trying to reach him," said General Patel. "But it's not possible given the situation. Even if it were, we can't find him."

"So you've tried?"

Patel nodded. "He was on the *Zheng He* when it sank. We've heard he's in the US but aren't certain. He could very well have returned to China. When we call his East-West Centers, the line always goes to an answering service, and when we've checked his offices, they're closed. I've personally looked at all of this with our intelligence services. It's as if he's disappeared."

"Have you called the Guoanbu?"

"We have."

"And?"

"They haven't been helpful. Keep in mind, we're on opposite sides of this conflict now, at least at the moment."

"Call them again," said Lily. "Tell them it's me calling and that I want to speak with Zhu De."

"Anything else?"

Lily planted her elbows on her desk. Not knowing the whereabouts of her son disturbed her. She could feel her emotions welling up from her stomach. She stared across her large office, to a bookcase on its far end. As she had aged, she'd lost a great deal but never her vision; it remained perfect. To calm herself, she began to read the titles on the spines of the books. Even the tiniest letters were clear to her.

21:47 Dec 22, 2084 (-5:00 GMT)
Fishers Island, NY

Jake Shriver was given an office two buildings down from the Death Rattlers' headquarters. Day and night, aircraft engines roared overhead and shook the windowpanes in their flimsy casements. Tick-Tock insisted they keep up an aggressive patrolling schedule. He presided over operations on the island like a feudal lord. Surrounded by his pilots, and with a battle inevitable, Tick-Tock seemed to

Shriver like a man who knew exactly who he was and what he was about.

As for himself, Jake Shriver was nursing doubts. His mission had been to help Tick-Tock and the Floridians establish themselves on the island. He'd accomplished this ahead of schedule. The Floridians now felt so welcome that one of the local real estate brokers had taken to offering tours of the island for off-duty pilots. Shriver could only marvel that the pilots thought they'd be alive long enough to enjoy one of the vacant homes, and that they believed the island would survive the battle. But hey, thought Shriver, a shred of optimism never hurt anyone, even if he was struggling to remain optimistic himself.

Eva Boucher had asked Shriver for a detailed report on the island's defenses, one she could present to Congress. Shriver had only to switch on the news to understand why the embattled Boucher needed this report. Each day more members of Congress joined the recently established Appeasement Caucus. To counter their efforts, Boucher needed to inspire confidence in the preparations her administration had overseen.

Jake was happy to work late into the night as he tabulated the impressive defenses on Fishers Island, not only the aviation assets at the airfield but also the tangle of missile defenses dug in like ticks along the shore and the destroyers and cruisers on patrol nearby in the Atlantic. As Jake combed through the reports Tick-Tock had provided, he became increasingly confident of two things: first, that the Floridians had done a remarkable job reinforcing the island and deploying their forces; and second, that this would make the coming bloodshed all the worse.

Shriver glanced up from his work, rubbing the heels of his palms against his tired eyes. No matter how he looked at the situation, it would come down to decisions made in Beijing. Recently, when he'd tried to reach Zhu De or any other official, his calls had gone unanswered. Shriver couldn't help but recall what Tick-Tock had told him days before: a person might be from two places but he's always more from one than the other. Shriver didn't want this to be true, but he was having an increasingly difficult time refuting the logic.

As Shriver worked, there was a knock at his door.

"Up late, I see . . ."

He glanced up, startled. It was Zhu De.

The island's defenses could use an upgrade, Zhu De explained. A lackadaisical air controller had cleared his jet for landing with only the most cursory of bone fides exchanged. "One never knows," he said, "I could have been a saboteur."

"Who says you aren't?" said Jake.

Zhu De laughed. He prowled the room, eventually sitting down without an invitation. "Come now," he said. "You must understand that it's been difficult to remain in touch. You wouldn't hold a lack of communication against me?"

"It seems as if Beijing has decided to turn its back on the Consortium."

"I wouldn't put it that way."

Shriver was exhausted. And although he prided himself on his diplomatic skills and self-control, he'd lost all patience with Zhu De's games. "How would you put it then?"

Zhu De rubbed the groove in his cleft chin. "I'd say that we're waiting until the right moment to allocate our military assets, that we're being strategic, that we're in no rush to escalate the situation."

"Escalate the situation?" Shriver came out of his seat. He stepped to the window, where another flight of Floridian J-19s was taxiing down the runway. "The situation has already escalated. Hundreds of ships are approaching landing beaches north of here. The Reparationists and the Consortium are set on a collision course. How can you wait any longer? The time to pick sides is now."

"Pick sides?" Zhu De laughed. "I never thought I'd hear you, 'Mr. East-West Center,' demanding that others pick sides."

"What's that supposed to mean?"

"You've always thought it was possible to reconcile both sides, to straddle two worlds."

"And you think I've been wrong?"

"That's not the word I would use," said Zhu De. "I think you've been *naïve*."

"Naïve . . ." Shriver said, squeezing out the word. "Maybe."

"Even your mother has picked sides. Under her leadership, the Tandava Group has allied itself with the Indians, who are supporting the Reparationists, who are coming here to kill you. Have you considered that?"

Shriver remained at the window. He had heard nothing from his mother. Just as his stubbornness wouldn't allow him to abandon the

Consortium, it wouldn't allow him to reach out to her—if that were even possible. "Would it be naïve of me to believe that Beijing will continue to provide support to the Consortium?"

"Beijing remains committed to the Consortium's best interests."

"I suspect you mean to Beijing's best interests. Have you communicated this to my mother?"

"I have."

Jake remained at the window. "And what does she say about my being here?"

"Nothing," answered Zhu De.

Jake turned away from the window and faced Zhu De. He needed to see if he was lying. Zhu De's expression was vacant.

The window behind Jake shuddered. Another flight of J-19s was taking off.

"How long will you stay with us?"

Zhu De stepped beside Jake at the window. He pointed to his private jet on the refueling pad. He'd return to Beijing momentarily.

"That's a short visit," Jake observed.

"We wanted to make sure we could count on you . . ."

A beat of silence passed between them. Jake hadn't realized this was a question. Zhu De added, "Can we? Can we count on you?"

"I remain committed to the Consortium's best interests," said Jake.

Zhu De laughed. "Well put." He shook Jake's hand and left his office.

Minutes later Jake heard the hollow whine of Zhu De's jet as it taxied down the runway.

08:25 Dec 25, 2084 (+7:00 GMT)
Java Sea

The resettlement fleet was underway, though Admiral Joko couldn't see a single ship through the heavy mist that had descended. His flag was once again situated on the Nigerian super destroyer *Aradu*, and looking out from its bridge he might as well have been sailing alone. To reduce their signature and avoid detection by the Consortium, they had their radars silenced. Joko had to take it on faith that the hundreds of ships were somewhere out there in the mist.

The crew of the *Aradu* led by Captain Gambo had more than proven their competence, and so Joko had little to do as they cruised westward, toward their rendezvous with the rest of their Nigerian, Indian, and Brazilian allies in the open Atlantic. Old habits die hard, and this first morning Joko stood on the bridge, scanning the horizon for no other reason than it filled him with a sense of calm.

The preparations of recent weeks had allowed little time for reflection. But now he had space to wonder why he'd been chosen for this task. Why had Beginner's Mind placed him in a position of such responsibility? Was it because of the loss of his family? Or perhaps it was because of his education? Few naval officers possessed his training in the environmental sciences. Ultimately, Joko couldn't say, though it suddenly occurred to him that he wasn't alone in having been chosen . . .

They'd all been chosen . . .

Each person under his command . . .

When viewed against the course of human history, those sailing west with him were so few, their number such a tiny fraction of all those who'd ever lived. For the first time in a long while, perhaps even since he'd lost his family, Joko knew he wasn't alone.

For the remainder of the morning, Joko stood on the bridge, searching for a break in the clouds, a seam of horizon. He felt as calm as the ocean he traveled over, consoled by this simple thought.

6

Red Sky at Morning

04:27 Dec 26, 2084 (-5:00 GMT)
Fishers Island, NY

Jake Shriver lay on a cot in the corner of his office, arms hanging over each side, like a corpse face down in a slow river. Someone had placed a nylon poncho liner over him as he slept. It covered him like a funeral shroud. He was dead drunk.

The night before, the Death Rattlers had thrown a Christmas party. They'd decked out their ready room in festive lights and hooked a karaoke machine to the A/V suite. A few requisitioned cases of high-end liquor from the Big Club fueled the evening, which featured an impressive number of Kenny Loggins songs in the karaoke lineup, belted out with intensifying gusto. After one particularly spirited rendition of "Danger Zone," Tick-Tock interrupted the karaoke. Two young lieutenants were about to serenade him with "You've Lost that Lovin' Feelin'," but he snatched the microphone instead.

“Listen up! Listen up, goddamn it!” Tick-Tock leaped onto the pair of desks pushed together to form the karaoke stage. The Christmas lights twinkled a sequence of primary colors against his face. Tick-Tock gestured to one of his pilots to bring him something. The pilot—a squat, muscly fellow, call sign Trash Panda in honor of his missing front tooth and the perpetual five-o’clock shadow that patterned his face—handed Tick-Tock a leather aviator’s jacket with shearling collar. “Snakes!” he shouted, bringing the squadron to order. “We’ll likely be seeing action soon. Before we do, it’s important to acknowledge someone who’s already played an important role in our inevitable victory.”

Tick-Tock called Shriver to the stage, presenting him the jacket. He was to become an honorary member of the Death Rattlers. “You’ve earned this,” Tick-Tock said. “You’re a Snake now.” Shriver smiled broadly at the honor. “As an honorary Snake,” Tick-Tock said, “you’ll need a call sign . . . Just so you know, we put a lot of thought into this one . . .” Shriver’s smile dimmed. Tick-Tock cleared his throat. “Jake Shriver, you’re a man of the world, a lawyer, a diplomat, a humanitarian who has committed his life to bridging cultures . . . You not only see the best in others but in our society, and what we might someday become . . . Reflecting on your sensibilities and accomplishments, on your firm character and indomitable spirit, your call sign became obvious to us . . . Let it be known among the Snakes that from this point forward and forever, you shall be known as . . .”

As if announcing the Best Picture winner at the Academy Awards, Tick-Tock read from a patch sewn onto the jacket’s left breast.

“Fancy Pants!”

A great cheer erupted. The Death Rattlers raised bottles aloft, drinking to the glory of Fancy Pants. Tick-Tock held the jacket open for Shriver, who slid his arms into it, tugging down the sleeves. It fit perfectly. They'd cheered again. Shriver didn't particularly like Fancy Pants, but he knew accepting an unflattering call sign was a rite of passage, a gesture of submission, that his individual ego could subordinate itself to the group. Then the squadron started chanting, "Fancy Pants! Fancy Pants! Drink, drink, drink!"

Growing up, precocious as he was, Shriver had struggled to know when the group was laughing *at* him or *with* him. His mother had tried to coach him on the difference between the two. Lily Bao had always understood how her son's intellectual gifts had proven both a blessing and burden, much like his dual American and Chinese heritage. Shriver had thought of her as he raised a bottle to his lips and began to drink. He knew that, as Fancy Pants, the Snakes were most definitely laughing with him. He knew the difference because she'd taught him. It felt good to belong.

It did not, however, feel good when Tick-Tock kicked the foot of his cot in the early morning darkness. "Shriver, get up."

No response.

"Shriver, wake up. We've got a holographic conference in thirty minutes."

Shriver rolled over on the cot. His vision came in and out of focus. When he turned his head he could feel his hungover brain sloshing around inside his skull. "Shriver?" He echoed his own name in a puzzled voice, as if not recognizing it. He stared up at Tick-Tock. "I thought I was Fancy Pants now . . ."

"You're gonna be late, that's what you are."

An email had come in to the watch officer only minutes before, Tick-Tock explained, an emergency meeting of the United States National Security Council Staff. It listed Eva Boucher as the meeting's chair. Other participants included the secretary of defense, chairman of the Joint Chiefs, and the heads of every operational command on the East Coast. That was all Tick-Tock knew.

"What about allies?" Shriver asked.

"Not many," said Tick-Tock. "Certainly no Chinese."

Shriver stood from his cot. He teetered across his office and into the hallway restroom. He turned on the tap. He brushed his teeth, washed his face, and shaved in the cold water. When he returned from the restroom, he dressed promptly, stepping into his trousers, tucking in his shirt. His tie was hanging from one of the blades of the ceiling fan slowly rotating overhead. Shriver pulled it down and struggled to knot it. He glanced over at Tick-Tock.

"Have you seen my jacket?"

Tick-Tock pointed to a gray blazer hooked to the back of the door.

"Not that jacket," said Shriver. "My new one."

Tick-Tock smiled. They found the leather aviator's jacket hanging on the back of a computer monitor in the corner. Shriver threw on the jacket. When he zipped it up to his throat, Tick-Tock pulled down the zipper a quarter of the way and popped the collar, how a fighter pilot would wear it.

"Looking good, Fancy Pants."

Tick-Tock glanced at his oversized aviator's watch, a vintage Breitling. If they left now, the two of them would make their meeting just in time. They strode out of Shriver's office and onto the airfield in their identical jackets. With each step Shriver took, he felt a little steadier on his feet.

09:42 Dec 26, 2084 (+5:30 GMT)
New Delhi

Each day since the fleet's launch, General Patel and Lily Bao had met in a cramped operations center buried on a low floor of the Indian defense ministry, the walls veined with circuits and wires, a thicket of downlinks and uploads and mainframes all tied into a frenetic discharge of information. From here, the two tracked the fleet's progress. The room was windowless, crowded with screens, and attended by a half dozen technicians.

The room reminded Lily of a photo from one of her elementary school history books. It'd been taken at the White House almost seventy-five years ago when the US had killed the terrorist leader Osama bin Laden. On that momentous day, one would've imagined the president, his cabinet secretaries, and his flag officers all gathering in a grand operations center to watch the mission. Instead, they'd huddled around a tiny conference table. The president hadn't even sat at its head, but in a chair off to the side.

The small operations center provided by the Indians also had a conference table in its center. At one end sat the technicians who toggled between a variety of overhead and holographic displays. On its other end sat Lily Bao, General Patel, and this morning's unannounced guest, Zhu De.

Zhu De was already at the head of the table when Lily Bao arrived. He'd been watching a satellite live feed of the resettlement fleet. Its first echelon of warship escorts was conducting an open-ocean rendezvous with a contingent of Brazilian ships four hundred miles south of Africa's Gold Coast. This rendezvous of destroyers, frigates, and cruisers, once successfully completed, would bring the resettlement fleet to full strength. They would then cross the Atlantic. Zhu De hardly acknowledged Lily Bao when she stepped inside. He was fixated on the minutia of this complex at-sea maneuver, even though he had no ability to affect its outcome from a conference room in New Delhi.

When Zhu De did eventually notice Lily Bao, he stood, offering her his seat at the head of the table. She coolly refused, saying, "I wouldn't have expected to see you here."

"Alliances change," said Zhu De. He again gestured to his seat. "Are you sure?"

"That's quite all right, you look comfortable where you are. How's the rendezvous going?"

"We're ahead of schedule," Zhu De said contentedly.

Lily Bao exchanged a look with General Patel. "We?"

There was an edge in her voice. She craned her neck forward, studying the satellite display. "I see Brazilian ships down there"—she made a theatrical gesture, sweeping her hand toward the screen—"some Indian ships too. Oh, those frigates look like our Indonesian allies . . . but, wait . . . are there Chinese ships down there? Did I miss those?"

"I take your point," said Zhu De dryly.

She resented any implication that the Chinese were allies, even if they had entered a nonaggression pact with the Reparationists. That nonaggression pact had required the Chinese to forfeit their Article 5 responsibilities to other Consortium nations in exchange for a promise that the Reparationists wouldn't attempt future landings on their shores in Asia. This policy decision was understandable. Beijing always had a flair for realpolitik, but it was difficult for Lily to respect; it was, after all, a betrayal.

"Any news from your son?" Zhu De replied.

"Shouldn't I be the one asking you?" said Lily. "Or are you through with him given that he's—"

"Enough," Patel interjected. "We've got more pressing matters to discuss." His disappointed gaze fell on Lily.

As Lily gradually became more and more enmeshed with Beginner's Mind, she started to lose a sense of where her personality, her consciousness, her choices ended and where the link to the entity began. If the emotions surrounding her son, their estrangement, and her inability to locate him existed in one room, then a different room contained her analysis of the resettlement fleet and its prospects for success. Patel was simply asking her to step from one room into the other.

Which she now did.

"These past few days," Lily began, "I've been running through landing models with Beginner's Mind. The resettlement fleet is making steady progress. Rendezvous have remained on schedule, and we've faced no major setbacks. Still, we're in a precarious position. No matter how I vary the inputs, the chance of a successful landing never exceeds thirty percent."

"Inputs like what?" asked Zhu De.

"We've got a pretty clear understanding of the Consortium's defenses," said Patel, "so there isn't much variance there. One of the main inputs that increases our odds of success is our direction of approach. After further analysis, Beginner's Mind has found a seam in their defenses."

Zhu De had removed his glasses. He was massaging their coin-sized lenses with a handkerchief. "What type of seam?"

"If we take a southern approach," Patel explained, "we can hit an area that isn't manned by US troops, but rather by the Floridians. If we bring the bulk of our combat power to bear on the Floridians, causing them to suffer heavy losses, it could undermine their alliance with the Consortium."

"What makes you so certain that heavy losses would cause the Floridians to break apart from the Consortium?" Zhu De asked. "It could have the opposite effect. After sustaining such losses, they could become more defiant."

"That's always a possibility," said Patel.

Zhu De crossed his arms over his chest and shifted uncomfortably in his seat. "What do you think?" he asked Lily Bao, who'd grown noticeably silent. "Will the Floridians collapse if we"—he cut himself off—"if *you* focus your attack on them?"

"It's unclear," she said.

"Unclear?" Zhu De was annoyed. "What do you mean it's unclear? What does Beginner's Mind say?"

"Beginner's Mind doesn't 'say' anything. It might allow me to see further down the path than you, but that doesn't mean I can predict how a group will react, or that I can see into people's souls. It doesn't mean that I'm God."

"No," said Zhu De. "I suppose not. It's been a long time since acts of God decided battles."

05:00 Dec 26, 2084 (-5:00 GMT)
Fishers Island, NY

The emergency meeting of the National Security Council staff convened by Eva Boucher occurred in a secure, metasphere-generated amphitheater. The stadium seating extended ten rows back. Tick-Tock and Jake Shriver—or rather, their avatars—sat in the seventh row. Their less-than-premium seating didn't bother Shriver; he understood how Beijing's duplicity had made him and his East-West Center an irrelevancy. What did bother Shiver, perhaps more than it should have, was that his digital avatar hadn't been updated. He wished he was wearing his newly acquired aviator's jacket in this meeting instead of his gray suit jacket.

Eva Boucher sat in the front row, dead center. At the top of the hour, she turned and addressed the crowd. Her avatar, fresh and well rested, didn't match her voice, which was thin, tight, and fatigued.

"We have confirmation," she began, "that a new and still sizable

Reparationist invasion fleet, a second armada, has gathered in the Atlantic. Their attempted landing is imminent and most likely to occur within the next five to seven days in southeastern Canada and on the northeastern seaboard of the United States. Everyone gathered in this meeting will play a critical role in what lies ahead. We're being called upon to defend something larger than our homes, our countries, or an alliance of nations. We're being called upon to save our planet. My heartfelt thanks to each of you."

Scattered and uncertain applause followed her comments. It sure wasn't Churchill, thought Jake. But who could fault her. Victory had made Churchill into Churchill, and victory might still work its same magic on Eva Boucher.

As Boucher sat, the first briefer, a rear admiral from the Canadian Intelligence Corps, took center stage. She spoke about the composition of the resettlement fleet, the disposition of its warship escorts and civilian barges. A combination of satellite imagery and hydrographic sensors confirmed that the Reparationists had deployed military and civilian vessels in distinct lines of battle. A slide flashed up on the screen depicting three rows of warships, followed by a fifty-nautical-mile gap, and then a half dozen rows of barges. The Canadian pointed out the size of the barges, some in the range of a million deadweight tons.

An American brigadier general in a flight suit raised his hand at the back of the amphitheater. He had a question. It was about rules of engagement. His command, an understrength fighter wing out of Hanscom Air Force Base near Boston, had only two dozen dilapidated F-22s at their disposal. "With our numbers, we're more of a squadron than a wing," he said, dropping the *r* from every word, a sign that he was native to the Northeast and would be defending his home beaches. "To have a chance at surviving," he added, "my pilots will need some standoff. We can't afford to come in close and try to figure out which ship is a resettler *Love Boat* and which one's a destroyer that's going to tear our heads off—you get me?"

The Canadian intelligence officer listened patiently. She understood. "All forces have been declared hostile within a two-hundred-nautical-mile exclusionary zone."

Boucher waved her hand, signaling the presentation forward a few slides, until arriving at a map of the Northeast. A band of red extended from the coast into the Atlantic. This was the exclusionary zone. Boucher turned left and right as she spoke, so she was addressing the entire auditorium. "Just so we're clear," she said, "if it's got a hull, and it's in that red band, and it's not flying a Consortium flag, send it to the bottom of the ocean." Boucher looked directly at the brigadier general. "Got that?"

"Yes, ma'am," he said crisply.

Boucher motioned for the Canadian intelligence officer to resume her briefing. While the officer cycled through slides on likely Reparationist approaches toward the landing beaches—all of them in the far Northeast, not anywhere near Fishers Island—Shriver leaned over to Tick-Tock. He whispered, "Why do you think they're keeping their warships apart from the civilian barges? If they mixed them all together, it'd make for a tougher target."

Tick-Tock raised an eyebrow. He felt the answer was obvious. "They're not mixing the warships with the barges because they want to protect the civilians."

"Understood," said Shriver. "But does it surprise you that they'd do that?"

"Do what?"

"Put themselves at greater risk and potentially risk the success of their landings to make sure that civilians don't wind up as targets."

"No," said Tick-Tock, clearly annoyed. "It doesn't surprise me. They're not monsters. They're just on a different side than you."

Shriver became defensive. "I guess that's something you know about," he said, "switching sides." He immediately regretted the words.

Tick-Tock turned away from Shriver to watch the rest of the presentation. A new briefer had taken the stage, a Marine lieutenant general who was describing the status of their shore defenses and the inadequate resources at their disposal. The Marine noted that if the Reparationists managed to land, it was unlikely current onshore defenses could push them back into the sea. This meant the brunt of responsibility for defense would fall to the navy and air forces. The Marine was saying something about the necessity of defeating the Reparationists on the waves, before they ever reached the shore, when Shriver leaned over again, this time to apologize to Tick-Tock.

"It's okay, Fancy Pants. I don't take this stuff personally. Not ever. If you stay in the war-fighting business long enough, you eventually learn that whether you wear one uniform your entire career or several, like me, you eventually wind up fighting on different sides for different causes. It comes with the job."

The Marine general finished his briefing. Four admirals—an American, a Brit, a Frenchman, and a Canadian—stepped to center stage. Their briefing on force readiness, on the most likely Reparationist approaches, and on possible deployment of those forces given a variety of contingencies—say, if the landings focused on Nova Scotia versus Maine, or if the Reparationists led their attack with a bombardment of hypersonics versus manned jets—was rehearsed down to the last beat, so that at every transition there was never a moment of unplanned silence or an errant "um" spoken. As their presentation gathered momentum, it became an elevated work of performance art, almost a form of music: the four admirals in their resplendent uniforms were as well tuned as a barbershop quartet.

About twenty minutes into their presentation, Tick-Tock leaned over to Shriver. "I'm pretty sure we're fucked."

Shriver looked at him blankly.

"No plan survives first contact with the enemy," said Tick-Tock, "and this plan is wired way too tight for my taste. These brass hats seem to think the enemy doesn't get a vote."

The admirals soon finished. The operations portion of the briefing was over. Everyone remained in their seats to listen to a rotation of secondary briefers who touched on resupply, communications, and other ancillary disciplines. Throughout the auditorium, sidebar conversations broke out as commanders dispatched subordinates to their various headquarters. The last briefing slide was a placeholder.

It gave Eva Boucher an opportunity to offer a few final—if ultimately forgettable—words. She ended her remarks with a stern "God be with you."

Shriver and Tick-Tock logged out of the metasphere and removed their headsets. They sat in the Death Rattlers ready room in the gray predawn light, seagulls moaning outside on the nearby beaches. They were exhausted, from the briefing and from the Christmas party the night before. Shriver asked if Tick-Tock wanted help waking up the pilots and ground crews. There was work to be done.

"It can wait," said Tick-Tock. "Let them sleep a little longer. You heard the briefing—the resettlement fleet is coming from the north. They could miss us entirely. What's a few more minutes of shut-eye?"

Tick-Tock slumped down in his chair, folded his arms over his chest, and kicked his heels up onto a nearby desk. He closed his eyes. Within seconds, he too was sleeping.

01:42 Dec 27, 2084 (+5:30 GMT)
New Delhi

Lily was working late, yet again. She was running scenarios through Beginner's Mind. The barrier between her and the interface had become increasingly porous, and she was struggling to understand where her consciousness ended and Beginner's Mind began. Lost as she was in her work, it took her a moment to notice that the lines of code on the interface had ceded to plaintext and then, suddenly, to Mandarin. The characters: 女儿, *daughter*, appeared. She paused.

Daughter? she typed into the interface.

You have been thinking of this all wrong came the reply in Mandarin. A cursor flashed beside the last word.

Who is this?

The Consortium, the Reparationists, their navies and armies, they aren't what's going to decide this war. They aren't what's going to determine the future of the planet.

Was this her father's intelligence uploaded? She typed: *Dad?*

There was no response. So she tried: *How have we been thinking of it wrong?*

If you are fighting for the future of the planet, doesn't it make sense that we should put the planet on our side? Victory isn't going to be determined by who has more ships, or aircraft, or the most cutting-edge military technology. Look at history.

Before he was murdered, her father, Admiral Lin Bao, had wanted to leave the navy behind. His great passion had always been history, and he'd dreamed of becoming a professor. A quiet life. A classroom filled with students instead of a warship manned by a crew. Her throat turned thick. *What history, Dad?*

In the Second World War, in certain battles, the US Navy lost more ships to storms at sea than to enemy action. Hundreds of years before that, during the Spanish Armada, the decisive blow wasn't delivered by the British, but by a North Atlantic low-pressure system. In ancient times, before battle, commanders would consult oracles. Why? Because they needed God on their side. If you put the planet on your side, who needs God? If you put the planet on your side, you win.

An image appeared on the interface, a triangle. Written onto each of its three sides was one of the following: *atmospheric carbon scrub, nuclear fusion, ice cap replenishment.* Drawn in its center was an unruly twist of lines.

What is this drawing in the center? Lily typed.

A storm . . . The cursor continued to blink, and then filled in: *A man-made storm. Tandava has been experimenting with those three technologies for years. None of them solve the climate crisis, not on their own. But the three combined could create a massive storm, the largest in our planet's history.*

Lily asked how.

The text came more rapidly now: *With ice cap replenishment, you can drop ambient air temperature in specific polar localities by up to five degrees for short periods. Atmospheric carbon scrubbers, though effective, are notoriously volatile. If they meet up with a low-pressure system, or high winds characterized by temperature variance, they turn cyclonic. If you perform a highly concentrated atmospheric carbon scrub in a small area while also dropping the ambient temperature in that area, it would create a localized superstorm—the seas would break open before your eyes, swallowing everything on the waves.*

Lily asked about the third side of the triangle.

A detonation, nuclear and precise.

Lily marveled at how casually this intelligence—whether it was her father, or Beginner's Mind, or a combination of the two—married those two words.

Create the storm over the Pole. Then, with an atmospheric blast, knock that storm south, into the Atlantic. The storm's size and speed will accelerate as it travels into increasingly warm waters. It will careen into the Atlantic at Category Five–plus speeds. Everything in its path will be destroyed.

Including the Consortium fleet, Lily added.

Above all, the Consortium fleet.

The cursor continued to flash, until another line of text was added.

Get to work, my daughter.

The interface shut down. Lily tried to reboot it, but soon gave up. She knew he wouldn't come back.

08:17 Dec 27, 2084 (-2:00 GMT)
500 nm west of Cabo Verde

The weather forecast for the next week was clear. This was a remarkable stroke of luck for Admiral Joko as his fleet crossed the Atlantic. The rendezvous on the open ocean had proven particularly complex. Not only had they needed to assemble the warships of three different nations, but they'd also had to arrange a dizzying array of civilian vessels into separate lines of convoy. During those days, Joko had been getting by on catnaps, fifteen-minute intervals of sleep he'd steal every second or third hour. Last night was the first in which he'd managed to sleep for several consecutive hours in his stateroom.

When Joko awoke, his head felt clearer than it had in days. He quickly dressed, grabbed a bite of breakfast and mug of tea in the wardroom, and then presented himself on the bridge of the *Aradu.*

He could see for miles. The ocean and sky, each an unblemished plane, seemed in competition as to which could achieve the purest shade of cerulean blue. Even though a suite of sensors—radar, infrared, sonographic—displayed the precise location of each ship in the fleet, Admiral Joko asked for a pair of binoculars. Captain Gambo, who'd also just arrived on the bridge, passed Joko his personal set.

Three well-spaced rows of warships came into focus, extending over the horizon in both directions. Their course was fixed, due west, while behind them six less-perfectly spaced rows of civilian ships followed.

Planners in Washington expected Joko to take a northern approach, and he would oblige them. Three hundred nautical miles from the East Coast, his fleet would hit a release point. From there, seven out of every nine of his ships would maneuver north, toward hundreds of miles of landing beaches. The Consortium might be able to keep him from landing in one or two places, but they couldn't keep him from landing in every place, which is what he intended to do.

A thousand local beaches and coves would play the role that Omaha and Utah beaches had played nearly 150 years before. Joko had conceived of this as a Dunkirk in reverse. His reliance on civilian shipping wasn't a weakness but a strength. Low-draught civilian ships could place the resettlers ashore almost anywhere, but their defenses were weak. To protect the main landing force, Joko would need to draw the Consortium's attention away. He needed a feint.

This is where the Brazilians would come in. Von Hütschler's protégé, Captain Duarte, would lead a separate flotilla. When the main body hit the release point, Duarte would maneuver two-thirds of the fleet's combat power to the south, attacking up through the mid-Atlantic. Given how heavily this attack would be weighted, Joko anticipated that the Consortium would commit the bulk of its forces to counter it. Joko would need the Consortium to take the bait and confuse this southern attack for the main landings. He thought it would work. Maybe.

Joko continued to scan the horizon with Gambo's binoculars. "Good distribution between ships," he said. "Looks like we're making nice progress."

He handed Gambo back his binoculars.

Joko stepped toward a holographic planner and Gambo followed. The Eastern Seaboard projected upward, suspended in a cone of three-dimensional light. Joko toggled on the map icons. In a flash, their entire battle plan appeared. Using his index finger, Joko rotated the coast so he could view this schematic from both a bird's-eye and then ground view. As he had again and again, he walked through the plan with Gambo—just as Gambo had done with his own subordinates. They did this not so they could rigidly adhere to that plan, but so they might adeptly deviate from it in a moment of crisis.

As Joko talked through hitting the release point—when the majority of the civilian ships would maneuver north while the bulk of the warships would hook south—he paused. Suddenly, something was off. Maybe it was the sleep he'd had that was allowing him to think more clearly, because his instincts were now telling him that this southward-hooking maneuver didn't look quite right.

"What don't you like about it, sir?"

Joko peered deeply into the holograph. "It looks phony and contrived; we're swinging too far south. Beginner's Mind might have orchestrated that move, but I'm not sure an actual person's going to buy it." He continued to manipulate the holograph, zooming in and out, scouring the waterways for a different axis of advance from the south. "What if Duarte's warships came up through here?" said Joko. "It's basically the same plan, just executed a little farther north. We'll still be far enough south to divert Consortium assets away from the landing beaches—except done this way, the feint is more convincing."

Gambo studied the proposed route, which had Duarte's ships approaching the coast at the border between New York and Connecticut. "The Consortium's defenses are definitely weakest down there, sir." Gambo reached for a tablet on a nearby desk. He opened a document, scrolling to its bottom. "Our intel section reports that there's a garrison nearby, several squadrons of fixed-wing fighters on Fishers Island."

Gambo and Joko carefully studied the little island that jutted inconveniently into the Atlantic. Joko made his decision; Duarte would take this new route. Although riskier, it would make the feint more convincing.

"What else do we know about that garrison?" Joko asked as an afterthought.

"The good news is they aren't regular US military," said Gambo.

"What are they then?"

"Floridians, sir."

"I wouldn't be so sure that's good news."

06:42 Dec 28, 2084 (+5:30 GMT)
New Delhi

Lily Bao, General Patel, and Zhu De were camped out in the operations center when an updated plan of action arrived from the resettlement fleet. Admiral Joko had decided to alter his direction of attack, deviating from the precise schematic created by Beginner's Mind. When Zhu De questioned Joko's decision, Lily Bao defended it. Altering battle plans was Joko's prerogative. After all, he was the fleet's commander, and it was Joko—not Beginner's Mind—who would be held accountable for the landings' success or failure.

First thing that morning, Zhu De left the defense ministry for a few hours. Lily assumed that he was at his embassy, reporting this development directly to Beijing. Which was understandable. Lily had her own concerns about Joko's decision, even if a lack of trust prevented her from voicing those concerns to Zhu De. She did, however, voice them to Patel. "Beginner's Mind chose Admiral Joko," said Lily. Her voice was just above a whisper. "I suppose his altering the battle plan shouldn't worry me. But his fleet is only a day out from the release point. It's a little late in the game to be making these changes."

Patel didn't disagree. The two of them spent the remainder of the morning reviewing the updates Joko had made to the landing plan. His rationale seemed sound. If his warships traveled too far south, their feint wouldn't be credible. If they traveled too far north, they wouldn't divert enough of the Consortium's combat power away from the main landing beaches. This new axis of attack seemed to strike the right balance—but who could know?

With that matter settled, Lily shut the door. It was only her and Patel in the room. She revealed the strange occurrence from the night before, her odd interaction with Beginner's Mind. "I'm not saying it was my father," she explained, "but it sure felt like him, or at least his intelligence." As Lily ran through the details of the three-pronged plan, Patel listened intently, nodding at times and at others looking confused. When Lily finished, he glanced once again at a holographic map of the Atlantic, as if he was seeing it for the first time. He turned back to Lily.

"So we create a storm?" asked Patel.

Lily could hear the skepticism in his voice. "Don't think of it as a storm."

"Then how should I think of it?"

"As a weapon," she said. "We make the earth a weapon."

23:46 Dec 28, 2084 (-4:00 GMT)
300 nm northwest of Bermuda

Julia Hunt lay awake four racks up in the berthing. It seemed a waste that she couldn't sleep, as she'd been lucky to find a place within the steel skin of the overcrowded *Sakura*, yet she was feeling unlucky that night as she lay in her rack.

Over the course of the day, she had wandered the decks of the massive civilian transport ship. The operations center, manned by a handful of Indonesian sailors, was left unguarded. She had settled in the back of the room and watched the ships on the displays. No one had noticed her as she observed the shifting course of the combatants arrayed ahead of the transports. It was clear the brunt of the fleet's combat power would hit the East Coast from the south, on a line of advance that ran directly into the Floridians' defensive positions. Directly into Tick-Tock.

Should she warn him? Lying awake, Julia was weighing her options. Perhaps she could prepare a message, something written and brief that she could transmit as data so no one would hear—a line or two to make sure the Floridians were ready, so they'd have a fighting chance, so Tick-Tock might survive?

And if she *didn't* deliver this warning . . . ?

Then she would be complicit in Tick-Tock's death . . . Because he would die, she felt certain of this. She could imagine the Reparationist warships striking his tiny garrison, their missiles cratering the runways, the aircraft turned to smoldering wrecks in their hangars.

And if she *did* warn Tick-Tock . . . ?

She'd be a traitor . . . she felt certain of this too.

Whichever choice Julia made would result in a betrayal. Her thoughts turned to her adoptive mother. Dilemmas like this had defined Sarah Hunt's existence. Her role in the nuclear devastation of fifty years before. The part she'd played in discovering the Singularity, only to suppress that discovery. Destruction and creation, those twin forces had shaped her mother's life.

Clearly, Julia wasn't going to get any sleep. She slid off her rack, tiptoeing over the resettlers sprawled in the overcrowded passageways. Some fresh air might clear her head. Above deck, it was no less crowded. She worked her way to the bow; here, a copper-wire HF radio link was hooked to the crane arm. It shone dully, and Julia's gaze followed the wire's sagging ascent from the crane to the bridge, where she could discern only a single silhouette framed against a dim blackout light.

The silhouette stretched its arms overhead, as a person does when yawning. It moved lazily about the bridge. While she observed the silhouette from the bow and weighed the decision before her, a well-trod phrase popped into her head like a nail banged into place with a single hammer stroke: *If you save a life, you save the world entire.*

How many times had Julia heard her mother repeat this? It wasn't life's cruelty that had defeated her mother but its logic. That logic of life—of the saving and taking of it—had also defined much of Julia's existence, from her adoption until now. The pain these words had caused her didn't rob them of their truth, particularly in this moment: she could save Tick-Tock's life.

Julia climbed up three decks and stepped onto the bridge. As she suspected, a lone member of the crew stood watch, a young sailor with a downy fringe of mustache shading his top lip. Aside from a few brief pleasantries, Julia ignored him. She went directly for the HF radio, which sat on the deck in a corner. She huddled over its interface. On a laptop attached to the radio by a cable, she typed up a note. Her message was succinct and to the point, a warning. From an international HF registry, she found a frequency associated with the Fishers Island airfield. She uploaded her message and switched the radio to data transmit. Her cursor hovered over the *send* button.

Click.

She then moved her message into the laptop's trash folder, which she emptied. She retuned the radio to its prior frequency. Everything was reset as if she'd never been there. The sailor—whether tired or simply incurious—seemed disinclined to ask Julia any questions; perhaps his time at sea had already taught him that unwanted questions typically lead to unwanted answers, which often lead to more work or serious trouble. Julia was leaving the bridge (she thought she might even get a little sleep belowdecks) when the captain of the *Sakura* appeared. He was with another sailor, a helmsman Julia recognized from earlier that day. They were blocking the hatch she needed to pass through.

"Dr. Hunt, what has you up here at this hour?" asked the captain.

The young sailor turned in her direction too, as if curious to hear the answer to a question he himself hadn't dared ask.

"I couldn't sleep, so thought I'd stretch my legs." She nodded at the computer and the wire running outside the porthole. "In the Marines, we used these old HF sets." She shrugged her shoulders. "I thought I'd take a look."

"I see . . ." The captain glanced at the young sailor, who glanced at Julia, who kept her gaze fixed on the captain. "Well," he added. "Did you get your look?"

Hunt nodded.

“Good,” said the captain. “You should probably get some rest.”

As Julia made her way off the bridge, she could hear the captain issuing a set of crisp orders to the junior sailor on watch as well as to the helmsman in Indonesian.

Julia had yet to climb down the three levels from the bridge when she felt the *Sakura* lurch to starboard. As they made this turn, the remainder of the resettlement fleet came into view. Civilian ships, twinkling with errant light, followed the *Sakura*’s starboard turn, traveling north. Interspersed between these civilian ships were the warships. Each was perfectly blacked out, invisible, their absence as ominous as silence in a conversation. These warships were turning to port, slipping into the southern darkness.

They had arrived at the release point.

07:47 Dec 28, 2084 (-5:00 GMT)
Fishers Island, NY

Tick-Tock arrived in Shriver’s office early in the morning. He had a single sheet of paper in his hands with two lines of text: *Attack against Floridian positions imminent.*

“It came in last night,” Tick-Tock explained. “What do you make of it?”

At the bottom of the sheet was an equipment identifier, the equivalent of an IP address for an HF radio. Shriver cross-referenced the number with an online registry. “It says this was sent from a Japanese ship under Indonesian charter, the *Sakura*." Shriver pulled up an image of the *Sakura* online.

"What's that crane on its front?" asked Tick-Tock.

"It's a maritime research vessel," said Shriver. "They use the crane to put submersibles and other equipment into the water. Its last logged position was in Nusantara, a week ago. No doubt it's part of the resettlement fleet. Why would someone on the resettlement fleet be sending us this message?"

Tick-Tock was silent.

"Unless it's a trap," Shriver added.

Tick-Tock remained lost in thought.

"Well . . . what do you think?"

"It's not a trap," said Tick-Tock. "I'm certain of that."

Within twenty minutes, Tick-Tock had a flight of two J-19s airborne and heading south. He and Shriver walked over to the Death Rattlers' ready room. Projected on the same screen where they'd sung karaoke a few nights before was the onboard display of the two J-19s, a map of their progress, and live feeds of their forward-looking infrared and thermal sensors. Internal communications from the two aircraft were piped in over speakers. Shriver felt as if he were in the cockpit with the two pilots and had a sudden rush of nausea—a residual Pavlovian response to his last flight in a J-19 with Tick-Tock.

"Red One, this is Red Leader . . . initial EW sensor sweep shows all clear. Descending to eight thousand feet for thermal sweep."

"Roger, Red Leader. Maintaining overwatch at twelve thousand feet."

The two pilots continued their easy, relaxed banter. The squadron's other pilots filtered in and out of the ready room, pouring coffee, bickering over a box of donuts and who'd get the last chocolate-frosted. No one wanted the old-fashioned or strawberry-frosted with sprinkles. Like their two comrades in the air, they seemed at ease. The only person who didn't seem relaxed was Tick-Tock. He was sitting on the edge of his seat, clutching his mug of coffee with both hands like a pilot trying not to lose control of his stick.

"Why would the resettlement fleet land this far south?" Shriver asked in a low, ponderous voice. "It doesn't make any sense."

"Unless it's a feint," said Tick-Tock, not taking his eyes off the screen. "If I were them, I'd hit us as hard as I could, and I wouldn't stop, not until I drew down forces from the north, leaving those landing beaches undefended."

"You think that's their plan, a feint in the south and a main landing in the north?"

Tick-Tock turned and faced Shriver. "If it is, all of us here are dead. We're just a speed bump, and not a very good one."

A staticky transmission interrupted them. "Red One, this is Red Leader . . . I've got a thermal signature moving at a high rate of speed on the surface . . . you tracking this?"

"Stand by . . ."

Red One, which as wingman was flying at a higher altitude, switched on his thermal sensors. A new live feed projected onto the ready room screen. In addition to the small, swiftly moving vessel—likely a surface drone—two large, rippling silhouettes appeared at the edge of the frame only to vanish. Like a shark glimpsed through a wave, or a jungle cat glimpsed through the trees, the implication was clear: something dangerous was out there. Something lethal. "You see that?" asked Red One.

Tick-Tock was on his feet. "Tell them to return to—" But before he could finish, a solid, piercing tone sounded from both aircraft.

"I've got radar lock on me! . . . Two . . . Three . . . Multiple radar locks!"

"Break right, Red One! Break right!" Red Leader delivered these instructions while breaking left. Onboard cockpit cameras piped in an image of the pilots as they began evasive maneuvers. Each was huffing into their oxygen mask as the Gs piled on. Shriver's mouth went dry as he watched. The pilots popped chaff and flares from the bellies of their barrel-rolling J-19s, making an incongruously festive display of daytime fireworks. A first missile—which was riding the tail of Red One—took the bait. With its sensors disoriented, it detonated on the chaff, exploding outward and then collapsing in on itself like a dark star. Red One still had two missiles riding its tail.

A second missile detonated on the chaff behind Red Leader, and he grunted like a pro tennis player. "Splash two," he said. "Red One! Go for the deck!"

The two J-19s, which had been in near vertical, corkscrewing climbs with afterburners blazing, now toppled nose over tail downward, in an equally punishing inverted dive. From the two cockpits there was no noise, only the continued, labored breathing of the pilots, who'd begun to sound fatigued and desperate, less like knights of the air and more like hunted animals.

Shriver counted three missiles still giving chase: two on Red One, the last on Red Leader. He didn't need Tick-Tock to explain this current maneuver, or its dangers. If the pilots charged violently enough toward the deck and pulled up at the last moment, they might confuse the tracking system of a lesser missile. The longer they waited to pull up, the greater chance they had of losing the missile and the greater chance they had of crashing into the ocean themselves.

Red Leader was in the lead, counting off altitude. "Two thousand feet . . . One thousand . . . Five hundred . . . Two hundred . . . Pull up! Pull up!"

The J-19 afterburners spat misty contrails across the surface of the ocean.

Shriver dipped his eyes. If the two pilots crashed, he didn't want to watch their deaths. He heard a first, then second explosion in quick succession, like the twin beats of a thunderclap. He thought he knew what this meant.

But then a joyous "Yeehaw!" came over the radio as Red Leader barrel-rolled up to altitude. Between panting breaths, he asked his wingman, "How you doing back there?"

"Still got one on me . . ." said Red One, who had also pulled into a climb.

Behind him, the first missile had plunged into the ocean. But the second had only skimmed its surface before reacquiring him as a target. It was rapidly closing. Red One popped his last half dozen chaff and flares as he again entered a punishing set of evasive maneuvers: he piled on more Gs; his grunts began to sound like whimpers; his head was lolling as if his helmet had become too heavy for his neck.

Shriver couldn't see Red One's face or eyes, covered as they were with a shaded visor and oxygen mask. He was glad for this, knowing that otherwise the face would haunt him.

"Red One, bail out, bail out!"

"I can hold it . . ." he muttered to his flight lead. "I can hold it . . ."

"Bail out!"

Red One's onboard live feed vanished in a flash of white light, then retuned to static. Silence fell over the ready room, and with it a threat of paralysis, inaction, which Tick-Tock wouldn't abide. He began barking out orders, one falling after the other in quick succession. "Red Leader, return to base . . . Scramble all available aircraft . . . Reorient shore defenses and dispatch all reconnaissance assets to the south . . ." Tick-Tock grabbed Shriver by the shoulder. "Get on the horn with Washington. Tell Boucher they're here . . ."

Shriver was still staring at the live feed turned to static. "Who'd we lose?"

"It doesn't matter . . . Did you hear what I said? I need you to tell Boucher that they're coming up from the south."

"You don't care who it was . . ." said Shriver in a dreamy voice. "Do you even know . . . ?" Shriver continued to stare into the static. His memories from the *Zheng He* came flooding back. The decomposition of the static was like a portal; it foretold only death.

"It was Trash Panda," said Tick-Tock. His expression betrayed no emotion, as if it were carved from stone. "He was flying Red One. Don't you ever fucking say that I don't know."

11:47 Dec 28, 2084 (-4:00 GMT)
200 nm off the coast of Maine and Nova Scotia

Joko and the bulk of his fleet were holding due east of the landing beaches when a report of initial contact arrived from Captain Duarte. His warships in the south had met the Consortium defenses in a successful engagement—or what Duarte termed a successful engagement. Joko was in the command center of the *Aradu* when he glanced over Duarte's SITREP: a pair of his guided-missile frigates had engaged a flight of Floridian J-19s, destroying one. The other had escaped, headed north. When Joko noted the location of the engagement, which had been off the Delaware coast, he became concerned.

He handed Gambo the SITREP. "It makes no sense," said Joko. "They shouldn't have picked us up so far south. Duarte still has hundreds of miles of ocean to cross. He'll be fighting all the way."

When Gambo offered the SITREP back to Joko, he waved it aside. Joko's irritation only seemed to grow the longer he considered the implications of being discovered so early. How had this happened . . . ? Had the Floridians simply gotten lucky . . . ? The right patrol, in the right place, at the right time . . . ? Joko would have to figure out that answer later. Battle had been joined. There was work to be done.

Although the second J-19 had broken contact, Duarte immediately deployed an orbital drone to track its return. From the edge of the atmosphere, the drone had done this undetected, following the

J-19's path up the East Coast of the United States to where it had just touched down on a small island airfield.

"What's the name?" Joko asked.

The technician manning the drone feed said, "Fishers Island." He pulled up the latest overhead imagery, which didn't seem to make much sense. There was only a single runway on the island with some recreational aircraft scattered about the taxiways, though these images were several weeks old. Joko told the technicians to get Nusantara on the line. He needed General Suharto's staff to re-task one of their high-resolution surveillance satellites to canvass the island. The technician made the appropriate calls. Suharto's staff would immediately implement the request. "The satellite's already in position," the technician reported. "We should have a half-meter resolution live feed up in the next"—he glanced at a digital clock in the middle of the command center—"seven minutes."

Joko nodded his satisfaction.

Gambo, who'd been deep in conversation with his weapons officer, turned to Joko and announced, "Captain Duarte has inputted all firing data for the island, sir. Time to target, eleven minutes. He's asking permission to begin his attack."

"Tell him to stand by."

"Sir?"

Joko shot Gambo an annoyed glance. "We don't know what's on that island, what the civilian presence is, whether that J-19 landed there because it's a military base or simply because it was the nearest airfield. I can wait seven minutes before deciding to crater an island that might have thousands of civilians on it."

"Very well, sir," said Gambo, clearly unconvinced. He nodded to his fires officer, who would relay the message to Duarte's command.

"Need I remind you," added Joko, "that when this is over, we will have to learn to live alongside these people."

"Very well," repeated Gambo, but he seemed even less convinced of this prospect.

The digital clock counted off the minutes. It hung above a blank screen where a live feed of the island would project as soon as the satellite had repositioned. Aside from procedures executed in low murmurs by the crew, the bridge remained silent. Unlike Gambo or Duarte, Joko understood that he had to wage the type of war that would allow the Reparationists to win the peace. Overwhelming and indiscriminate force—of the type he could tell Gambo and Duarte longed to unleash—would assure them victory on the battlefield, but little else. Joko was playing for higher stakes. A longer game.

Before the satellite live feed had a chance to flicker on, Joko's instinct for restraint was proven wrong. The vanguard of Duarte's fleet reported at least two dozen aircraft approaching at low altitude and a high rate of speed. They must've come from Fishers Island. Duarte didn't wait for orders to scramble his interceptor aircraft. Duarte did, however, ask if he now had permission to fire his missiles at the island.

Joko glanced at the clock. A minute left until the live feed, an eternity.

"Sir . . . ?" said Gambo, demanding an answer on Duarte's behalf.

"Fire," said Joko.

11:02 Dec 28, 2084 (-5:00 GMT)

Fishers Island, NY

Dozens of Floridian pilots had taken to the air. They seemed to chase each other off the runway, one charging down its near end before the other could take off from its far end. Shriver had never seen anything like it. Before Tick-Tock had sprinted to his own aircraft, he'd left Shriver clear instructions. He was to remain in contact with Washington and help coordinate the shore-based defenses, including the missile batteries.

Along with a handful of technicians, Shriver sat in the Death Rattlers' ready room. Empty flight lockers lined the walls. He would monitor the progress of each pilot and their aircraft from here. Sets of wedge formations, each five fighters strong, pealed across the sky. They formed into a phalanx and immediately headed south, flying as if possessed by instinct, by the ancient, winged migratory patterns of the fighter pilot, which today carried them at twice the speed of sound at under one thousand feet toward their targets.

Shriver felt overwhelmed. He was monitoring the progress of these aircraft, tracking the readiness of the on-island missile batteries as they reoriented southward, and preparing an updated SITREP to send to Eva Boucher in Washington. This was interrupted when one of the pilots cursed over their internal network, "Did you fucking see that!"

The pilot's voice, which was being piped into the ready room, was met by Tick-Tock, who admonished him. "Silence on the net."

A live feed of Tick-Tock's cockpit was also being transmitted into the ready room. Shriver was watching now, and he saw a flash of dark jags pass overhead. Calmly, Tick-Tock announced, "Looks like we got a spread of missiles headed back toward home. Fancy Pants, you tracking? Missiles inbound."

Shriver swallowed, wetting his throat. "This is Fancy Pants . . . Copy all."

He sprinted out the door, stepped on the airfield, and faced south. The day was clear and bright. Passing through a mantle of blue, he glimpsed the missiles skimming the curvature of the earth. They were coming straight toward him. To run seemed ridiculous—he didn't want to run anymore. So he just stood there watching.

21:42 Dec 28, 2084 (+5:30 GMT)
New Delhi

Lily Bao observed the day's events with a deepening sense of dread. The setbacks began when a flight of J-19s had spotted Duarte's southern advance. Both she and Beginner's Mind had predicted that Duarte's maneuver would catch the Consortium unaware, granting the resettlement fleet the crucial advantage of surprise. Except the opposite had occurred. For the past few hours, a contingent of Floridian aircraft had stalled Duarte's progress. The Floridians were taking heavy casualties, but they were doling out the same.

Along with General Patel and Zhu De, Lily had watched from

their command center at the defense ministry as the Floridians scored successive hits—a destroyer, followed by two cruisers. The first ship to sink, an unmanned reconnaissance frigate, went down in eight minutes after its magazine ignited. The damaged destroyer and two cruisers soon sank as well. When the radio operator at the far end of the command center tuned to the destroyer's internal network, it was bedlam: the dazed voice of the lieutenant who now held command reporting that the captain and executive officer were dead; him pleading for aid from other ships; and the screams of the wounded in the background. General Patel, with a flick of his wrist, signaled for the radio operator to tune to a different frequency.

Wave after wave of aircraft pummeled the Reparationists. The Floridian pilots swept in over the horizon in groups of five, coming in low and fast. They would pop high, piling on the necessary altitude to deliver their ordnance. Duarte threw drone swarms, interceptor aircraft, anything and everything at the Floridians. This cost them at least two or three aircraft on every pass, but they typically scored at least one hit.

The math wasn't adding up for the Reparationists. Duarte couldn't continue swapping ships to aircraft at a 1:3 or 1:4 ratio. He'd already launched an ineffectual missile strike on the Floridian air base, the one on Fishers Island. The air base had launched an equally ineffective missile strike in return. Duarte needed to disable that runway so the Floridians couldn't rearm and refuel. This would shift the math to his advantage. It would also require him to get in closer, so he could deploy heavier cratering charges against the runway.

"Another one hundred seventy-five to two hundred nautical miles should do the trick." Duarte was explaining this when his executive officer rushed up beside him, whispering into his ear. No noticeable change came over Duarte. He nodded and uttered the name of another fatally damaged destroyer and frigate. "I've given the order for those crews to abandon ship."

Lily Bao glanced at Zhu De, who shifted uncomfortably in his seat. Even though his country had declared neutrality, in doing so they'd cast their lot in with the Reparationists. If these landings didn't work, if it turned out the Chinese had backed the wrong side, it wasn't the luminaries on the Politburo Standing Committee who would pay the price. They'd find a scapegoat—Lily knew this well. Fifty years ago, her father had played that role; it had cost him his life.

"How many more ships will they lose before they take out that airfield?" asked Zhu De, anxiously blurting out the question to no one in particular.

As if in response, a series of sonic booms transmitted over the radio. Duarte momentarily disappeared from the frame. Shouts for updates from damage control could be heard in the background. Right as the first reports came in—all of which were negative, no ship had been struck—eight Floridian J-19s popped up into their angle of attack fifty miles behind Duarte's vanguard. Due to the political sensitivity surrounding Indian military involvement, given that the Indians weren't technically part of the Reparationist alliance, they'd sent only a half dozen ships along with Duarte. An older-generation carrier, the INS *Vikrant*, was the largest of them.

Little gallant clusters of black smoke from the *Vikrant*'s antiair guns puffed around the eight predatory Floridian aircraft. Three aircraft lost sections of their wings and turned flaming pinwheels into the ocean. When the *Vikrant* got its lasers into action, two more aircraft dissolved into beams of light that flashed across the sky. But three vaulted over the lasers, their missiles impacting bow, amidships, and stern along the *Vikrant*, in a devastating one-two-three. As the last aircraft came out of its attack, it swung into a roll, wagging its tail section in a celebratory pirouette.

The *Vikrant* cracked into three pieces, thousands of tons of flaming steel bobbing on the water. Lily Bao watched the live feed with a horror that was only made worse when she glanced at General Patel, whose unblinking eyes had turned wide as twin moons. His mouth was open and when he spoke, he didn't close it, but instead only huffed the inept words, "Damage report . . ."

Lily leaned over the conference table, toward a speaker box at its center. "Captain Duarte, damage report?"

No response.

"Duarte!" Lily shouted.

Joko came up on the net. "Ma'am, he's likely got his hands full right now . . ."

"Are you seeing this?"

Joko was irritatingly calm. "Yes, ma'am."

Lily glanced back at Patel, who'd pulled himself together. He had his personal headsUp out. He was furiously tapping a message. To Lily, the implications were clear. Nothing had gone to plan. This tenuous alliance—between the Chinese, the Indians, and the Reparationists—could collapse under continued heavy and sustained losses. Patel was, in Lily's estimation, asking some ministerial colleague whether the time had come to dissolve that alliance, whether the Indians should change course and send their ships home.

"Admiral Joko," Lily said in a flat, almost mechanical voice. "What is the plan?"

"We're almost in range of the Floridian airfield," he said. "Once we eliminate that as a base of operations, our progress north should be smoother—"

She cut him off. "Smoother until we meet fighters from another airfield . . ."

"That's right," said Joko. There was no emotion in his voice. If anything, he sounded surprised that Lily, Patel, and even Zhu De hadn't anticipated these types of losses. "That's our only option, ma'am."

"Use your cratering charges against their airfield once in range," said Lily. "Wipe that island off the map." She glanced at Patel, a slight gesture of deference to him in this military matter. He nodded his approval.

Lily switched off the radio.

"Let's not forget," she said in an aside to General Patel. "We do have other options." They sat around the conference table, wordlessly considering not only the situation but the decisions each might take. It was Patel who broke this silence, saying to Lily, "I suppose I have a bomb to get to you."

He dipped his head and began to peck at the keys of his headsUp.

12:13 Dec 28, 2084 (-5:00 GMT)
Fishers Island, NY

The first salvo of Reparationist missiles proved surprisingly ineffective. Only one had struck the airfield, punching out a pothole that ground crews filled within minutes. The other missiles had landed around the outbuildings, killing two aircraft maintainers and wounding several dozen more. Once the smoke had cleared, Shriver was feeling optimistic. He even allowed himself to think that if this was the best the Reparationists could do, he and the Floridians might survive this ordeal.

Shriver's optimism wilted when he reentered the ready room. The radio operator, who remained crouched under a desk, had Eva Boucher on the holographic uplink. Shriver popped up the collar on his leather flight jacket and told the radio operator to get out from under the desk. Hesitantly, he did.

Errant rockets struck outside in ones and twos, their impacts rattling the windowpanes. The radio operator had just managed to raise Boucher when a rocket landed close enough to knock the holographic projector off its desk, which the radio operator dove under again. Shriver picked up the projector.

"Is everything all right there?" asked Boucher. "What's your status? Report . . ."

"Fine," said Shriver. "We're taking intermittent and largely ineffective rocket fire. The airfield remains operational . . ." He proceeded to update Boucher on the situation off the Delaware coast, referencing a small whiteboard where he'd kept a tally of their aircraft losses as well as the number of Reparationist ships damaged and destroyed. "As of this moment, we've scored thirty-seven hits, sunk thirteen ships, at the cost of forty-two aircraft . . . that's roughly a one-to-one hit ratio and a three-to-one aircraft-to-ships-destroyed ratio . . . at that rate, we're winning. But we're running out of aircraft down here. When can we expect reinforcements?"

Boucher offered hefty words like "historic" and "valorous" as she described the deeds of those Floridian pilots who had held the line against "the invaders." Shriver appreciated the rhetorical flourishes, but he needed an answer on when reinforcements would arrive and in what numbers. "Hopefully soon," said Boucher. But when Shriver pushed harder, she said, "Reinforcements remain limited." Shriver, who wasn't a military man, didn't understand. How could reinforcements remain limited? Had the Reparationists attacked somewhere else?

"We believe this is a feint," said Boucher, "designed to divert our forces. The main landings will occur in the north. It's important we don't take the bait. Hold your position. Eventually, the Reparationists will break contact. When they do, that's when we strike." Boucher excused herself. She had other matters to attend to. She finished the call with more lavish praise. Soon another transmission was coming into the airfield, this one from Tick-Tock. Shriver hung up while Boucher was in mid-sentence.

Tick-Tock immediately asked about the status of reinforcements. Shriver summarized his conversation with Boucher.

"Not surprising," answered Tick-Tock with a resignation that

Shriver couldn't help but admire. "I'm inbound to the airfield, ETA six minutes. Have ground crews ready to refuel and rearm my section . . . three aircraft in my flight."

Tick-Tock had left to sink an Indian carrier with eight aircraft . . . so they'd lost five . . . five aircraft yielded them one carrier—that was the math.

Minutes later, Tick-Tock landed, reappearing in the ready room with his helmet clutched under his arm. "What's the latest?" he asked. While Shriver posted him on the current disposition of Reparationist ships, Tick-Tock rifled through the box of donuts from earlier that morning. All that was left was a single old-fashioned. His pilots—more than half of them now captured or dead—had eaten the rest. As Tick-Tock was finishing off the donut, a report came in. The Reparationist ships were reversing course, headed back out to sea. When Shriver asked what this meant, if perhaps they'd fought off the resettlement fleet, Tick-Tock seemed skeptical, offering a curt "I wouldn't bet on it."

Before running out to the airfield to get back in the cockpit, Tick-Tock shouted over his shoulder, "Hey, Fancy Pants . . . be careful."

"You too," Shriver shouted as Tick-Tock scrambled up the ladder.

As Tick-Tock's aircraft taxied, Shriver walked down to the near end of the runway. He visored his hand above his eyes and watched as his friend's flight of three aircraft turned south and disappeared into a pile of clouds. Even if Tick-Tock was cautious, Shriver remained optimistic that the hour of victory was at hand. The Reparationists were turning around, heading back out to sea . . . a retreat.

What other meaning could this have?

Shriver jammed his hands in the pockets of his flight jacket. Through his boots, he could feel a triumphant heat smoldering up from the asphalt where all day the Death Rattlers had blasted their engines onto the runway in a ceaseless parade of takeoffs and landings. Shriver walked with his head down, scanning the runway's surface. He was looking for a souvenir, something to remember what they'd accomplished. If this was an overly optimistic projection of the battle's outcome, Shriver would gladly be guilty of optimism.

Pessimism . . .

Cynicism . . .

A failure to believe in others . . . He thought again of his mother. It had been foolish, he realized, to judge her so harshly. When this was over, he'd patch things up. Whether she agreed with his choices or not hardly mattered. He could love her all the same. He imagined telling her about everything that had happened here . . . but he didn't know where to start. His attention turned once more to finding that souvenir. Maybe he'd start there, by showing her something from this place, something taken from the battlefield.

Shriver continued to walk, his head down, searching for this special something he couldn't seem to find . . .

He didn't hear or feel the first of the five cratering charges as they impacted all around him, destroying the runway. Shriver vanished in a cloud of dust.

16:47 Dec 29, 2084 (-4:00 GMT)
200 nm off the coast of Maine and Nova Scotia

All day, Admiral Joko had coordinated the withdrawal of his ships to the east, to a series of rendezvous positions on the open Atlantic. When Joko had contacted Nusantara about these orders, which made little sense, General Suharto said they'd come directly from New Delhi and without explanation. Joko couldn't quite understand it. Although Duarte's forces in the south had sustained heavy losses, they'd inflicted the same. Yesterday, they'd been poised to advance farther up the Eastern Seaboard after having destroyed the airfield on Fishers Island. Very few of those Floridian pilots had escaped north. By Joko's count, it'd been only three.

Of those three, one pilot had managed to make a final pass on a Brazilian cruiser, scoring a hit. The pilot had even executed an obnoxious little pirouette as he pulled out of his dive. Joko wished they'd shot that pilot out of the sky. In the end, Duarte would get the better of them. When those pilots returned to their airfield, they'd find it destroyed, razed to the ground.

Confused as Admiral Joko was by these orders to withdraw, he'd asked Suharto what he was supposed to do once the resettlement fleet arrived at the rendezvous. He would have hundreds of ships spread across the open ocean; they couldn't simply drop anchor. Suharto said, "If I were you, I'd assume a good defensive posture and establish a strong rear guard. The Consortium will likely follow in pursuit."

"Anything else?"

"That's all from me," Suharto had said. "But New Delhi did have an additional request . . . this also made little sense, but I've had my staff confirm it. As your fleet gets underway, all ships are to assume extreme storm conditions. Batten down every hatch. Secure aircraft and equipment belowdecks. Minimize crew movements outside."

Joko had checked the forecast. Conditions would remain clear all week. He was perplexed.

He protested, but Suharto said, "Just do it," and so Joko passed the order to set storm conditions and begin redeploying hundreds of ships, peeling them back one by one, starting with the resettlement barges and then his warship escorts.

A day later, he was almost finished. Throughout this ordeal, he'd kept a close eye on the weather, which had remained clear up into the North Atlantic. It was only when he gave the final order for his flagship, the *Aradu*, to change course that he noticed something on his meteorological display:

A gathering low-pressure system. Nothing dramatic, but it was definitely there, a wisp of cirrus in the high north. And it was growing.

07:00 Dec 30, 2084 (+5:30 GMT)
New Delhi

The centermost monitor inside the command center displayed the rapidly deteriorating weather conditions around the Pole. The Tandava Group, with the aid of General Patel, had requisitioned dozens of cargo planes to perform an aerosol carbon scrub across a two-hundred-mile radius. Already, this was resulting in increasingly high winds, so that those aircraft could likely fly only one or two more sorties before conditions became too dangerous. Simultaneously, the Tandava Group had, through the marathon pumping of groundwater, replenished a significant portion of the polar ice cap, dropping local temperatures by nearly five degrees centigrade.

The temperature variance along with the carbon scrub was building a formidable storm in the north, but for the next hour, they would turn their attention elsewhere. That evening, at nine p.m., Eva Boucher would address the American people. She would be doing this in lieu of the president. Already, she was touting recent events as the "nation's greatest military victory in a generation" and framing herself as the architect of that victory.

Lily Bao, Zhu De, and General Patel sat at the far end of the conference table as the address began. Boucher indulged in every protocol: she stood in the East Room of the White House behind a podium with the presidential seal affixed to its front; gold brocaded curtains draped the walls behind her; portraits of George and Martha Washington flanked either side. The audacity, that Boucher would appear in the trappings of the presidency . . . it was remarkable. But it'd been many decades since dignity as opposed to audacity had galvanized the American voter. Given recent losses at sea, an audacious victory was Boucher's only pathway to political survival. A successful defense of the United States would no longer suffice; no, she would have to annihilate the Reparationists once and for all, destroy their ships—military and civilian alike—so they could never again menace Consortium shores.

It was this vision of carnage that Boucher began to articulate in her address.

"With the Reparationist invaders withdrawing in disarray, some might say our work is done, our mission accomplished, that we've executed a successful defense." Boucher leaned over the podium, glowering through the camera's lens to the entire nation. "It would be a grave mistake to believe this. So long as the resettlement fleet exists, our shores remain under threat. So long as misguided leaders in Nusantara, Lagos, and Brasília refuse to confront the problems of climate in their nations and instead seek solutions by appropriating territory, this conflict will persist. Already, too much blood has been spilled . . ."

Boucher turned to anecdotes at this point, singling out the brave pilots who'd fought in the south, particularly the Floridians on Fishers Island who'd endured the heaviest losses, with their airfield and most of the island annihilated. In one squadron, the Death Rattlers, only three pilots had survived the ordeal, managing to escape north in their J-19s.

"Those three pilots, as well as many others," Boucher continued, "remain committed to this fight. Right now, they're awaiting orders to pursue the resettlement fleet. What about each of us? Are we similarly committed? Our families, our homes, our country, our planet, the defense of these is nonnegotiable; it is our highest calling . . ."

She looked up from her script and paused a beat. "In the difficult days ahead, I trust that I can count on your continued, unwavering support. God bless our allies. Our troops. And God bless these United States."

The broadcast cut.

Seated around the command center's conference table, Lily Bao, Zhu De, and General Patel exchanged glances.

"Boucher has clearly taken the bait," said Zhu De. "Well done."

Lily nodded, but this wasn't the moment for congratulations. She asked one of the technicians to bring up the latest meteorological report from the Pole. When it projected on the screen, Lily began to study the reams of data. Reading through it had a strange, calming effect on her, the equivalent of concentrating on a single point on the wall to regain one's balance. Her prolonged silence caused General Patel to ask if she was all right.

"Yes, fine. Why do you ask?"

"Your son," he said softly. "I know you must be worried about him."

"Yes, of course." Lily Bao turned back to the screen.

Truthfully, she seldom thought of Jake, not since her work with Beginner's Mind. This realization upset her. Had she lost grasp of that most primal of instincts: a mother's concern for her child? If her father's intelligence was blended with the artificial intelligence that powered Beginner's Mind, did that mean her father had contrived a plan that would kill his own grandson? What type of mother, what type of human, would enter into the bargain she'd made with Beginner's Mind? She thanked General Patel for his concern but couldn't allow personal considerations to distract her. Lily finished studying the meteorological data.

"What's your conclusion?" Patel asked.

"Tell your colleagues it's time to blow the storm south."

06:32 Dec 31, 2084 (-3:00 GMT)
300 nm northwest of Bermuda

The captain of the *Sakura* had received strict orders to run his ship under storm conditions. Only the most essential crew could come above deck. For the past two days, Julia had remained trapped in the berthing, breathing the stale air. The *Sakura* was going nowhere, and she could feel it. They were cutting squares into the middle of the Atlantic, to what purpose Julia couldn't say. This direction from on high sounded far-fetched to Julia until the morning of the second day, when, unable to take being cooped up anymore, she'd snuck outside and stood on the wet gray deck, staring north.

It was near dawn, and she thought she'd stay topside long enough to watch the sunrise, to breathe the air, and then to disappear below-decks before anyone noticed her missing. When she climbed through a small, seldom-used hatch aft of the anchor, near the crane arm, she was dumbfounded when she first glimpsed the sky. She'd never seen it so red.

The striations of cloud seemed backlit in the north, as if a sun were rising there as well as in the east. Her mother, a sailor who later in life avoided the sea, had nevertheless taught her the old ditty about storms: *Red sky at night, sailors delight. Red sky at morning, sailors take warning.* As Julia recalled these words, the sky began to transform. An ominous glow pulsated in the north. The fringe of clouds that had reflected this mysterious light thickened dramatically, tumbling in growing coils southward. The clouds came on with the velocity of an avalanche, their approach so quick that to Julia it seemed as if she were observing a piece of time-lapse photography. A steady, cold wind accompanied them. She could smell snow on the wind, and freezing rain had begun to pelt her face.

Before Julia could return belowdecks, an alarm for general quarters looped from every corner. A half dozen members of the crew sprinted topside. Julia wasn't supposed to be outside, so she hid from them at the base of the crane arm, inside its control box, which was the size of a telephone booth. When she glanced at the horizon, she saw the reason for the alarm.

A line of attack aircraft was approaching, their dark V formations stitching a seam across the sky. These pilots also seemed to observe the storm bearing down. At first, one broke west toward land. Then a second followed. Their formations grew more ragged by the second. They began aborting their attack in whole batches, desperate it seemed to return to their airfields or aircraft carriers while they could.

A few fighters continued doggedly toward their targets. Among them was a particularly stubborn flight of three, headed right at the Nigerian super destroyer *Aradu*, which was a few ships abreast from the *Sakura*. These three aircraft were J-19s and close enough that when they vaulted into their angle of attack, Julia could see their fuselage markings: the St. Andrew's cross. Floridians.

The flight lead descended, strafing the deck of the *Aradu* with his minigun as an antiship missile corkscrewed from his wing. The *Aradu* began evasive maneuvers, skidding its hull across the ocean's surface. While rounds from the minigun tore up the bow section, causing mostly superficial damage, the *Aradu* was popping chaff and flares from amidships, so in appearance its hull became indistinguishable from a fireworks barge. The confused missile from the J-19 locked onto the chaff and flares, plunging into the ocean.

As the flight lead pulled out of his attack, a lasso of antiaircraft fire followed, lashing at the sky. It clipped his starboard wing. His aircraft entered a flat spin. As Julia was watching, her stomach leaped into her throat, propelled by a protective instinct for the pilot. A lesser pilot might not have recovered, but the flight lead brought his J-19 under control.

The second pilot now entered his attack. An antiship missile sailed off his wing at a fortuitous moment, right in those seconds when the *Aradu* was resetting its defensive countermeasures. The missile took advantage of this gap, scoring a hit and puncturing a molten hole in the side of the *Aradu* just aft of the bridge. Opposite the missile's impact, a jet of blue flame shot out the other side of the ship, scattering debris across the ocean's surface.

As the second pilot climbed out of his attack, he was followed by the same antiaircraft fire that'd chased the flight lead. His aircraft was damaged in much the same way, with chunks bitten off his starboard wing that also sent him into a spin. Unlike the flight lead, he couldn't manage to recover. As his J-19 tumbled end over end, he ejected. Julia couldn't discern his parachute through the storm clouds. There was just the flash of the booster in his ejection seat. A nearby frigate immediately broke off from the main fleet to recover the pilot, who would now become a prisoner of war.

The third pilot entered his attack. The rearmed *Aradu*, as well as two frigates who'd rushed to its defense, unleashed a full complement of defensive weapons, a multilayered phalanx of missiles and lasers backed up by a curtain of armor-piercing tungsten from the sea-wiz of each ship. This combination incinerated the third aircraft before a single missile left its wing. Julia watched as little pieces of its fuselage plunked into the ocean.

Only the flight lead remained. His aircraft, badly damaged, was making a wide arcing turn back toward the resettlement fleet for a second pass. Crouched in the crane arm's control booth, Julia couldn't observe any other aircraft in the sky. When the pilot stopped his turn, his aircraft was nosed right at the *Sakura*. Julia couldn't help it: alone and afraid, it felt personal. Like the pilot was coming for her.

The *Aradu* and other warships fired lasers and a spread of missiles at the approaching J-19, but these systems were designed for self-protection, not the defense of adjacent ships, and weren't as effective at these ranges. Even with his aircraft damaged, the lead pilot was able to juke and dodge his way past. He was climbing now, again gathering altitude, entering his angle of attack.

On the deck of the *Sakura*—while the captain attempted evasive maneuvers, sluggishly turning the ship in a slow, unconvincing arc—the crew scrambled for cover. The flight lead was piling on altitude, disappearing for seconds at a time in the descending layers of cloud. Julia caught a glimpse of his J-19 as it bellied over, brandishing its racks of missiles as it speared out through the clouds and toward the *Sakura*.

Julia was crouched in the crane arm's control booth, her gaze fixed skyward, when one of the crew flung open its door, clambering inside. It was the helmsman she'd encountered before on the bridge. "What are you doing in here?" he asked breathlessly while squeezing himself inside the booth, pushing her against the controls. This caused the white crane, which had been folded on the bow of the ship, to suddenly deploy, reaching forward over the ocean like a welcoming arm. As the helmsman crammed himself inside and secured the booth's door, Julia's entire body was crushed against the control panel.

The lead pilot was coming directly at them, the tips of his missiles poking from beneath the wings like teeth. His descent was met with the absurd swaying of the crane arm, as if the *Sakura* were waving a good-natured hello to its murderer. Pinned against the controls, Julia was staring upward, demanding that the helmsman get off of her. The crane arm kept waving side to side. That these would be the last moments of Julia's life seemed preposterous.

She shut her eyes.

A jet of water struck the booth's window, followed by a supersonic roar.

Julia glanced up, into the white-hot glow of two afterburners in ascent.

The J-19 was climbing, fully armed, its missiles unfired in their racks beneath the wings. Even with a badly damaged aircraft, the pilot managed to execute a celebratory pirouette as he climbed skyward, hurrying for the safety of the clouds.

"Holy fuck, we're alive!"

As the helmsman uttered this, the *Aradu* fired a single missile.

The J-19 entered the clouds as the missile gave chase. But already it had locked on, following close behind and gaining. A muzzled, gauzy flash followed. The growing storm was already spun so thick that Julia could see little, except for the few pieces of debris that drizzled from the clouds like rain.

Violent, gale-force winds battered the *Sakura*, playing the ship like an instrument, blowing a maniacal anthem into every crevasse and hollow compartment, whining louder and louder. After twenty minutes or so, once the helmsman seemed convinced that no other aircraft would appear, he levered himself around in the control booth and opened its door. Both he and Julia toppled clownishly onto the rain-soaked deck. When Julia turned to leave, the helmsman grabbed her by the wrist.

"Where you going?"

"Belowdecks," said Julia, her voice raised against the wind. "Back to the berthing."

"No, you're not."

"No?"

The helmsman gripped her wrist tighter.

Julia tugged her arm away, but the helmsman still held her. "Let go of me."

"Captain's been looking for you."

Julia stopped her pulling away. "Am I in some sort of trouble?"

"Yes," said the helmsman. "Quite a bit, I'd say."

07:46 Dec 31, 2084 (-3:00 GMT)
300 nm northwest of Bermuda

Admiral Joko's flagship, the *Aradu*, had suffered a direct hit. The single missile had impacted on the port side, punching a narrow entrance wound while blowing out an exit wound two decks tall. Remarkably, the missile had destroyed no critical systems and caused few casualties, having lanced its way through storage areas and the ship's potable water supply. Captain Gambo and his crew had repairs well in hand, which freed Admiral Joko to concentrate on more pressing matters, the storm that was bearing down on them having appeared from seemingly nowhere.

On the bridge, Joko hovered over a display of the weather along with the fleet's chief meteorologist. They'd overlaid the storm's path on a tactical map, which showed their position versus the latest intelligence reports of the Consortium navy. Despite only being on the fringes of the storm, the *Aradu* tossed and pitched violently through curtains of white rain seamed with lightning. Joko could hardly imagine conditions inside the storm, at its epicenter, which is exactly where the Consortium navy found themselves. Joko asked the meteorologist whether he thought any of the Consortium aircraft from before, the ones that had turned around, had managed to land safely.

"Doubt it, sir . . . That storm's metrics are double a Category Five. Call it a Cat Ten. It'll destroy anything in its path."

Joko glanced out a window, through a wedge cleared by a pair of furiously working wipers. At first, he was disoriented. Their ship was supposed to be pointing north, but for a moment it appeared as if it was headed in the direction of the rising sun, due east. Except sunrise had passed more than an hour before.

Joko double-checked the time and their heading.

They were definitely headed north. So what was this ominous red glow off his bow? He couldn't say but felt certain it had something to do with this storm, which was, at this very moment, consigning thousands of enemy sailors to watery graves.

19:14 Dec 31, 2084 (+5:30 GMT)
New Delhi

All day Lily Bao, Zhu De, and General Patel kept close watch on the storm's progress through the western Atlantic. In addition to Admiral Joko's updates sent from the eastern fringes of the storm, they also monitored its progress through satellite imagery and signals intercepts from within the Consortium navy.

Although Lily couldn't see into the dense brocade of clouds, she could hear the sailors describe the conditions and she could hear their terror and desperation. Winds so powerful they tore superstructures from the decks of ships, tossing crew members overboard as if yanked by an unseen tether into oblivion, their names shouted uselessly after them. Waves building to the size of small mountains, crashing in white avalanches of water that wiped out two, three, even four ships. Panicked changes in heading transmitted from bridge to bridge. Ship captains colliding in their desperate attempts to stay afloat, cursing one another in their final breaths as these collisions sparked fires that burned with an intensity no rain could extinguish.

The order to abandon ship was given again and again. Few obeyed an order so superfluous; no lifeboat could survive the storm. Like a game of "would you rather," the decision for most had devolved into stay on board and burn or abandon ship and drown. As the day wore on, instead of "abandon ship," the order most often heard in the moments before the storm consigned another destroyer, frigate, or carrier to the depths was "every sailor for themselves."

While Lily listened, she peered into the satellite video feed. When the camera zoomed in on the storm's periphery, she could make out the resettlement fleet. Unlike days before, when they'd sailed in neatly ordered rows, those ships—which appeared like so many insect-sized specks—were arranged in a disordered swirl. But they continued to float, sailing in a churning sea.

Lily and the others remained in direct contact with Admiral Joko, so they knew how desperately he was trying to hold his own fleet together even at the storm's edge. That a skilled naval officer like Joko was struggling this way, even when he wasn't directly in the storm's path, spoke to its power. It also spoke to how desperate Lily's gamble had been. Two hundred or one hundred miles in another direction, and this storm might have wiped out the resettlement fleet as well.

As the day progressed, the radio traffic between Consortium ships petered out. Occasional, staticky transmissions came through. Most of these were SOS calls from a handful of lifeboats that had, through some miracle, survived. The storm continued its rampage south, but it began to dissipate almost as quicky as it had appeared. To the east, Admiral Joko reformed the resettlement flotilla into neatly ordered rows. Sea conditions were returning to normal levels. The clouds began to hollow, each gap a window into the scope of devastation below.

Lily, along with Zhu De and Patel, peered anxiously into these gaps, searching the waves for evidence of the Consortium navy. They couldn't find any. The ocean had consumed them.

"They're gone," said Zhu De. Enthusiasm lifted his voice, as if he could already imagine reporting this news to the grim eminences of the Politburo Standing Committee. He could hardly conceal his relief. Their gamble had succeeded.

Lily glanced at Patel to validate this assessment. With rather less enthusiasm, he said, "It would appear you've done it," but the way he gave Lily the credit made her uneasy, as if he wasn't quite certain himself whether he wanted his share of responsibility for what they had done.

An HF radio transmission interrupted them. The technicians explained that it was the captain of the *Sakura*. He was requesting to speak "directly to New Delhi." Lily had little patience for such interruptions and asked the technician to find out what he wanted. "I already tried that, ma'am. He said he needs to speak directly to 'the chairman.'"

Lily reached out her hand. The technician placed the receiver in her palm. She held it to her ear, saying only, "This is the chairman of Tandava." When the captain answered, Lily had to pull the receiver away from her ear by an inch or so given his animated reply. He explained that he'd taken Julia Hunt into custody for espionage. He had proof that she'd warned the Floridians of their approach. He also explained that as a sea captain in a time of war, he had a right, if not an obligation, to execute Julia Hunt on the spot for treason.

"We'll have none of that," said Lily curtly.

She continued watching the satellite feed. The clouds were clearing, each layer unclasping from the next as quickly as they'd first seized together. The ocean was calming too.

"You'll keep Dr. Hunt on board the ship with you," Lily said. "Understood?"

There was a long pause.

"Yes, ma'am."

"Stand by for your orders," Lily added. "They'll arrive shortly." She handed the technician back the old HF receiver and asked him to raise Admiral Joko holographically. Moments later, Joko's avatar appeared in a cone of light. He was also conducting a post-storm battle damage assessment, scanning not only the satellite live feed but also hydrographic and sonographic data, all of which he did from the bridge of the damaged *Aradu*. Lily asked about the status of his ship and its crew first, and then the disposition and preparedness of his fleet.

"We're ready, ma'am. We've been waiting for this moment a long time."

"Very well," said Lily. She swallowed hard. "Prepare to land."

"Aye, aye," he said with a smile.

"And Admiral Joko . . . Happy New Year."

14:46 Jan 01, 2085 (-5:00 GMT)
5 nm east of Landing Beach 17E

In the night, a new year had arrived. Julia Hunt would spend its first hours detained on the bridge of the *Sakura* listening to news coverage of the "historic . . . unprecedented . . ." landings they were about to embark upon. The superfluous use of such adjectives by Reparationist leaders bothered her. Once the political hyperbole starts, she thought, it never stops . . . and never ends well.

Events hadn't ended well for Eva Boucher, who until yesterday had assured her country of their impending victory over the Reparationist invaders. She had resigned in disgrace that next morning. Her decision to pursue the resettlement fleet had resulted in the loss of nearly 70 percent of the Consortium navy. What made this staggering number even worse was that the US Navy was overrepresented; they'd lost 85 percent of their ships to the storm. When it came to historical parallels, this loss wasn't Churchill in the Dardanelles for Boucher; it was Tojo in the Pacific. Total defeat. Unconditional surrender. Politically, there would be no coming back. The news anchors, who were covering a vote in Congress to invoke the Twenty-Fifth Amendment, speculated as to Eva Boucher's whereabouts. Like those ships in the western Atlantic, she seemed to have vanished.

By that afternoon, the newly established resettlement authority had assigned thousands of settlers to a landing craft and landing beach. Hours before the first of them embarked for their cold parcel of northeastern shoreline, the vice president of the United States took to the airwaves. A ceasefire between the Consortium and Reparationists had been agreed upon. It would take effect immediately, followed by negotiations to create resettlement enclaves, in which resettlers as well as Americans would live and work side by side. It seemed the landings would occur unopposed, and for the first time, the acting president referred to those embarked on the resettlement fleet as "immigrants" instead of "invaders," the type of remarkable concession a nation could only make when facing up to defeat.

The first wave of landing craft was underway, the *Sakura* receding behind them. A mile off the coast, they encountered a ribbon of debris that had gathered short of the beach, driven by the tide, remnants of the navy their escorts had destroyed. A life jacket. A plastic slat painted gray. A blanket. An empty boot. Photographs. Whatever floated. Fortunately, no bodies. Not yet.

On one of the boats were two settlers, a newly married couple expecting a child. Their landing craft was piloted by an impossibly young Indonesian coxswain who struggled to steer the slightly overloaded boat ashore. He threaded their launch through this debris field, being mindful not to plow through the sad little clutter of objects. Try as he might to steer clear of these obstacles, the coxswain had to pause when his outboard motor fouled, groaning as smoke billowed up from the stern. The coxswain killed the motor and raised it from the water. The husband left his pregnant wife in the bow to lend a hand, untangling a uniform shirt that had coiled around the prop. Before tossing the knotted shirt into the ocean, he couldn't help but read the name tape embroidered on the chest: *Cole.*

A mile out from shore, the coxswain pointed the bow straight at the beach. He shouted, "Five minutes!" and the man, who was once again perched on the gunwale beside his wife, took her hand and squeezed it. When the coxswain shouted, "One minute!" she squeezed his back. They could both smell the shore, the pungent scent of land.

The coxswain revved the engine, powering the launch forward so its hull scraped onto the sand. The husband vaulted over the side. He helped his wife into the thigh-deep water. The sand was even whiter and the water even colder than they could have imagined. Gathered on the dunes one hundred yards away, as if they'd been waiting some time, was a cluster of spectators.

The woman lunged forward with a first, second, and then third step, holding her arms high above her. She was plowing through the surf, leaving her husband behind, determined to cover that last little distance to shore, no matter how difficult. She had one more step to take when she clutched her stomach and gasped. She made a little half pirouette and turned toward her husband. She said his name in a panicked exhalation, then she toppled face-first into the sand.

Her husband charged through the breakers, collapsed onto his knees, and flipped his unconscious wife onto her back. Her face had turned deathly pale. He looked up to the bystanders on the dunes. He screamed to them for help. He began slapping her on both cheeks. "Wake up . . . c'mon . . . you gotta wake up . . ."

He cried for help again. At that instant, she awoke.

She coughed as she choked on little gulps of inhaled salt water. "Your hands," she said. "Give me your hands." She clasped his hands by the wrists and placed his palms on her stomach. "There, hold them there. Do you feel the baby?"

A determined little push, like a wild thing trying to escape.

"There . . . right there . . . the baby kicked," she said with delight. "I'm sorry . . . it so surprised me . . . I must've . . ."

"You blacked out," he said.

"Yes, I suppose I did." She smiled. "It kicked so hard . . . like it's dead set on being the first to step ashore . . ."

She rolled onto her side and her husband took her by the arm. He helped her to her feet as the onlookers from up on the dunes arrived. She was covered in sand, coated head to toe in this new land.

CODA

Santorini Grapes

14:46 Apr 12, 2086 (-5:00 GMT)
Massachusetts General Hospital

Lily Bao waited alone in a conference room on the seventeenth floor, in the pediatric oncology department. She stood in the corner, where the floor-to-ceiling windows met at a right angle. With her hands clasped behind her back, she studied the view. The Charles River unspooled beneath her, spanned by the Longfellow Bridge. Rowers attired in bright collegiate colors plied their oars against the wind-scalloped water, slipping beneath the center of the bridge's eleven archways. Charming as the view was, Lily thought it was cruel that the children treated on this floor had to look out at others practicing for a race—and for a life—that they would surely never join.

This would be the second time Lily would meet with Penelope, a fifteen-year-old girl diagnosed with a glioblastoma, but it was, perhaps, her hundredth such meeting with a child who had only months to live and whose parents wanted to find some way to preserve their life, even if it wasn't their biological life.

"Very sorry to keep you waiting," said a nurse as she backed into the room, pulling Penelope in her wheelchair. The nurse pushed aside the nearest seat at the conference table, which happened to be at its head, and installed her patient in this spot. After placing a bottle of water and some tissues on the table so Penelope might easily reach them, the nurse stepped to the door.

"Aren't her parents coming?" Lily asked.

Penelope answered before the nurse could. "I told them I wanted to speak with you alone." Her voice came out in a rasp. She took a sip of water.

"I'll be right down the hall," the nurse said, and ducked out the door.

The congenital bone disease that had ultimately morphed into brain cancer had slowed Penelope's physical development, dramatically stunting her growth. This caused her to appear four or even five years younger. It was only when Penelope spoke that Lily was reminded that she was fifteen.

"My parents say it's my decision."

"Is there anything else I can do to help you make that decision?" Lily sat beside Penelope at the conference table. Not even Penelope's jaundiced skin nor the dark half-moons beneath her eyes could hide the immutable fact—as immutable as the cancer coded into her DNA—that if nature had given her the opportunity to reach adulthood, she would've grown into a woman of formidable beauty and intelligence.

"I either participate in your trial program or this disease kills me," said Penelope. "That's my choice, right? Although it's not much of a choice."

"Your diagnosis doesn't have to be a death sentence," Lily explained. "By blending the biological and technological, by uploading your intelligence, your life continues."

"Sure," said Penelope. "But I could lose other things . . . Like my parents."

"You'll be able to interact with your parents anytime you like."

"But I won't be like I am now . . . I'll be different."

A silence fell between them.

"I heard you had a son once."

"Yes," said Lily. "I did."

"I heard he was killed."

Lily stood from the table. She stepped to the corner of the conference room, where its two windows met and looked out at the river.

"I also heard you could've stopped it," said Penelope. "Is that true?"

"Beginner's Mind doesn't have to change you like it changed me."

"But it did change you."

"What if I promised you?" asked Lily.

"Promised me what?"

"That even if this technology changes you, even if you're different, you will still recognize you."

"You can promise that?"

Lily crouched down to eye level with Penelope. "Yes."

That night, in her hotel suite, Lily couldn't sleep. She'd never made a promise like that before.

Buried in her desk in New Delhi was a letter, a single page she'd penned to her son before she'd unleashed Beginner's Mind years before. The letter had been her way of saying goodbye to him, though she'd never mailed it. Contained within its lines, Lily thought she might recognize this old version of herself.

Two days later, alone at her desk, she read the letter:

Dear Son,

I love you.

And I am sorry.

Those two sentences are perhaps the truest sentences any parent can offer to a child, and I hope you will accept them from me.

My love for you requires little explanation. You are my son. All the good that I have to offer this world, I recognize in you—I love you.

And I am sorry because I am imperfect, as are all parents. I recognize how my imperfections have and will affect you, including recent decisions I've made.

This is the nature of life, I suppose. We pass down everything to our children, all that is good and far too often all that is bad. We can only hope the balance tilts in our favor.

I know we haven't been speaking much lately, Jake. I'm not sure where you are, or whether you'll even get this letter. But I wanted to write it now, before anything has changed with me.

I don't feel the need to explain my choices, or to ask you to explain yours, or to rehash the specifics of where and how I fell short. All of that is in the past. With this letter, I simply wanted to say those two sentences to you clearly and with my whole heart, one final time:

I love you. And I am sorry.

Mom

When Lily finished reading the letter, she refolded it and slid it back in its envelope. Everyone she'd ever loved was gone, from her son to her husband to her mother, stretching back to her father, Rear Admiral Lin Bao, killed by the very same Chinese authorities her son sought to understand and with whom she had ultimately cooperated in the climate war. Loss and betrayal had underpinned so much of Lily's life. What was she offering this girl? Was she offering Penelope the same type of life, one defined by loss, in which she'd fuse herself with Beginner's Mind and cheat death, but in exchange would have to watch everyone she ever loved destroyed? What type of life was that?

Lily gazed at the unsent letter sitting on her desk. The more she thought of it, the more she concluded that, yes, watching everything you care about and everyone you love destroyed is in fact the very definition of a life—at least any long one.

Lily could recognize this truth: that life takes what it gives, that we love imperfectly and therefore with apology. It was like recognizing the person she'd once been, not only before Beginner's Mind but all the way back to when she was a child, when she'd lost her father. It was proof that Lily hadn't lost herself because she could still recognize herself in this letter.

She knew what to do, how to keep her promise to Penelope.

The letter went out in the next morning's post, priority mail. If this letter hadn't saved her son, perhaps it would save this girl.

14:46 Nov 06, 2087 (-5:00 GMT)
Resettlement District 32

Admiral Joko had retired the year before. Generals Suharto and Patel, and even Lily Bao, had pleaded with him to reconsider. His best years were ahead of him, they argued. He still had much to contribute to the Reparationist cause. The Chinese were rearming, unconvinced of the assurances they'd received that the resettlement enclaves would remain solely on American soil. The Chinese navy, which had avoided the losses inflicted on the Consortium navies, was now the most powerful on earth. Chinese ships often sailed into the territorial waters of Green Zone nations, particularly the Floridians, whom they loved to provoke.

Joko had politely listened to the pleadings of his former colleagues. Popular and competent admirals were tough to come by, they'd said. But Joko wouldn't be moved. A rumor had begun to spread that the reason Joko had left uniform was because he had political ambitions. He found this particularly amusing. His greatest ambition was to be left alone.

The resettlement authority had granted Joko its standard forty acres. Joko had made a special request: that his land have a view of the ocean. The resettlement authority had done him one better, placing him on a rocky outcropping surrounded by water on three sides. If the location was perfect, the land as it existed was not. A sewage treatment facility had preceded Joko's tenancy, pumping its filth into the North Atlantic. Fortunately for Joko, the resettlement authority had allocated funds for his property's cleanup. It had also authorized modest funds for the construction of a new home, a project that was nearing completion.

That morning, Joko was scheduled to meet the project foreman for a walk-through of the house. The foreman arrived uncharacteristically late. He found Joko sitting in the kitchen, which was finished aside from the installation of its appliances.

"Sorry to have kept you waiting, Admiral Joko."

"Not a problem. And please, just call me Joko. Everything okay?"

"Yeah, everything's fine. I stayed up too late last night watching the news."

"Something happen?" asked Joko.

The foreman glanced up from the plans he'd already laid across the kitchen counter, a puzzled look on his face. "Last night was the debate . . ."

"The debate?"

"For the election of resettlement zone administrator."

Joko laughed. "Oh, that's right . . . I must've missed it."

The foreman, who'd built houses his entire life up and down the coast of what was now known as Resettlement District 32, shook his head with a mixture of disappointment and disbelief. But he held his tongue, and the two of them spent some hours walking through Joko's house. They inspected the progress and quality of the last few weeks' work, checking on everything from electrical outlets to window seals and crown moldings. Joko made a note of how impressed he was by the quality of the construction, particularly as most of the workers were volunteers brought in by the resettlement authority in a new government program that blended resettlers with residents, the idea being to ease social tensions through shared labor. Side by side, they would rebuild and develop this new community.

"I've heard a rumor that you've been volunteering on construction projects a couple of times a week," said the foreman as they returned to the kitchen.

This rumor was true. It had taken Joko a few months to get on his feet, but now that his new home was almost finished, he'd returned to the type of volunteerism that'd kept him in the navy after the loss of his family. He explained to the foreman how rewarding he found this work and how much he was learning. When he'd started, he could barely drive a nail straight and didn't know the difference between a hex driver and screwdriver. The foreman listened politely, nodding along, and then paused before asking, "And do you think you're doing *enough*?"

"Enough?" asked Joko.

"Yeah, are you doing enough? Is some volunteer construction work really all you have to offer? If you'd watched the debate last night, you would have seen how weak the candidates are. There's no front-runner. Some are even saying that Eva Boucher sees an opening and might throw her hat in the ring. Jesus, that's all we need. Lately, she's been spewing all sorts of anti-resettler garbage. Still, she's getting more and more traction. You must've seen the graffiti and stickers in town, the ones with Boucher's picture that say *Miss me yet?* Boucher's support is real. The Tandava Group has opened three new innovation zones, but this stuff with Beginner's Mind . . . I dunno. Technology and biology merging together . . . where's that end? People are getting scared. Politicians are telling them that more resettlers are coming to replace them. People need someone they've got confidence in, someone to lead them—someone like you."

"I'm retired," said Joko. He looked around his unfinished house. He inhaled deeply and could smell the freshly hung drywall. "I'm not a politician."

"We all know who you are—or were," said the foreman.

"I've earned the right to a little peace and quiet," Joko said brusquely. "I've done my share."

"That you have." The foreman gazed down at the schematic on the kitchen counter, as if referencing the blueprints for a way to corner Joko in his own house. "It certainly wouldn't be *fair* to ask you to do more than your share."

"No . . ." said Joko, "I don't suppose it would."

"It certainly wouldn't . . . but let me ask you something else, Admiral. When has what's been asked of you ever been fair?"

Joko couldn't find an answer.

The foreman was well-connected in the resettlement authority. His request from Joko was simple, that he agree to a couple of preliminary conversations. The foreman thought Joko should start small. It was already too late for him to enter the upcoming election, but given Joko's popularity among resettlers, who owed their very lives to his skill as a naval officer, the announcement that he was exploring a bid for office—even a lesser office—would upend the political landscape.

"You announcing your candidacy for anything," the foreman concluded, "would dump the wind right out of Eva Boucher's sails. Let me make a couple of introductions. Whaddya say?"

Joko crossed his arms over his chest. "I'll think about it."

"You'll think about it?"

"Yes, I'll think about it."

And true to his word, Joko did.

10:15 Oct 06, 2089 (+9 GMT)
New Delhi

Julia Hunt was among the several dozen attendees at the funeral of Major General Patel. Others who'd come to pay respects were Lily Bao, retired Admiral Joko—who'd recently won election as the administrator of the resettlement authority—and several retired military officers of some renown, including Suharto. It was a relatively small and somber gathering, held at the Gymkhana Club in New Delhi where Patel's family had spent decades—first as servants, then as members.

During the small reception afterward, the conversation turned to prisoners of war. The Floridians, whose economy had entered a tailspin, still held several hundred. They were demanding ransoms for their release from both Consortium and Reparationist nations, even forgoing prisoner swaps in cases where they thought they could elicit a ransom. Among the retired officers gathered, the attention focused on a Brazilian rear admiral, a man Julia had met years ago, von Hütschler; he'd been playing a role in negotiating the release of some of the prisoners, though he seemed reluctant to discuss the subject in detail and eventually excused himself from the conversation.

Julia had been happy to linger out of sight, particularly as the conversation turned to the war. She worried that some of those gathered might remember how she'd betrayed the resettlement fleet. She was sitting by herself when von Hütschler found her. "It's been a while," he said. "Do you remember me?"

"Of course."

"Might I join you?"

She gestured to the seat next to her. An awkward silence passed between them, filled only by the sound of quiet conversations around the room and the clinking of glasses and utensils as the guests found their way to the refreshments.

"They certainly like to talk," von Hütschler eventually said.

"That they do."

The silence between them returned.

"I hear you moved to a farm outside of Nuuk."

"A vineyard, in Sarqaq."

When von Hütschler inquired about her life on the vineyard, Julia explained that shifts in the climate, which included increasingly high winds and exhausted viticultural conditions in the soil, had caused her last two grape harvests to fail.

"Have you ever heard of Santorini grapes?"

Julia hadn't.

"They're from Greece, the volcanic island of Santorini," von Hütschler explained. "The vine grows to the side instead of vertically, low to the ground, out of the wind. They're adapted to survive in the harshest conditions, in the barest soils."

"I'll have to look into it," said Julia, and then changed the subject. "How did you know Sandeep?"

"Sandeep?"

"General Patel . . ."

"Sorry, of course," said von Hütschler. "We didn't really know one another."

"Then what's brought you here?"

"A mutual friend of ours," said von Hütschler. "He thought you'd be here."

At that moment, from a PA system across the room, the Patel family began their remarks, a series of eulogies that went on for the better part of an hour. By the time they'd finished, von Hütschler had migrated to the door. Before he left, Julia found him and asked about their mutual friend. Who exactly was this? Von Hütschler was putting on his coat. He didn't answer her question; instead, he said, "Let's stay in touch on the matter."

Julia had returned to Sarqaq. Not even a week later, she awoke to the sound of one of her dogs barking. Someone was at her door. When

Julia opened it, there he stood. Skinnier. Older. His hair cropped short. His mustache shaved. She'd never entirely believed he was dead but hadn't allowed herself to cling to the hope that he was alive either. Whatever ordeal he'd passed through, it hardly mattered.

When she reached for him, he stopped her. First, he wanted to show her something that he'd brought, a gift from von Hütschler, who had helped broker his release. He reached into his tattered old flight bag. Sitting on top of his folded blue pajamas was a bundle, swaddled in a damp white rag. He held it between them and carefully untied the edges of the fabric, revealing a web of delicate roots and green shoots, growing to the side.

"It's a new vine."

Julia took him by the hand and led him around the back of the house, into their vineyard. The two of them wandered around in the wind, searching for the perfect place to plant it.